D0900339

FIC

Cuentos Chicanos

Cp 2   *19 95*

DATE			
	APR	1988	

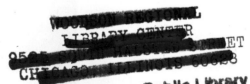

~~WOODSON REGIONAL~~
~~LIBRARY CENTER~~
~~9525 SOUTH HALSTED STREET~~
~~CHICAGO, ILLINOIS 60628~~

Chicago Public Library
Clearing Branch
6423 West 63rd Place
Chicago, Illinois 60638-5005

© THE BAKER & TAYLOR CO.

Cuentos Chicanos

Cuentos Chicanos

A Short Story Anthology

REVISED EDITION

CEO Edited by
Rudolfo A. Anaya
and Antonio Márquez

Published for NEW AMERICA
by the University of New Mexico Press
Albuquerque

This issue of *New America* has been funded in part by The New Mexico Arts Division, National Endowment for the Arts, The Coordinating Council of Literary Magazines, The University of New Mexico, and the Graduate Student Association of the University of New Mexico.

FIC
cop2

Library of Congress Cataloging in Publication Data
Main entry under title:

Cuentos Chicanos

   1. Short stories, American—Mexican-American authors.
2. American fiction—20th century. I. Anaya, Rudolfo A.
II. Márquez, Antonio, 1940-
PS647.M49C8   1984   813'.01'0886872073   84-13066
ISBN 0-8263-0771-X
ISBN 0-8263-0772-8 (pbk.)

©1984 by the University of New Mexico Press. All rights reserved. Manufactured in the United States of America.
Library of Congress Catalog Number 84-13066
International Standard Book Number 0-8263-0771-X (cloth)
                                0-8263-0772-8 (paper)
Revised edition.

Permission to reproduce these stories has been secured from the authors and their original publishers, where applicable.

Contents

Chicago Public Library
Clearing Branch
6423 West 63rd Place
Chicago, Illinois 60638-5005

Introduction

Chicano literature has undergone a phenomenal growth during the past two decades. Working both within and outside the context of the social-political movement known as El Movimiento, contemporary Chicano writers have created a body of work that has rightfully taken its place in American and world literature. The Chicano Movement was not only a declaration of Chicanos' right to their heritage within the American society, it was also an avenue for literary creativity. Writers and artists have attempted to give form to the aspirations of the Movement in poetry, drama, story, film, song, and other aesthetic media, and Chicano writers seized the impetus of the movement to forge a contemporary literature. This role required a responsibility and commitment on the part of the writer as he sought to capture the dimensions, nuances, subtleties, and paradoxes of Chicano life and culture. The writers of the movement met the challenge, and the literary upsurge brought forth accomplished writers whose unique voices, intrepid visions, and passionate intensity created the literature of El Movimiento.

The first anthology of contemporary Chicano literature, *El Espejo/The Mirror* (Quinto Sol Publications, 1969), boldly announced that "to know themselves and who they are, there are those who need no reflection other than their own." Chicano literature has come a long way from this impassioned but now rather narrow literary credo. The past two decades have seen important developments in Chicano literature. Liberated from the constraints of "social protest literature," Chicano writers vigorously explored new thematic and stylistic modes to express their literary conceptions of the Chicano experience. So it was that Rolando Hinojosa created his own world in Belken County, Texas, and peopled it with complex characters, not only to explore cross-cultural relationships between Chicanos and Anglos, but also to dramatize the Chicano's unique quest for identity and to affirm the Chicano's history, language, and cultural values. So it was that Ron Arias imaginatively transported the Quijote legend to an East

vii

Los Angeles barrio and, with his memorable character Fausto, magically and realistically gave vitality to the life-death theme. And so it was that Tomas Rivera caught the harsh realities of life in migrant communities and illuminated the want, despair, hopes and heart-breaking dreams of migrant workers and their children as they struggled to survive and retain their dignity and humanity. What distinguishes these and other writers who stand at the vanguard of contemporary Chicano literature is their mastery of the craft, their insight into the world of the Chicano, and their ability to expand specific Chicano characters and themes to universal comprehension and significance.

We were gratified by the purpose, vitality, and diversity of the material submitted for this anthology. In compiling it, we wanted to demonstrate that the Chicano short story has reached new levels of maturity and sophistication. What is notable about these stories is that they offer highly personalized visions of the world presented in styles unique to each writer. In form they range from the oral narrative patterns of the traditional cuento to experimentation with stream-of-conciousness; in tone they range from the visceral and tragic to lighthearted musing; in attitude they range from cynicism to exuberant celebration of cultural values and personal worth. Overall, they cannot be easily categorized; however, they verify that exploratory literary voices and energetic currents are creating the contemporary Chicano short story.

In collecting these stories, we were moved by the joy of discovery. Regrettably, it was impossible to publish an exhaustive collection, so it will fall to other editors to collect and publish in this area. This is a task that is more easily defined than accomplished, primarily because the greatest impediment in the dissemination of Chicano literature continues to be the lack of attention from large, commercial publishers. For that reason we were happy to work with *New America* in publishing the first edition in 1980, and we are grateful to the University of New Mexico Press for publishing this revised edition of *Cuentos Chicanos*. We are honored to bring these writers to the attention of the reading public, and we hope that the authors will be appreciated for their contribution to Chicano literature.

Rudolfo A. Anaya
Antonio Márquez

B. Traven is Alive and Well in Cuernavaca

Rudolfo A. Anaya

I didn't go to Mexico to find B. Traven. Why should I? I have enough to do writing my own fiction, so I go to Mexico to write, not to search out writers. B. Traven? you ask. Don't you remember THE TREASURE OF THE SIERRA MADRE? A real classic. They made a movie from the novel. I remember seeing it when I was kid. It was set in Mexico, and it had all the elements of a real adventure story. B. Traven was an adventurous man, traveled all over the world, then disappeared into Mexico and cut himself off from society. He gave no interviews and allowed few photographs. While he lived he remained unapproachable, anonymous to his public, a writer shrouded in mystery.

He's dead now, or they say he's dead. I think he's alive and well. At any rate, he has become something of an institution in Mexico, a man honored for his work. The cantineros and taxi drivers in Mexico City know about him as well as the cantineros of Spain knew Hemingway, or they claim to. I never mention I'm a writer when I'm in a cantina, because inevitably some aficionado will ask, "Do you know the work of B. Traven?" And from some dusty niche will appear a yellowed, thumb-worn novel by Traven. Thus if the cantinero knows his business, and they all do in Mexico, he is apt to say "Did you know that B. Traven used to drink here?" If you show the slightest interest, he will follow with, "Sure, he used to sit right over here. In this corner. . . ." And if you don't leave right then you will wind up hearing many stories about the mysterious B. Traven while buying many drinks for the local patrons.

Everybody reads his novels, on the buses, on street corners; if you look closely you'll spot one of his titles. One turned up for me, and that's how this story started. I was sitting in the train station in Juárez, waiting for the train to Cuernavaca, which would be an exciting title for this story except that there is no train to Cuernavaca. I was drinking beer to kill time, the erotic and sensitive Mexican time which is so different from the clean-packaged, well-kept time of the Americanos. Time in Mexico can be cruel and punishing, but it is never indifferent. It permeates everything, it changes reality. Einstein would have loved Mexico because there time and space are one. I stare more often into empty space when I'm in Mexico. The past seems to infuse the present, and in the brown, wrinkled faces of the old people one sees the presence of the past. In Mexico I like to walk the narrow streets of the cities and the smaller pueblos, wandering aimlessly, feeling the sunlight which is so distinctively Mexican, listening to the voices which call in the streets, peering into the dark eyes which are so secretive and proud. The Mexican people guard a secret. But in the end, one is never really lost in Mexico. All streets lead to a good cantina. All good stories start in a cantina.

At the train station, after I let the kids who hustle the tourists know that I didn't want chewing gum or cigarettes, and I didn't want my shoes shined, and I didn't want a woman at the moment, I was left alone to drink my beer. Luke-cold Dos Equis. I don't remember how long I had been there or how many Dos Equis I had finished when I glanced at the seat next to me and saw a book which turned out to be a B. Traven novel, old and used and obviously much read, but a novel nevertheless. What's so strange about finding a B. Traven novel in that dingy little corner of a bar in the Juárez train station? Nothing, unless you know that in Mexico one never finds anything. It is a country that doesn't waste anything, everything is recycled. Chevrolets run with patched up Ford engines and Chrysler transmissions, buses are kept together, and kept running, with baling wire and home-made parts, yesterday's Traven novel is the pulp on which tomorrow's Fuentes story will appear. Time recycles in Mexico. Time returns to the past, and the Christian finds himself dreaming of ancient Aztec rituals. He who does not believe that Quetzalcoatl will return to save Mexico has little faith.

So the novel was the first clue. Later there was Justino. "Who is Justino?" you want to know. Justino was the jardinero who cared for the garden of my friend, the friend who had invited me to stay at his home in Cuernavaca while I continued to write. The day after I arrived I was sitting in the sun, letting the fatigue of the long journey ooze away, thinking nothing, when Justino appeared on the scene. He had finished cleaning the swimming pool and was taking his morning break, so he sat in the shade of the orange tree and introduced himself. Right away I could tell that he would rather be a movie actor or an adventurer, a real free spirit. But things didn't work out for him. He got married, children appeared, he took a couple of mistresses, more children appeared, so he had to work to support his family. "A man is like a rooster," he said after we talked awhile, "the more chickens he has the happier he is." Then he asked me what I was going to do about a woman while I was there, and I told him I hadn't thought that far ahead, that I would be happy if I could just get a damned story going. This puzzled Justino, and I think for a few days it worried him. So on Saturday night he took me out for a few drinks and we wound up in some of the bordellos of Cuernavaca in the company of some of the most beautiful women in the world. Justino knew them all. They loved him, and he loved them.

I learned something more of the nature of this jardinero a few nights later when the heat and an irritating mosquito wouldn't let me sleep. I heard music from a radio, so I put on my pants and walked out into the Cuernavacan night, an oppressive, warm night heavy with the sweet perfume of the dama de la noche bushes which lined the wall of my friend's villa. From time to time I heard a dog cry in the distance, and I remembered that in Mexico many people die of rabies. Perhaps that is why the walls of the wealthy are always so high and the locks always secure. Or maybe it was because of the occasional gunshots that explode in the night. The news media tell us that Mexico is the most stable country in Latin America and, with the recent oil finds, the bankers and the oil men want to keep it that way. I sense, and many know, that in the dark the revolution does not sleep. It is a spirit kept at bay by the high fences and the locked gates, yet it prowls the heart of every man. "Oil will create a new revolution," Justino had told me, "but it's going to be for our people. Mexicans are tired of building gas stations for the Gringos from Gringolandia." I understood what he meant: there is much hunger in the country.

I lit a cigarette and walked toward my friend's car, which was parked in the driveway near the swimming pool. I approached quietly andd peered in. On the back sear with his legs propped on the front seat-back and smoking a cigar sat Justino. Two big, luscious women sat on either side of him running their fingers through his hair and whispering in his ears. The doors were open to allow a breeze. He looked content. Sitting there he was that famous artist on his way to an afternoon reception in Mexico City, or he was a movie star on his way to the premiere of his most recent movie. Or perhaps it was Sunday and he was taking a Sunday drive in the country, towards Tepoztlán. And why shouldn't his two friends accompany him? I had to smile. Unnoticed I backed away and returned to my room. So there was quite a bit more than met the eye to this short, dark Indian from Ocosingo.

In the morning I asked my friend, "What do you know about Justino?"

"Justino? You mean Vitorino."

"Is that his real name?"

"Sometimes he calls himself Trinidad."

"Maybe his name is Justino Vitorino Trinidad," I suggested.

"I don't know, don't care," my friend answered. "He told me he used to be a guide in the jungle. Who knows? The Mexican Indian has an incredible imagination. Really gifted people. He's a good jardinero, and that's what matters to me. It's difficult to get good jardineros, so I don't ask questions."

"Is he reliable?" I wondered aloud.

"As reliable as a ripe mango," my friend nodded.

I wondered how much he knew, so I pushed a little further. "And the radio at night?"

"Oh, that. I hope it doesn't bother you. Robberies and break-ins are increasing here in the colonia. Something we never used to have. Vitorino said that if he keeps the radio on low the sound keeps thieves away. A very good idea, don't you think?"

I nodded. A very good idea.

"And I sleep very soundly," my friend concluded, "so I never hear it."

The following night when I awakened and heard the soft sound of music from the radio and heard the splashing of water, I had only to look from my window to see Justino and his friends in the pool, swimming nude in the moonlight. They were joking and laughing softly as they splashed each other, being quiet so as not to awaken my friend, the patrón who slept so soundly. The women were beautiful. Brown skinned and glistening with water in the moonlight they reminded be of ancient Aztec maidens, swimming around Chac, their god of rain. They teased Justino, and he smiled as he floated on a rubber mattress in the middle of the pool, smoking his cigar, happy because they were happy. When he smiled the gold fleck of a filling glinted in the moonlight.

"¡Qué cabrón!" I laughed and closed my window.

Justino said a Mexican never lies. I believed him. If a Mexican says he will meet you at a certain time and place, he means he will meet you sometime at some place. Americans who retire in Mexico often complain of maids who swear they will come to work on a designated day, then don't show up. They did not lie, they knew they couldn't be at work, but they knew to tell the señora otherwise would make her sad or displease her, so they agree on a date so everyone would remain happy. What a beautiful aspect of character. It's a real virtue which Norteamericanos interpret as a fault in their character, because we are used to asserting ourselves on time and people. We feel secure and comfortable only when everything is neatly packaged in its proper time and place. We don't like the disorder of a free-flowing life.

Some day, I thought to myself, Justino will give a grand party in the sala of his patrón's home. His three wives, or his wife and two mistresses, and his dozens of children will be there. So will the women from the bordellos. He will preside over the feast, smoke his cigars, request his favorite beer-drinking songs from the mariachis, smile, tell stories and make sure everyone has a grand time. He will be dressed in a tuxedo, borrowed from the patrón's closet of course, and he will act gallant and show everyone that a man who has just come into sudden wealth should share it with his friends. And in the morning he will report to the patrón that something has to be done about the poor mice that are coming in out of the streets and eating everything in the house.

"I'll buy some poison," the patrón will suggest.

"No, no," Justino will shake his head, "a little music from the radio and a candle burning in the sala will do."

And he will be right.

I liked Justino. He was a rogue with class. We talked about the weather, the lateness of the rainy season, women, the role of oil in Mexican politics. Like other workers, he believed nothing was going to filter down to the campesinos. "We could all be real Mexican greasers with all that oil," he said, "but the politicians will keep it all."

"What about the United States?" I asked.

"Oh, I have traveled in the estados unidos to the north. It's a country that's going to the dogs in a worse way than Mexico. The thing I liked the most was your cornflakes."

"Cornflakes?"

"Sí. You can make really good cornflakes."

"And women?"

"Ah, you better keep your eyes open, my friend. Those gringas are going to change the world just like the Suecas changed Spain."

"For better or for worse?"

"Spain used to be a nice country," he winked.

We talked, we argued, we drifted from subject to subject. I learned from him. I had been there a week when he told the story which eventually led me to B. Traven. One day I was sitting under the orange tree reading the B. Traven novel I had found in the Juarez train station, keeping one eye on the ripe oranges which fell from time to time, my mind wandering as it worked to focus on a story so I could begin to write. After all, that's why I had come to Cuernavaca, to get some writing done, but nothing was coming, nothing. Justino wandered by and asked what I was reading and replied it was an adventure story, a story of a man's search for the illusive pot of gold at the end of a make-believe rainbow. He nodded, thought awhile and gazed toward Popo, Popocatepetl, the towering volcano which lay to the south, shrouded in mist, waiting for the rains as we waited for the rains, sleeping, gazing at his female counterpart, Itza, who lay sleeping and guarding the valley of Cholula, there, where over four-hundred years ago Cortés showed his wrath and executed thousands of Cholulans.

"I am going on an adverture," he finally said and paused. "I think you might like to go with me."

I said nothing, but I put my book down and listened.

"I have been thinking about it for a long time, and now is the time to go. You see, it's like this. I grew up on the hacienda of Don Francisco Jimenez, it's to the south, just a day's drive on the carretera. In my village nobody likes Don Francisco, they fear and hate him. He has killed many men and he has taken their fortunes and buried them. He is a very rich man, muy rico. Many men have tried to kill him, but Don Francisco is like the devil, he kills them first."

I listened as I always listen, because one never knows when a word or phrase or an idea will be the seed from which a story sprouts, but at first there was nothing interesting. It sounded like the typical patrón-peón story I had heard so many times before. A man, the patrón, keeps the workers enslaved, in serfdom, and because he wields so much power soon stories are told about him and he begins to acquire super-human powers. He acquires a mystique, just like the divine right of old. The patrón wields a mean machete, like old King Arthur swung Excaliber. He chops off heads of dissenters and sits on top of the bones and skulls pyramid, the king of the mountain, the top macho.

"One day I was sent to look for lost cattle," Justino continued. "I rode back into the hills where I had never been. At the foot of a hill, near a ravine, I saw something move in the bush. I dismounted and moved forward quietly. I was afraid it might be bandidos who steal cattle, and if they saw me they would kill me. When I came near the place I heard a strange sound. Somebody was crying. My back shivered, just like a dog when he sniffs the devil at night. I thought I was going to see witches, brujas who like to go to those deserted places to dance for the devil, or la Llorona."

"La Llorona," I said aloud. My interest grew. I had been hearing Llorona stories since I was a kid, and I was always ready for one more. La

Llorona was that archetypal woman of ancient legends who murdered her children then, repentant and demented, she has spent the rest of eternity searching for them.

"Sí, la Llorona. You know that poor woman used to drink a lot. She played around with men, and when she had babies she got rid of them by throwing them into la barranca. One day she realized what she had done and went crazy. She started crying and pulling her hair and running up and down the side of cliffs of the river looking for her children. It's a very sad story."

A new version, I thought, and yes, a sad story. And what of the men who made love to the woman who became la Llorona, I wondered? Did they ever cry for their children? It doesn't seem fair to have only her suffer, only her crying and doing penance. Perhaps a man should run with her, and in our legends we would call him "El Mero Chingón," he who screwed up everything. Then maybe the tale of love and passion and the insanity it can bring will be complete. Yes, I think someday I will write that story.

"What did you see?" I asked Justino.

"Something worse than la Llorona," he whispered.

To the south a wind mourned and moved the clouds off Popo's crown. The bald, snow-covered mountain thrust its power into the blue Mexican sky. The light glowed like liquid gold around the god's head. Popo was a god, an ancient god. Somewhere at his feet Justino's story had taken place.

"I moved closer, and when I parted the bushes I saw Don Francisco. He was sitting on a rock, and he was crying. From time to time he looked at the ravine in front of him, the hole seemed to slant into the earth. That pozo is called el Pozo de Mondoza. I had heard stories about it before, but I had never seen it. I looked into the pozo, and you wouldn't believe what I saw."

He waited, so I asked, "What?"

"Money! Huge piles of gold and silver coins! Necklaces and bracelets and crowns of gold, all loaded with all kinds of precious stones! Jewels! Diamonds! All sparkling in the sunlight that entered the hole. More money than I have ever seen! A fortune, my friend, a fortune which is still there, just waiting for two adventurers like us to take it!"

"Us? But what about Don Francisco? It's his land, his fortune."

"Ah," Justino smiled, "that's the strange thing about this fortune. Don Francisco can't touch it, that's why he was crying. You see, I stayed there, and watched him closely. Every time he stood up and started to walk into the pozo the money disappeared. He stretched out his hand to grab the gold, and poof, it was gone! That's why he was crying! He murdered all those people and hid their wealth in the pozo, but now he can't touch it. He is cursed."

"El Pozo de Mondoza," he said aloud. Something began to click in my mind. I smelled a story.

"Who was Mendoza?" I asked.

"He was a very rich man. Don Francisco killed him in a quarrel they had over some cattle. But Mendoza must have put a curse on Don Francisco before he died, because now Don Francisco can't get to the money."

"So Mendoza's ghost haunts old Don Francisco," I nodded.

"Many ghosts haunt him," Justino answered. "He has killed many men."

"And the fortune, the money. . . ."

He looked at me and his eyes were dark and piercing. "It's still there. Waiting for us!"

"But it disappears as one approaches it, you said so yourself. Perhaps it's only an hallucination."

Justino shook his head. "No, it's real gold and silver, not hallucination money. It disappears for Don Francisco because the curse is on him, but the curse is not on us." He smiled. He knew he had drawn me into his plot. "We didn't steal the money, so it won't disappear for us. And you are not connected with the place. You are innocent. I've thought very carefully about it, and now is the time to go. I can lower you into the pozo with a rope, in a few hours we can bring out the entire fortune. All we need is a car. You can borrow the patrón's car, he is your friend. But he must not know where we're going. We can be there and back in one day, one night." He nodded as if to assure me, then he turned and looked at the sky. "It will not rain today. It will not rain for a week. Now is the time to go."

He winked and returned to watering the grass and flowers of the jardín, a wild Pan among the bougainvillea and the roses, a man possessed by a dream. The gold was not for him, he told me the next day, it was for his women, he would buy them all gifts, bright dresses, and he would take them on vacation to the United States, he would educate his children, send them to the best colleges. I listened and the germ of the story cluttered my thoughts as I sat beneath the orange tree in the mornings. I couldn't write, nothing was coming, but I knew that there were elements for a good story in Justino's tale. In dreams I saw the lonely hacienda to the south. I saw the pathetic, tormented figure of Don Francisco as he cried over the fortune he couldn't touch. I saw the ghosts of the men he had killed, the lonely women who mourned over them and cursed the evil Don Francisco. In one dream I saw a man I took to be B. Traven, a grey-haired distinguished looking gentlemen who looked at me and nodded approvingly. "Yes, there's a story there, follow it, follow it. . . ."

In the meantime, other small and seemingly insignificant details came my way. During a luncheon at the home of my friend, a woman I did not know leaned toward me and asked me if I would like to meet the widow of B. Traven. The woman's hair was tinged orange, her complexion was ashen grey. I didn't know who she was or why she would mention B. Traven to me. How did she know Traven had come to haunt my thoughts? Was she a clue, which would help unravel the mystery? I didn't know, but I nodded. Yes, I would like to meet her. I had heard that Traven's widow, Rosa Elena, lived in Mexico City. But what would I ask her? What did I want to know? Would she know Traven's secret? Somehow he had learned that to keep his magic intact he had to keep away from the public. Like the fortune in the pozo, the magic feel for the story might disappear if unclean hands reached for it. I turned to look at the woman, but she was gone. I wandered to the terrrace to finish my beer. Justino sat beneath the orange tree. He yawned. I knew the literary talk bored him. He was eager to be on the way to el Pozo de Mendoza.

I was nervous, too, but I didn't know why. The tension for the story was there, but something was missing. Or perhaps it was just Justino's insistence that I decide whether I was going or not that drove me out of the house in the mornings. Time usually devoted to writing found me in a small cafe in the center of town. From there I could watch the shops open, watch the people cross the zócalo, the main square. I drank lots of coffee, I smoked a lot, I daydreamed, I wondered about the significance of the pozo, the fortune, Justino, the story I wanted to write about B. Traven. In one of these moods I saw a friend from whom I hadn't heard in years. Suddenly he was there, trekking across the square, dressed like an old rabbi, moss and green algae for a beard, and followed by a troop of very dignified Lacandones, Mayan Indians from Chiapas.

"Victor," I gasped, unsure if he was real or a part of the shadows which the sun created as it flooded the square with its light.

"I have no time to talk," he said as he stopped to munch on my pan dulce and sip my coffee. "I only want you to know, for purposes of your story, that I was in a Lacandonian village last month, and a Hollywood film crew descended from the sky. They came in helicopters. They set up tents near the village, and big-bosomed, bikined actresses emerged from them, tossed themselves on the cut trees which are the atrocity of the giant American lumber companies, and they cried while the director shot his film. Then they produced a grey-haired old man from one of the tents and took shots of him posing with the Indians. Herr Traven, the director called him."

He finished my coffee, nodded to his friends and they began to walk away.

"B. Traven?" I asked.

He turned. "No, an imposter, an actor. Be careful for imposters. Remember, even Traven used many disguises, many names!"

"Then he's alive and well?" I shouted. People around me turned to stare.

"His spirit is with us," were the last words I heard as they moved across the zócalo, a strange troop of near naked Lacandon Mayans and my friend the Guatemalan Jew, returning to the rain forest, returning to the primal, innocent land.

I slumped in my chair and looked at my empty cup. What did it mean? As their trees fall the Lacandones die. Betrayed as B. Traven was betrayed. Does each one of us also die as the trees fall in the dark depths of the Chiapas jungle? Far to the north, in Aztlán, it is the same where the earth is ripped open to expose and mine the yellow uranium. A few poets sing songs and stand in the way as the giant machines of the corporations rumble over the land and grind everything into dust. New holes are made in the earth, pozos full of curses, pozos with fortunes we cannot touch, should not touch. Oil, coal, uranium, from holes in the earth through which we suck the blood of the earth.

There were other incidents. A telephone call late one night, a voice with a German accent called my name, and when I answered the line went dead. A letter addressed to B. Traven came in the mail. It was dated March 26, 1969. My friend returned it to the post office. Justino grew more and more morose. He was under the orange tree and stared into space, my friend complained about the garden drying up. Justino looked at me and scowled. He did a little work then went back to daydreaming. Without the rains the garden withered. His heart was set on the adventure which lay at el pozo. Finally I said yes, dammit, why not, let's go, neither one of us is getting anything done here, and Justino cheering like a child, ran to prepare for the trip. But when I asked my friend for the weekend loan of the car he reminded me that we were invited to a tertulia, an afternoon reception, at the home of Señora Ana R. Many writers and artists would be there. It was in my honor, so I could meet the literati of Cuernavaca. I had to tell Justino I couldn't go.

Now it was I who grew morose. The story growing within would not let me sleep. I awakened in the night and looked out the window, hoping to see Justino and women bathing in the pool, enjoying themselves. But all was quiet. No radio played. The still night was warm and heavy. From time to time gunshots sounded in the dark, dogs barked, and the presence of a Mexico which never sleeps closed in on me.

Saturday morning dawned with a strange overcast. Perhaps the rains will come, I thought. In the afternoon I reluctantly accompanied my friend to the reception. I had not seen Justino all day, but I saw him at the gate as we drove out. He looked tired, as if he, too, had not slept. He wore the white shirt and baggy pants of a campesino. His straw hat cast a shadow over his eyes. I wondered if he had decided to go to the pozo alone. He didn't speak as we drove through the gate, he only nodded. When I looked back I saw him standing by the gate, looking after the car, and I had a vague, uneasy feeling that I had lost an opportunity.

The afternoon gathering was a pleasant affair, attended by a number of affectionate artists, critics, and writers who enjoyed the refreshing drinks which quenched the thirst.

But my mood drove me away from the crowd. I wandered around the terrace and found a foyer surrounded by green plants, huge fronds and ferns and flowering bougainvillea. I pushed the green aside and entered a quiet, very private alcove. The light was dim, the air was cool, a perfect place for contemplation. At first I thought I was alone, then I saw the man sitting in one of the wicker chairs next to a small, wrought iron table. He was an elderly white-haired gentlemen. His face showed he had lived a full life, yet he was still very distinguished in his manner and posture. His eyes shone brightly.

"Perdón," I apologized and turned to leave. I did not want to intrude.

"No, no, please," he motioned to the empty chair, "I've been waiting for you." He spoke English with a slight German accent. Or perhaps it was Norwegian, I couldn't tell the difference. "I can't take the literary gossip. I prefer the quiet."

I nodded and sat. He smiled and I felt at ease. I took the cigar he offered and we lit up. He began to talk and I listened. He was a writer also, but I had the good manners not to ask his titles. He talked about the changing Mexico, the change the new oil would bring, the lateness of the rains and how they affected the people and the land, and he talked about how important a woman was in a writer's life. He wanted to know about me, about the Chicanos of Aztlán, about our work. It was the workers, he said, who would change society. The artist learned from the worker. I talked, and sometime during the conversation I told him the name of the friend with whom I was staying. He laughed and wanted to know if Vitorino was still working for him.

"Do you know Justino?" I asked.

"Oh, yes, I know that old guide. I met him many years ago, when I first came to Mexico," he answered. "Justino knows the campesino very well. He and I traveled many places together, he in search of adventure, I in search of stories."

I thought the coincidence strange, so I gathered the courage and asked, "Did he ever tell you the story of the fortune at el Pozo de Mendoza?"

"Tell me?" the old man smiled. "I went there."

"With Justino?"

"Yes, I went with him. What a rogue he was in those days, but a good man. If I remember correctly I even wrote a story based on that adventure. Not a very good story. Never came to anything. But we had a grand time. People like Justino are the writer's source. We met interesting people and saw fabulous places, enough to last me a lifetime. We were supposed to be gone for one day, but we were gone nearly three years. You see, I wasn't interested in the pots of gold he kept saying were just over the next hill, I went because there was a story to write."

"Yes, that's what interested me," I agreed.

"A writer has to follow a story if it leads him to hell itself. That's our curse. Ay, and each one of us knows our own private hell."

I nodded. I felt relieved. I sat back to smoke the cigar and sip from my drink. Somewhere to the west the sun bronzed the evening sky. On a clear afternoon, Popo's crown would glow like fire.

"Yes," the old man continued, "a writer's job is to find and follow people like Justino. They're the source of life. The ones you have to keep away from are the dilettantes like the ones in there." He motioned in the general direction of the noise of the party. "I stay with people like Justino. They may be illiterate, but they understand our descent into the pozo of hell, and they understand us because they're willing to share the adventure with us. You seek fame and notoriety and you're dead as a writer."

I sat upright. I understood now what the pozo meant, why Justino had come into my life to tell me the story. It was clear. I rose quickly and shook the old man's hand. I turned and parted the palm leaves of the alcove. There, across the way, in one of the streets that led out of the maze of the town towards the south, I saw Justino. He was walking in the direction of Popo, and he was followed by women and children, a rag-tail army of adventurers, all happy, all singing. He looked up to where I stood on the terrace, and he smiled as he waved. He paused to light the stub of a cigar. The women turned, and the children turned, and all waved to me. Then they continued their walk, south, towards the foot of the volcano. They were going to the Pozo de Mendoza, to the place where the story originated.

I wanted to run after them, to join them in the glorious light which bathed the Cuernavaca valley and the majestic snow-covered head of Popo. The light was everywhere, a magnetic element which flowed from the clouds. I waved as Justino and his followers disappeared in the light. Then I turned to say something to the old man, but he was gone. I was alone in the alcove. Somewhere in the background I heard the tinkling of glasses and the laughter which came from the party, but that was not for me. I left the terrace and crossed the lawn, found the gate and walked down the street. The sound of Mexico filled the air. I felt light and happy. I wandered aimlessly through the curving, narrow streets, then I quickened my pace because suddenly the story was overflowing and I needed to write. I needed to get to my quiet room and write the story about B. Traven being alive and well in Cuernavaca.

Lupe

Ron Arias

In the morning Tiburcio's wife Isabel gave birth to a nine-pound, eight-ounce hermaphrodite. Isabel immediately asked to see the child. She pushed up on both elbows, smiling, eyes alert. It had been her easiest birth, so easy that Cuca the midwife hardly did more than hold Isabel's hand.

Isabel's pregnancy had almost gone unnoticed. To her other children she appeared the same, perhaps rounder, her eyes more affectionate. She had told them that one day soon their new brother or sister would arrive from her womb, clean and innocent—not "bought" at some mysterious store, as some of her neighbors liked to say.

Cuca hesitated, then held up the naked infant, its combination of boy and girl protruding before the mother's happy inspection. Isabel counted the fingers and toes. "Any birthmarks?" she asked.

"No," the old woman said, raising a brow.

"He looks like his father, wouldn't you say?"

"He . . .? Isabel, it's just as much a he as a she."

"Then *she* looks like her father." Isabel blinked and lay back on the pillow. Before she dozed off, she asked that Tiburcio and the children be allowed to see her creation. They had been waiting in the kitchen for more than an hour, and the pot of Wheatena Isabel had been cooking was still on the burner, lumpy and hardly mixed. The contractions had come so fast that calling the hospital was out of the question; even Cuca—two blocks away—almost missed the event.

Tiburcio entered the sunlit room first. He patted the small, bald head, smiled and nodded to his wife. The eldest son Robert moved close and said all newborn babies look alike. Eventually the other children touched the tiny hands, made faces and wondered if the birth meant they didn't have to go to school today.

"Yes, go to school," Isabel whispered, closing her eyes.

Isabel was soon flooded with sympathy. Some called the baby a "he," others maintained it was a girl because of one very long strand of hair

14

above the left ear, and still other neighbors switched back and forth, sometimes saying the baby was muy chulo, sometimes muy chula.

"What about a name?" Tiburcio asked. "We just can't keep calling it *it*."

Her husband was right, Isabel thought. "Any suggestions?"

No one spoke. Tiburcio became nervous and opened a telephone directory.

"Tiburcio," Isabel said, "go ask the priest. He should know."

Tiburcio jogged around the block to the sacristy behind the church and quickly explained the predicament. After a moment's meditation, the young Spanish priest shook his head, shrugged and advised him to pick a name before the baptism.

Cuca was more positive. There was only one solution: an operation. Afterward, naming the baby would be no problem.

"Absolutely not!" Isabel cried. "Nobody's going to touch my baby."

In the afternoon, Fausto and Carmela—neighbors from across the street—stopped by to congratulate Tiburcio and Isabel. The baby was asleep in its crib, Isabel was propped up with pillows, and Tiburcio was scribbling names on a pad and just as quickly crossing them out. Fausto, an oldtimer from Chihuahua, studied the baby, circling the crib and stroking his own hairless chin.

"Well, what do you think?" Tiburcio shouted in a nervous pitch.

"Lower your voice," Isabel said. "You'll wake the baby."

"Well, Fausto? You're the man with all the books, give us a name."

Carmela, Fausto's niece, reminded them that her uncle wasn't a magician.

"Lupe," Fausto said suddenly, "Guadalupe. It's perfect. Either way it fits."

Tiburcio raised his heavy body and looked at his wife. "What do you think?"

"Fine."

"Tio," Carmela said, "I think we'd better go. You need your nap, and Isabel has to rest."

Carmela kissed Isabel on the cheek, then led her uncle out the door and through the living room. The unopened presents were still piled on a table in one corner; the baby shower had been planned for today, but Lupe had arrived two weeks early.

"Poor woman," Carmela said when they were outside. "All those kids and one more to take care of. God, I'd hate to be in her place. She says her mother can't even help her."

"Why not?"

"She lives in Texas, and they don't have the money to send for her."

"She'll survive, Isabel's a strong woman."

"She has to be. Did you take a look at Tiburcio? He's like a walrus. She must spend all day cooking for him."

"He's nervous. Some people eat when they're nervous."

Carmela steadied Fausta's arm as they crossed the street. "Yeah, I'd be nervous too. Six kids and a lousy job . . ."

"That's why he's nervous. He lost his job."

The two entered Fausto's house and the old man sat down next to a bookcase jammed with paperbacks, magazines and hardcover discards from the county library. "Carmela, that man is desperate. A strange baby's one thing . . . but giving it up to some circus—"

"You're kidding!"

"He told me this morning. What could I say? It's his kid."

Two days later Tiburcio—fear in his eyes—stumbled up the stairs and banged on Fausto's door.

¿Qué pasa?" Fausto asked, flipping up the latch.

"My kids, they won't eat."

"So? It happens—"

"I mean a whole day and a half now. Nothing! All except for Lupe. He doesn't stop eating."

The two men walked into the kitchen. Fausto sat down at the table and turned on the radio. The cracked dial knob was loosely held together with a Band-Aid and kept slipping off the metal rod.

"What'll I do?" Tiburcio pleaded.

Fausto finally stopped the dial on the station he wanted. The announcer was giving the day's astrology reading. "Maybe," Fausto said, "your food is bad. Is that it?"

"I tried everything, even capirotada. They've never turned that down."

Fausto leaned forward and listened for Sagittarius. After a moment he looked up and told his sallow-faced friend not to worry. "You know children, they probably planned this weeks ago. On the other hand, it might be the weather. It does funny things . . . Or maybe they're like me. Sometimes I get tired of eating—todo me da asco. You ever feel that way?"

Tiburcio slapped his paunch. "That's another thing. I haven't eaten all afternoon. It doesn't even bother me."

"Tiburcio, go on home and I'll try to read up on this. Maybe I'll find an answer."

For two days more days the children of Elysian Valley fasted, then one by one the adults were afflicted by the same indifference to all forms of food. School was closed, some parents straggled to work for a few days, and by Sunday only the most faithful of the Church were able to listen to the dark, weary figure seated on a stool behind the pulpit. By the fourth day most of the children lay in bed with vague, limp expressions, their parents not much better. Even Fausto, searching his books, could barely stand any reference to food.

As for Lupe, the baby had quickly sucked his mother dry, and Isabel was forced to fill the hungry little mouth with bottles of milk, tea, chicken broth, juices, even soft solids. Hour after hour Isabel trudged between the kitchen and the crib, stepping around her reduced husband, occasionally stopping to rouse an eyelid of one of her other children.

It wasn't long before Lupe and his emaciated neighbors captured instant national attention. Reporters wandered freely through the homes, describing the scene; full cupboards, untouched freezers, blank faces and the usual skeletal forms buried under the bed blankets. Television crews marched in with their portable units, pinching pale cheeks, trying in vain to provoke a few intelligible words for their viewers. Nothing worked; they were left with silence or the continuous slurpings of one voracious eater—little Lupe.

Fate, the state governor announced, rested in the hands of medical knowledge. The teams of doctors and nurses moved in with their tubes, bottles, needles, machines, medicines and advice.

Most of the tests were run on the healthy infant. A hermaphrodite was unusual, but of course not impossible. What was strange was the baby's appetite, and they could only admire its phenomenal digestive development.

By the second week the neighborhood had been placed under quarrantine. Reserve troops from the Glendale Armory guarded all exits and entrances, while overhead two Sheriff's helicopters watched for any suspicious movement.

About this time Fausto lifted his eyes from a worm-eaten page, crawled past a dozing Carmela to the door and feebly shouted: "I know! I know!"

A male nurse stationed outside stared through the rusty screen at the decrepit figure on the floor. "You say something?"

"Yes," Fausto cried, "take me to the baby's house."

"Sure, but they ain't gonna let you in." The young man then carried Fausto across the street to Tiburcio's house. Reporters and medical people were sprawled on the yellowed lawn.

"Hold on!" a soldier shouted. "You can't take him in there."

Fausto wagged a crooked finger at the helmet. "I know something."

The soldier hesitated. "Alright, but just for ten minutes."

A man with camera cables looped around his arm moved up on one knee. "What's happening?"

"Hey, who's the old man?" another asked, shouldering a camera.

Inside the house, Fausto was set down. He moved aside a microphone and hobbled through the crowd of nurses and doctors. "Get me a banana," he said.

"What did he say?" someone asked.

"Said he wants a banana."

Upstairs, Fausto found Tiburcio lying under the sheets of his bed. Tiburcio's eyes were closed and his hands were folded over his once great belly. Fausto shook his friend by the shoulder.

"Shh," a voice said, "he's going to say something."

"Fred, get the lights on."

"Hey, quiet!"

"Dammit, get the lights on."

"Shhhh!"

"Make room! Cable comin' through."

"Make room yourself—"

"Shut up, you guys! The old man's trying to speak."

Suddenly the room turned quiet. "Bring the baby," Fausto said. "And the banana—a ripe one, not too green."

After Lupe was brought in, Fausto had him placed beside his father. Tiburcio smiled at his chubby bedmate.

Fausto now placed Tiburcio's hand on the baby's stomach. "Watch," Fausto said, moving the hand to Tiburcio's mouth. "First it goes in the mouth, then you chew it, then you swallow it, then it goes down to your stomach." Again, Fausto carefully repeated the motions.

After the third lesson Fausto took the ripe banana, peeled it and gave some to the baby. Tiburcio watched Lupe open and swallow.

"Now do the same," Fausto instructed, nudging the fruit between his friend's quivering lips. The cavernous eyes blinked twice, and Tiburcio bit down. Yes—the taste of bananas.

Everyone cheered, cameras popped, and one TV reporter snatched up the banana peel to dangle before the lens. "Could you tell our viewers what you did, Mister—"

"Fausto, Fausto Fejada."

"Mister Fajada, what exactly did you do?"

Fausto, now munching his own banana, cleared his throat. "A remedy for curses and lost appetite. It's the fruit of Capricorn, the goat . . ."

The reporter frowned and waited a moment longer. "Is that it—a banana?"

"A ripe one," Fausto said with a mischievous glance at the group of doctors. "The Tarahumaras of Chihuahua believe that goats eat everything. Grass, leaves, hierbas—"

"What?"

"Herbs!" a Chicano cableman shouted over the crowd of heads.

Fausto had bitten down to the peel stem. "And if you want a cure for the mysterious, you eat some . . . you know. But I knew Tiburcio wouldn't eat *that,* so I gave him a banana, like the horoscope says. Actually one book said goats only like banana leaves."

"Bananas? Leaves? Mister Fajado, are you serious?"

"I know, I was taking a chance, pero más vale ser caprichudo que ser mudo."

"What was that?"

The Chicano cableman laughed, then shouted: "Better to take a chance with a banana than to keep quiet and be ignored."

"Oh, sure, that explains everything."

Tiburcio now tugged at Fausto's sleeve and whispered: "Ask them if they've got anything else to eat."

The ordeal over, donations soon poured in for the hungry people of Elysian Valley. And it wasn't long before Tiburcio could be seen parading around his newest offspring, swearing that Lupe would never work in a circus.

El Tonto del Barrio

José Armas

Romero Estrado was called "El Cotoro" because he was always whistling and singing. He made nice music even though his songs were spontaneous compositions made up of words with sounds that he liked but which seldom made any sense. But that didn't seem to bother either Romero or anyone else in the Golden Heights Centro where he lived. Not even the kids made fun of him. It just was not permitted.

Romero had a ritual that he followed almost every day. After breakfast he would get his broom and go up and down the main street of the Golden Heights Centro whistling and singing and sweeping the sidewalks for all the businesses. He would sweep in front of the Tortillería America, the XXX Liquor Store, the Tres Milpas Bar run by Tino Gabaldon, Barelas' Barber Shop, the used furniture store owned by Goldstein, El Centro Market of the Avila family, the Model Cities Office, and Lourdes Printing Store. Then, in the afternoons, he would come back and sit in Barelas' Barber Shop and spend the day looking at magazines and watching and waving to the passing people as he sang and composed his songs without a care in the world.

When business was slow, Barelas would let him sit in the barber's chair. Romero loved it. It was a routine that Romero kept every day except Sundays and Mondays when Barelas' Barber Shop was closed. After a period of years, people in the barrio got used to seeing Romero do his little task of sweeping the sidewalks and sitting in Barelas' Barber Shop. If he didn't show up one day someone assumed the responsibility to go to his house to see if he was ill. People would stop to say hello to Romero on the street and although he never initiated a conversation while he was sober, he always smiled and responded cheerfully to everyone. People passing the barber shop in the afternoons made it a point to wave even though they couldn't see him; they knew he was in there and was expecting some salutation.

When he was feeling real good, Romero would sweep in front of the houses on both sides of the block also. He took his job seriously and took great care to sweep cleanly, between the cracks and even between the sides of buildings. The dirt and small scraps went into the gutter. The bottles and bigger pieces of litter were put carefully in cardboard boxes, ready for the garbage man.

If he did it the way he wanted, the work took him the whole morning. And always cheerful—always with some song.

Only once did someone call attention to his work. Frank Avila told him in jest that Romero had forgotten to pick up an empty bottle of wine from his door. Romero was so offended and made such a commotion that it got around very quickly that no one should criticize his work. There was, in fact, no reason to.

Although it had been long acknowledged that Romero was a little "touched," he fit very well into the community. He was a respected citizen.

He could be found at the Tres Milpas Bar drinking his occasional beer in the evenings. Romero had a rivalry going with the Ranchera songs on the jukebox. He would try to outsing the songs using the same melody but inserting his own selection of random words. Sometimes, like all people, he would "bust out" and get drunk.

One could always tell when Romero was getting drunk because he would begin telling everyone that he loved them.

"I looov youuu," he would sing to someone and offer to compose them a song.

"Ta bueno, Romero. Ta bueno, ya bete," they would tell him.

Sometimes when he got too drunk he would crap in his pants and then Tino would make him go home.

Romero received some money from Social Security but it wasn't much. None of the merchants gave him any credit because he would always forget to pay his bills. He didn't do it on purpose, he just forgot and spent his money on something else. So instead, the businessmen preferred to do little things for him occasionally. Barelas would trim his hair when things were slow. The Tortillería America would give him menudo and fresh-made tortillas at noon when he was finished with his sweeping. El Centro Market would give him the overripe fruit and broken boxes of food that no one else would buy. Although it was unspoken and unwritten, there was an agreement that existed between Romero and the Golden Heights Centro. Romero kept the sidewalks clean and the barrio looked after him. It was a contract that worked well for a long time.

Then, when Seferino, Barelas' oldest son, graduated from high school he went to work in the barber shop for the summer. Seferino was a conscientious and sensitive young man and it wasn't long before he took notice of Romero and came to feel sorry for him.

One day when Romero was in the shop Seferino decided to act.

"Mira, Romero. Yo te doy 50 centavos por cada dia que me barres la banqueta. Fifty cents for every day you sweep the sidewalk for us. Qúe te parece?"

Romero thought about it carefully.

"Hecho! Done!" he exclaimed. He started for home right away to get his broom.

"Why did you do that for, m'ijo?" asked Barelas.

"It don't seem right, Dad. The man works and no one pays him for his work. Everyone should get paid for what they do."

"He don't need no pay. Romero has everything he needs."

"It's not the same, Dad. How would you like to do what he does and be treated the same way? It's degrading the way he has to go around getting scraps and handouts."

"I'm not Romero. Besides you don't know about these things, m'ijo. Romero would be unhappy if his schedule was upset. Right now everyone likes him and takes care of him. He sweeps the sidewalks because he wants something to do, not because he wants money."

"I'll pay him out of my money, don't worry about it then."

"The money is not the point. The point is that money will not help Romero. Don't you understand that?"

"Look, Dad. Just put yourself in his place. Would you do it? Would you cut hair for nothing?"

Barelas just knew his son was putting something over on him but he didn't know how to answer. It seemed to make sense the way Seferino explained it. But it still went against his "instinct." On the other hand, Seferino had gone and finished high school. He must know something. There were few kids who had finished high school in the barrio, and fewer who had gone to college. Barelas knew them all. He noted (with some pride) that Seferino was going to be enrolled at Harvard University this year. That must count for something, he thought. Barelas himself had never gone to school. So maybe his son had something there. On the other hand . . . it upset Barelas that he wasn't able to get Seferino to see the issue. How can we be so far apart on something so simple, he thought. But he decided not to say anything else about it.

Romero came back right away and swept the front of Barelas' shop again and put what little dirt he found into the curb. He swept up the gutter, put the trash in a shoe box and threw it in a garbage can.

Seferino watched with pride as Romero went about his job and when he was finished he went outside and shook Romero's hand. Seferino told him he had done a good job. Romero beamed.

Manolo was coming into the shop to get his hair cut as Seferino was giving Romero his wages. He noticed Romero with his broom.

"What's going on?" He asked. Barelas shrugged his shoulders. "Qué tiene Romero? Is he sick or something?"

"No, he's not sick," explained Seferino, who had now come inside. He told Manolo the story.

"We're going to make Romero a businessman" said Seferino. "Do you realize how much money Romero would make if everyone paid him just fifty cents a day? Like my dad says, 'Everyone should be able to keep his dignity, no matter how poor.' And he does a job, you know."

"Well, it makes sense," said Manolo.

"Hey. Maybe I'll ask people to do that," said Seferino. "That way the poor old man could make a decent wage. Do you want to help, Manolo? You can go with me to ask people to pay him."

"Well," said Manolo as he glanced at Barelas, "I'm not too good at asking people for money."

This did not discourage Seferino. He went out and contacted all the businesses on his own, but no one else wanted to contribute. This didn't discourage Seferino either. He went on giving Romero fifty cents a day.

After a while, Seferino heard that Romero had asked for credit at the grocery store. "See, Dad. What did I tell you? Things are getting better for him already. He's becoming his own man. And look. It's only been a couple of weeks." Barelas did not reply.

But then the next week Romero did not show up to sweep any sidewalks. He was around but he didn't do any work for anybody the entire week. He walked around Golden Heights Centro in his best gray work pants and his slouch hat, looking important and making it a point to walk right past the barber shop every little while.

Of course, the people in the Golden Heights Centro noticed the change immediately, and since they saw Romero in the street, they knew he wasn't ill. But the change was clearly disturbing the community. They discussed him in the Tortillería America where people got together for coffee, and at the Tres Milpas Bar. Everywhere the topic of conversation was the great change that had come over Romero. Only Barelas did not talk about it.

The following week Romero came into the barber shop and asked to talk with Seferino in private. Barelas knew immediately something was wrong. Romero never initiated a conversation unless he was drunk.

They went into the back room where Barelas could not hear and then Romero informed Seferino, "I want a raise."

"What? What do you mean, a raise? You haven't been around for a week. You only worked a few weeks and now you want a raise?" Seferino was clearly angry but Romero was calm and insistent.

Romero correctly pointed out that he had been sweeping the sidewalks for a long time. Even before Seferino finished high school.

"I deserve a raise," he repeated after an eloquent presentation.

Seferino looked coldly at Romero. It was clearly a stand-off.

Then Seferino said, "Look, maybe we should forget the whole thing. I was just trying to help you out and look at what you do."

Romero held his ground. "I helped you out too. No one told me to do it and I did it anyway. I helped you many years."

"Well, let's forget about the whole thing then," said Seferino.

"I quit then," said Romero.

"Quit?" exclaimed Seferino as he laughed at Romero.

"Quit! I quit!" said Romero as he walked out the front of the shop past Barelas who was cutting a customer's hair.

Seferino came out shaking his head and laughing.

"Can you imagine that old guy?"

Barelas did not seem too amused. He felt he could have predicted that something bad like this would happen.

Romero began sweeping the sidewalks again the next day with the exception that when he came to the barber shop he would go around it and continue sweeping the rest of the sidewalks. He did this for the rest of the week. And the following Tuesday he began sweeping the sidewalk all the way up to the shop and then pushing the trash to the sidewalk in front of the barber shop. Romero then stopped coming to the barber shop in the afternoon.

The barrio buzzed with fact and rumor about Romero. Tino commented that Romero was not singing anymore. Even if someone offered to buy him a beer he wouldn't sing. Frank Avila said the neighbors were complaining because he was leaving his TV on loud the whole day and night. He still greeted people but seldom smiled. He had run up a big bill at the liquor store and when the manager stopped his credit, he caught Romero stealing bottles of whiskey. He was also getting careless about his dress. He didn't shave and clean like he used to. Women complained that he walked around in soiled pants, that he smelled bad. Even one of the little kids complained that Romero had kicked his puppy, but that seemed hard to believe.

Barelas felt terrible. He felt responsible. But he couldn't convince Seferino that what he had done was wrong. Barelas himself stopped going to the Tres Milpas Bar after work to avoid hearing about Romero. Once he came across Romero on the street and Barelas said hello but with a sense of guilt. Romero responded, avoiding Barelas' eyes and moving past him awkwardly and quickly. Romero's behavior continued to get erratic and some people started talking about having Romero committed.

"You can't do that," said Barelas when he was presented with a petition.

"He's flipped," said Tino, who made up part of the delegation circulating the petition. "No one likes Romero more than I do, you know that Barelas."

"But he's really crazy," said Frank Avila.

"He was crazy before. No one noticed," pleaded Barelas.

"But it was a crazy we could depend on. Now he just wants to sit on the curb and pull up the women's skirts. It's terrible. The women are going crazy. He's also running into the street stopping the traffic. You see how he is. What choice do we have?"

"It's for his own good," put in one of the workers from the Model Cities Office. Barelas dismissed them as outsiders. Seferino was there and wanted to say something but a look from Barelas stopped him.

"We just can't do that," insisted Barelas. "Let's wait. Maybe he's just going through a cycle. Look. We've had a full moon recently, qué no? That must be it. You know how the moon affects people in his condition."

"I don't know," said Tino. "What if he hurts . . . ."

"He's not going to hurt anyone," cut in Barelas.

"No, Barelas. I was going to say, what if he hurts himself. He has no one at home. I'd say, let him come home with me for a while but you know how stubborn he is. You can't even talk to him any more."

"He gives everyone the finger when they try to pull him out of the traffic," said Frank Avila. "The cops have missed him, but it won't be long before they see him doing some of his antics and arrest him. Then what? Then the poor guy is in real trouble."

"Well, look," said Barelas. "How many names you got on the list?"

Tino responded slowly, "Well, we sort of wanted you to start off the list."

"Let's wait a while longer," said Barelas. "I just know that Romero will come around. Let's wait just a while, okay?"

No one had the heart to fight the issue and so they postponed the petition.

There was no dramatic change in Romero even though the full moon had completed its cycle. Still, no one initiated the petition again and then in the middle of August Seferino left for Cambridge to look for housing and to register early for school. Suddenly everything began to change again. One day Romero began sweeping the entire sidewalk again. His spirits began to pick up and his strange antics began to disappear.

At the Tortillería America the original committee met for coffee and the talk turned to Romero.

"He's going to be all right now," said a jubilant Barelas. "I guarantee it."

"Well, don't hold your breath yet," said Tino. "The full moon is coming up again."

"Yeah," said Frank Avila dejectedly.

When the next full moon was in force the group was together again drinking coffee and Tino asked, "Well, how's Romero doing?"

Barelas smiled and said, "Well. Singing songs like crazy."

Sterile Relationships

Kathleen M. Baca

"Do you do this often?" she asked. Russell shrugged. "My God, you're twenty-five years old. You know it's only going to get worse?" Norma took a deep breath. "I suppose you also watch dirty movies and stand around magazine racks staring at pictures of nude women?" He nodded. Norma picked up a hose that was coiled near the orangutan cages and gave it a good hard pull before turning on the water. She motioned for her son to move out of the way before she aimed the water at the semen on the cement slab. Wally, the orangutan, slapped at the water as it splashed up into his cage.

Russell stepped back and shook the water off his sneakers. His hairy ankles made Norma cringe. "Why aren't you wearing socks?" she demanded.

"I hate socks," he said. He lifted up his pant leg and wiggled his foot in front of her.

"You hate socks, you like apes; God knows I've tried, Russell." She looked at his soiled tennis shoes, green army pants, and oversized sweatshirt and took a deep breath. It hadn't been easy for her to raise a son. He had been difficult to potty train, and in spite of all her efforts to teach him otherwise, he continued to pee standing up. "It's uncomfortable for a man to sit and pee," he told her. "It's unnatural for a woman to constantly be wiping piss off the back of a toilet seat," she argued. Still, he persisted in leaving his mark on the uplifted seat. This convinced her that he was a victim of the very organ that made him stand at attention when he urinated. Norma was certain the penis ruled the man, and because it was a proud organ, it refused to hang limply between his legs while he relieved himself. That was the theory she explained over and over again to the mothers of the little girls Russell had exposed himself to. "I can cure him," she assured them.

Now as she rinsed off the slab, she doubted her abilities. She had a feeling Russell was at the zoo when she entered the ladies' room and saw urine splattered on an uplifted seat. But she dismissed the idea when she saw a young mother washing her little boy's hands. Her first reaction was

27

to run up to the woman and tell her it was useless to try and change him. Instead, she said, "Pray, honey, that his stays small." She had just finished drying off her hands and was about to begin her rounds at the Mead Town Zoo where she was head keeper, when a frantic call came over the walkie talkie that a pervert was jacking off in the ape building. She patted the woman sympathetically on the back. As Norma neared the building she could hear the high pitched screams of the orangs mixed in with the sounds of laughter and cries of outrage. She unsnapped the billy club which hung haphazardly from a thick leather belt around her waist and smiled wickedly as she fondled the club. This wasn't the first time she had encountered a man who enjoyed performing for an audience. When she jerked open the door the smell of apes and fresh sperm made ner nauseous.

"Ok, you," she said. "Come with me." She reached out and grabbed the young man by the collar. Russell turned and smiled. "Oh my God!" she cried. Her son's deflated penis hung apologetically out of his unzipped pants.

"Mom!" Russell pulled out his shirt tails to cover himself.

"Put that thing back in your pants!" she said.

"Norma, Norma," hissed a voice over the giraffe-shaped walkie talkie, a gift commemorating ten years of service, "did you catch the pervie? What's he look like?"

Disgustedly she turned her back on her son who was fumbling with his pants and spoke sternly into the box. "I said I'll take care of this," she snapped. She pushed in the antenna cutting off the voice at the other end and shoved the plastic giraffe into her back pocket. It's black pin-head eyes seemed to be laughing at Russell as it swayed back and forth with each step Norma took.

"Oh, Russell," she said softly.

"Mom, I."

Norma interrupted. "God, how you must suffer. Look what it has you doing." Russell glanced down at his crotch. "Now don't you wish it hadn't grown so big?"

Russell sighed. "I know. I can't explain it. It's as if I'm being pulled by something I have no control over, and the bigger it gets, the stronger it gets."

He wondered if Norma knew that he had read most of her notes on REPIT. Ever since she had caught his father and her sister stuck together like two prison escapees on an electrical fence, she had become interested in the sexual behavior of men. A year later she developed what she called the Ronald Evertt Penile Independence Theory. REPIT, she bragged, would someday make her more notable than Freud. Her theory that a man had no control over his organ, once it became erect, delighted him. He relished in telling his dates that he was the son of a sex therapist, whose findings, once published, would prove that men were victims of their "masculinity" rather than insensitive creatures who indulged in sex purely for self-gratification. If his date seemed to be believing what he was saying, he would lie back and a sigh would escape his slightly parted lips. Then, slowly, he would unzip his pants.

"Look at this," he would say, nodding toward his penis. "It's disgusting the way it leaps up at you. Vicious, that's what it is." He would stop at this point and look at his date. He had used these lines several times and knew by the expression on the woman's face if he should continue. The next three lines were his favorite.

"God, why was I saddled with this thing? I wish I could just lie here and watch TV or go get something to eat, but 'IT' won't let me. You have no idea what it's like to be a man." With that remark, he would motion for the woman to remove her underwear.

That was his favorite fantasy and the one he had been thinking about fulfilling when he went to the zoo. He thought about going back to the women's restroom to relieve himself, but he liked the idea of an audience. When the women around him began screaming, so did he. He tightened the grip around his penis and as he rhythmically built up momentum, he imagined that he was making love to his first grade teacher, Miss Welch, who let him stay after school with her to erase the blackboards.

But now he had to face his mother, a woman who kept a journal with over three hundred names in it of men she used in her experiments. After reading it, he thought of Mrs. Mitchell, a neighbor who had once called him and his mother sexual perverts. He wanted to xerox the page with her husband's name on it and mail it to her, but instead he telephoned her and asked for Mr. Mitchell. When he came to the phone, he asked him how Ralphy was. Mr. Mitchell didn't respond. Russell had burst out laughing. Alex Mitchell's name was starred twice in Norma's book because he called his penis by name. Under the letter M, in small print, she had written: "Alex Mitchell, age 37, father of three. Says he loves his wife and wants to be a devoted husband but can't control REPIT. Calls his penis Ralphy." The fact that many men had a name for their organ was an important part of Norma's theory.

Russell watched in silence as his mother ushered people out of the building. She was attractive but stocky, like a wrestler. Her green catlike eyes were outlined by thick dark eyelashes and eyebrows. Her curly black hair was beginning to streak with age. One curl was completely white and hung down the front of her forehead. This pleased her because she thought it made her look distinguished. She told Russell that when she became famous and appeared on The Johnny Carson Show, or gave an interview to *Time* magazine, she would look more credible. "People respect you," she'd say, "if you have white hair. It's a fact."

For a moment he felt a twinge of guilt. Norma believed in REPIT. It was the only way she could justify sleeping with other women's husbands. She was obsessed with the male organ and how it functioned. Russell looked down at his untied sneakers. Norma turned and smiled at her offspring. She loved him, and she wanted to free him from the disease that had consumed her own life since the day she caught her husband with her sister.

"Russell," she said. "I want you to see a therapist." She pointed at his untied shoes. He bent down to tie them. "If you don't see someone I'll turn you in to the authorities."

He straightened up. "C'mon ma, you're kidding right?" Norma shook her head. "You know damn good and well that there is no cure for me. You've said it yourself, I'm cursed to be a victim of my organ."

"That's beside the point. Do you know where you'd be this very second if I hadn't been the one on duty?" Russell held his hands up to his face, spread his fingers, and pretended to be peering out from behind bars. "Be serious, Russell. Jail is no fun. They make you sleep on narrow beds and feed you instant food."

"I don't care, I'm not seeing a therapist. You're a therapist, you help me! You even took in a guy who liked flashing mannequins last year, remember? And I'm your son!"

Norma hesitated. "I know that, but I just finished with the married men of Crest and Cedar Street, and already the men from Elm have been calling to set up appointments. I just don't have the time." Russell looked away. "Beside you look too much like your father. It would feel weird to me."

"Well, I'm not Dad, and I won't see anyone. I don't trust someone who makes a living off of other people's problems." His eyes shifted from the orangutans back to Norma. "Anyway, I think there's something perverted about a person who encourages one-sided relationships."

"Oh, and I suppose you and Wally shared something here today?" The orangutan curled up its bottom lip and flicked its head from side to side. "Damn it, Russell, I'm not talking about going to confession. I'm talking about seeing a trained professional, a social servant like myself."

"Social servant? Really, Mom. Do you know how much some of those servants make a year?" A man and a woman stopped to watch Wally swing back and forth on an old tire. Russell was certain they had been eavesdropping. When they turned to leave he moved his hips suggestively behind the woman and winked at the man. Norma slapped him on the back. She smiled apologetically at the couple. The man put his arm around the woman and hurried her away.

"That's it, Russell. You're seeing someone. I don't care how much they make a year."

"What if they strap me to a couch until I scream out that I'm suffering from an ediface complex. You know what that is, don't you?"

Norma wiped her hands on the front of her brown trousers. She looked to him like the victor who had just left her opponent for dead.

"Of course I know what that means," she said, "and it's Oedipus, not ediface." She opened the door and waved for him to follow her. He stuck his tongue out at Wally who lay on his back playing with his toes.

The receptionist greeted him with a warm smile. "I'm here to see Dr. Tamask," he said. She nodded and flipped through an appointment book.

"Russell Evertt?" she asked without looking up.

"That's right," he said.

"You're early, have a seat. She'll be with you shortly."

He took a seat near the gurgling aquarium. Doctors certainly like fish, he thought. They must remind them that they work with living specimens. He wondered if doctors had aquariums in their homes. A large orange fish with black stripes on its tail pressed its face against the glass and opened and closed its mouth. A smaller fish swam above it and shit. Russell reached for a magazine and noticed that his new shoes had been splattered with mud. He licked the tips of his fingers and wiped it off. He stretched out his legs as far as they would go and tried to catch the reflection of the aquarium light on the tips of his shoes.

He was embarrassed he had come so early. This was his twelfth session. He rather enjoyed talking about himself. His favorite session had been when he told her how his father died. "He slipped on a pair of panties," he said matter of factly. It had amused him to watch Dr. Tamask's eyes widen in disbelief. He found her attractive, despite the fact that she never changed the tone of her voice or her perpetual look of concern; except when he told her about his father. Norma had told him that his father's death was caused by a pair of panties tossed carelessly on the floor in a moment of passion. She had come home early one afternoon, she said, and found his father in bed with her sister. Ronald Evertt had jumped out of bed, slipped on the underwear and hit his head on the side of the bed. The impact had killed him instantly. His father had never respected his marriage vows. As a child Russell often came home from school to find his father entertaining in bed. He never told Dr. Tamask about that.

He liked Lillian Tamask. A few weeks earlier he had asked her for her phone number; she wasn't listed in the book, he had already checked. He told her he needed it in case an emotional emergency should arise. That night when he called her number a voice on the other end told him to leave his name and number and the doctor would get right back to him. "Just tell her I'm going to kill myself," he said. He kept the phone off the hook just long enough to hear the woman at the other end frantically pleading with him to tell her who he was. It was her loss, he thought, as he ran his fingers through his hair. Obviously, she doesn't know I'm hung like my father. Suddenly he realized his penis had become hard. He looked at the receptionist before picking up a magazine and laying it across his lap. He blamed his father for his sexual prowess.

A woman seated across the room looked at him as she turned a page in the magazine she was reading. Russell stiffened. He hadn't been aware of the other people in the room. He studied every face for signs that someone knew what he was hiding under the magazine. But no one seemed to suspect as he stood up, still keeping the magazine in front of him, and walked up to the receptionist. "Oh, excuse me," he said politely, "is there a bathroom I can use?" She pointed down the hall. "Thank you," he said. As he walked toward the bathroom, he held the magazine at his side; he could feel every eye on him.

The bathroom was a pinkish-orange color, the same color of the petitions that periodically were circulated in his neighborhood. Each petition, neatly typed, was signed by the "Concerned Parents of Film Street," and suggested that Russell and his mother find another place to live. Norma never took the petitions seriously. Instead she'd ask to meet with the committee, because she wanted to educate women on the seriousness of the disease which afflicted the male population. She had devoted the last fifteen years of her life to this illness. In fact, most of the men who accompanied their wives to these meetings had sought a cure from Norma. Russell remembered that when the concerned fathers of Crest Street saw Norma approaching the podium with her notes, several left, while others developed an uncontrollable cough. It was the men of Crest Street that finally coerced their wives into forgetting about him and his mother.

Dr. Tamask was waiting for him when he returned. She smiled and told him to go on in her office. Her perfume made him uncomfortable.

The inside of her office smelled of books and leather; he thought it belonged on the cover of *Offices Today*. There was a couch in her office, but he refused to lie on it. He was afraid it was rigged with electrodes or something that would shock him into impotency. I'm only here, he thought, because my mother promised to turn me in if I didn't come. Before seating himself, he brushed off his pants. The tops of his socks were visible when he sat down. Russell pretended not to notice that Dr. Tamask had taken her place across from him. He watched out the corner of his eye as she took out a legal size pad and a pen. She never spoke first. She was a Freudian therapist, but he wasn't in the mood for any psychoanalytical crap. He would wait until she spoke.

"How was your week?"

"Fine."

"Do you want to talk about what you did?"

He shrugged. There was an uneasy feeling in the pit of his stomach. Dr. Tamask looked away from him for a moment. "I sense some hostility in you." He rolled his eyes. "Is something making you uncomfortable?"

Russell folded his arms across his belly. He smiled at her. Neither one spoke. He enjoyed the silence. There had always been silence in his home when he had done something wrong. Norma would seat herself across from him and wait for him to tell her what he had done wrong. It seemed to him that he was always in trouble. He would refuse to volunteer any information that could result in his being punished. Sometimes he and Norma sat and stared at each other for hours. Finally he'd make something up.

He glanced at the digital clock on the desk. Bitch, he thought. She makes seventy dollars an hour and she watches the clock. He felt like telling her to buy one of those stick-them-anywhere clocks and attach it to her note pad so that her concern would seem more genuine. He remembered the time he had come home early from third grade and Mr. Burrows was pulling out of the driveway. He had turned and smiled at Russell. Norma was in the study writing in her journal. He tapped lightly on the door. "I'm sick," he said. She looked up, nodded, and wrote something in her journal. "Mom, I said I'm sick." She held up a hand to silence him. Then she put down her book, grabbed him by the hand and pulled him into the kitchen. She handed him an orange, an aspirin, and a glass of water before disappearing back into her study. His cold had lasted two weeks.

"Russell," Dr. Tamask's voice broke through his thoughts. "Can you tell me what you're thinking about?"

"You think I'm a pervert, don't you?"

"What do you mean?"

"I'm not stupid. I know that's why you gave me the number to your answering service and not your home."

Dr. Tamask thought for a moment. "What if I had answered the phone? What then?"

"You probably would have found out what a nice guy I am, and we'd be somewhere else right now."

"Russell, what you're feeling for me is natural, and your feelings for me may change from week to week. It's okay, we can talk about those feelings in here. Am I making sense?" She tilted her head to one side and the stale look of concern that crept over her face made him angry. He bit his lip.

"You didn't like what I said, did you?" Her voice resounded in his ears.

"Jesus," he said. "I can't believe you. You're acting like I asked you to have my children." Like his mother, he too had developed theories. He had suspected that therapists were a miserable lot whose own feelings of inadequacy made them dependent on the admiration of the poor souls who turned them into numina and their offices into sanctum sanctorums. Those destitute souls gave them a hefty bank account and a meaningful occupation they could talk about at cocktail parties.

"I bet you think you're a real social servant, huh?" He strained to see what Dr. Tamask had just underlined three times. Why hadn't he worn his glasses? It had to be the word pervert, he just knew it. His new shoes were beginning to hurt his feet, and he was beginning to dislike Dr. Tamask. Who in the hell does she think she is, anyway, he thought. She didn't know why he liked jerking off in public places, any more than she knew why she wrote down bits and pieces of his life. She was seducing him, and they had never touched. He looked away from her long slender legs.

"Do you know why I jacked-off at the zoo?" He leaned forward. "Because I like the way it smells. It smells good to me." His voice was getting louder. "It smells real." Maybe that was why he had done it. The realization of that made him feel better about himself.

He pointed at the therpist's note pad. "You know my mother keeps notes on all the men she sleeps with because she wants to find a cure for a disease she's invented. And you? You keep files on all the men and women you seduce into participating in a sterile relationship. Hell, I'm not the one who is sick."

Russell stood up. Every muscle in his body was tense. "This damn office," he said, "is as sterile as my mother's bedroom." He made a fist and contemplated knocking the pad out of her hands; instead he walked toward the door. In a half-hour it would be feeding time at the zoo.

The Manuscript

Bruce-Novoa

The package arrived by registered mail Monday morning. Immediately the handwriting identified the sender as Robert Olma, a good friend and fellow author who for some time now has formed part of the circle of writers who gather at my home every Thursday night to read, listen to each other's work, and then talk into early Friday about literature, art, women or any other subject. It seemed unusual for Robert to have sent a registered package when he could have dropped it off anytime; but as it's my custom to write all morning without allowing interruptions, I placed the manila envelope on the hall table and returned to my desk in the library.

Words began to fill a page, but the unopened envelope distracted my mind, necessitating several pauses to scratch out phrases that were not developing as I wanted. Why had Robert sent what was obviously a manuscript without so much as a call or a mention of it Friday? I tried to write again, but instead began to recall the last few months in which our constant theme had been the relationship of literature to life, or so-called reality, and Robert's intense interest in the endless discussions, his almost disturbing habit of returning to the subject even after the conversation had decidedly swayed towards other topics, and the way he had drawn even nearer to me. Of all those who agreed with him, I was the closest to his own position and maybe even more extreme. It must have all begun when Robert mentioned that he had been rereading Borges.

Robert had come to the United States from Mexico, originally on a Ford Foundation grant, and had managed to stay on with the small income from his publishing in Latin America and his teaching of literature and creative writing at the university, finally achieving financial stability with the help of his wealthy wife. Maybe our common heritage drew us together; although many people around him spoke Spanish besides myself, they weren't Mexican, nor had they read the authors Latin Americans consider important. We had spent hours discussing Borges, Cortázar, García Márquez, and others when we first met, but gradually the interests of the larger part of the group, mostly devotees of French or German literature, dominated the conversations. Only some three months ago had Robert said he was reading Borges. I responded that I had just read García Ponce, a Mexican author intensely involved in creating alternate reality in literature, similar to Borges but tending more to themes of love. This interested him, and though he didn't speak of either writer again for some weeks, several times he arrived at our meetings with their books in hand. About a month or so later the relationship of literature to life dominated the Thursday evening meeting.

"What fascinates me most," Robert explained, "is Borges' creation of the Aleph, that point where all reality is concentrated at once, independent of contingency. What a marvelous tool for retrieving whatever time or error has deprived us of!"

"Like what?" asked one of the group.

"Anything. Youth, happiness, lost opportunities," he responded, staring at his cognac as if searching for an awaited apparition, then laughingly added, "women, or yesterday's price of filet."

"Ah," I interposed, "but Borges only retrieves a few obscene letters and Beatriz's dried bones from the Aleph. Not exactly a desirable image to perpetuate eternally, Robert."

"That's not the point. The Aleph is only a metaphor for literature itself. It's not to be found, but created, and then you don't extract images, but take them there; and if Borges cares to laugh at himself and his women that's his affair. Argentines are strange that way. No. But your Ponce, he clearly understands literature as a world apart, where whatever is created goes on endlessly reflecting an independent reality in itself and projecting even upon life, in life, opening a new space in the fabric of reality."

"Literature is the reflection of life," interrupted Kollins, a dull Spanish professor someone had invited once and who had now hung on past his welcome, "not the opposite," he concluded with a self-satisfied grin and a glance around the room where he expected to meet approving eyes. Most, however, were trying to find some point in the large study on which to concentrate the embarrassment that each of his pompous clichés spread over the conversation, embarrassment compounded by the fact that no one accepted the blame for having invited him the first time, and all shared it equally for not having already thrown him out.

"Don't be such an ass," Robert cut him off, and I suppose this uncharacteristic discourteousness, coupled with the unusual and consciously well-aimed vulgarity—Robert always reverted to Spanish for such expressions, adding injury to insult by addressing himself in English to this so-called Spanish teacher—should have alerted me: the subject was more than just a passing interest.

"What a man *is* means little compared to what he is said to be in writing. History, truth is determined by the best writer, or in the present day, by the one lucky enough to combine a pleasant style, an intelligent editor, and a name publisher. It's all fiction, just fiction."

"Absolutely, Robert," I agreed. "The past is a fiction. I don't much care for the *just* but definitely a fiction by the best authors regardless of the realities, at least after those realities have disappeared. And the present? A neutral zone up for grabs, gentlemen."

The conversation drifted into examples of countless heroes, wars, and movie idols, expanding the topic globally as we vengefully buried Kollins under the weight of his unacceptable presence.

The following meetings found us examining the issue from all angles. Liberated now of Kollins, who forced everyone to side against him on any point, the group broke up into those who actually assumed Kollins' position, some who agreed with Robert in theory, but whose tone revealed the weightless quality the idea had in the balance of their thought, and finally Robert and me, both of us insisting on the idea's almost exceptionless truth. After all, we two were the only ones dedicated solely to the writing of fiction, staking our existence on the ability of well-constructed lies to open a crack in the smooth surface of contingency, widen a space large enough to expand the logic of their premise into a closed, self-supporting structure, indistinguishable, except in the intensity of its will to survive, from the surrounding surface.

I don't remember at what point the memory of those conversations forced me back out to the hall to where the envelope waited unopened. I stared at my name and address in Robert's unmistakable handwriting on the otherwise blank surface. The weight revealed more than the unyielding color—more than a short story, maybe the novel to which Robert had once vaguely alluded.

I poured my first drink of the day, took a sip, then passed the letter opener through the end of the envelope.

"Querido amigo," the letter began, but before reading any further, I laid it aside to see the manuscript. Even with a friend, my belief that the work is more important than the author dominated my actions. It surprised me to find not a novel nor even a collection of short stories, but a diary: *El diario de Roberto Olma N.* I scanned a few pages, slowed to the rhythm of the prose, then settled to a concentrated pace, finding the writing disturbingly but pleasantly normal, with none of the flourish of style nor characteristic undermining irony that distinguishes Robert's fiction. The diary began with his university years, moving smoothly though his first attempts at writing, his success, his break with his family who expected more from a supposedly intelligent son, his winning of the Ford grant and his first years in the U.S., his romance with one of his students and the beginning of their life together . . . .

It was all too well-written to be wasted on a diary, clearly the best piece he had produced. All excesses had been pruned completely or subtly reduced to a perfect balance of style and content.

I had read over half of the manuscript before pausing, though still not to read the letter, to pour another drink. Back at my desk I picked it up:

> Dear friend:
> Whether or not this manuscript ought to be published, I leave to you. You know most of the people in it. But if you have it published, I'd rather it didn't have an introduction.
> I exist now in a most unhappy happiness. But strangely without remorse. I only feel sorry for those who had me as husband, father, son.
> Last I leave this manuscript to you feeling that you knew me better than anyone else (the skin of this cosmopolitan me stripped away).
> Roberto Olma N.

Immediately I recognized the letter as Akutagawa's preface to *A Fool's Life,* his literary suicide note. The manuscript, the registered mail, the total circumstance focused as if each been a scarce degree out of phase, needing only this simple turn to clear the haze, revealing the delicate outline of a deadly image.

The phone rang only twice before an unfamiliar voice answered, and in reply to my questions, responded quite unemotionally.

"Yes, Sir, this morning. Mrs. Olma found him in the study . . . . Yes, veronal or something similar . . . . would you care to speak to her?"

"Yes."

Anne's voice was only slightly less controlled, though the tautness of it seemed to convey a lack of firm ground beneath her, as if she were suspended over a sudden void, but was determined not to fall into or even acknowledge it. She confirmed the type of poison and asked if it was the same as Akutagawa had taken. Her awareness of Roberto's predilections surprised me and almost moved me to an indiscreet expression of sympathy; but I only answered, "yes." I didn't mention the manuscript, not caring to risk any abrupt change in the balance of her precarious perch over the new, unfathomed absence. It wasn't apparent which words would strengthen her hold and which would threaten it; in truth I had always been neutral in regard to her (though I suppose I could be accused of siding with Roberto), never moving beyond the expected etiquette of polite greetings and trivial cocktail conversation at first. Then later, of course, I hadn't seen her at all. I muttered a last "yes" to a question or an affirmation I no longer recall, or perhaps never really heard, and hung up.

My drink was warm and tasteless. I reread the letter and then took up the manuscript, beginning anew, moving once more through the university years, the first attempts at writing, the break with a family that expected more from an intelligent son, the winning of the Ford grant and the first years in the U.S., the romance with a student and their life together until the break with society. In these last two sections there was the beginning of a subtle change in tone, a barely discernible concentration of vision, a gradual heightening of intensity, accompanied by a paradoxical dispersal of definition, and finally brief lapses into poetry within the prose, taking me back to see that the change had actually begun much earlier, but only in isolated words, even sound clusters in the beginning, expanding slowly at measured intervals to occupy more and more space in a rhythmic take over until the genre metamorphosed plainly into the poetic; and it coincided with the appearance of love almost in a perturbingly too polished, too delicately interlaced manner, but the motion of the words avoided the feeling of planned structure. Their life together was a poem in content as well as form, its essence a free-floating openness suspended in the neutral space where a plurality of possibilities vies for attention, keeping the love ever moving, changing, allowing each free motion, separately or together as they, the moment, or the circumstance suggested, sometimes forming dual configurations, at others a single profile or even a total absence of form expressed in the presence of the absence of definition; and always, whatever form it took, the figure was found at the margins of the social, refusing to allow itself to become part of any movement other than that of the tensions exerted by their own relationship, one to the other. The image would split, multiply, and vary, as if kaleidoscoped in space, multifaceted and toned, but always revolving around an invisible center, underscoring the free spontaneous movement whose lines of relationship formed the fluid center.

The reading left me exhausted but quite excited, sure that the book would be an artistic success, if only on a small scale; definitely not a best seller, it was too good for that, but a solid contribution to the finest in

Latin American literature; and I would have the privilege of making it a reality: an elegant format, quality paper, maybe the photograph of Roberto and Margarita I had taken on the boat, and another at the cabin, perfect visual companions to the verbal description of their love, a facsimile of the handwritten first page, all in keeping with the essential truth of a sublimely achieved autobiography.

El Patrón

Nash Candelaria

My father-in-law's hierarchy is, in descending order: Dios, El Papa, y el patrón. It is to these that mere mortals bow, as in turn el patrón bows to El Papa, and El Papa bows to Dios.

God and the Pope are understandable enough. It's this el patrón, the boss, who causes most of our trouble. Whether it's the one who gives you work and for it pay, the lifeblood of hardworking little people—or others: Our parents (fathers affectionately known as jefe, mothers known merely as mama, military commanders el capitán), or any of the big shots in the government el alcalde, el gobernador, el presidente and never forget la policía).

It was about some such el patrón trouble that Señor Martínez boarded the bus in San Diego and headed north toward L.A.—and us.

Since I was lecturing to a midafternoon summer school class at Southwestern U., my wife, Lola, picked up her father at the station. When I arrived home, they were sitting politely in the living room talking banalities: "Yes, it does look like rain. But if it doesn't rain, it might be sunny. If only the clouds would blow away."

Lola had that dangerous look on her face that usually made me start talking too fast and too long in hope of shifting her focus. It never worked. She'd sit there with a face like a brown-skinned kewpie doll whose expression was slowly turning into that of an angry maniac. When she could no longer stand it, she'd give her father a blast: "You never talk to me about anything important, you macho, chauvinist jumping bean!" Then it would escalate to nastiness from there.

But tonight it didn't get that far. As I entered Señor Martínez rose, dressed neatly in his one suit as for a wedding or a funeral, and politely shook my hand. Without so much as a glance at Lola, he said, "Why don't you go to the kitchen with the other women."

"There are no other women," Lola said coldly. She stood and belligerently received my kiss on the cheek before leaving.

41

Señor Martínez was oblivious to her reaction, sensing only the absence of "woman," at which he visibly relaxed and sat down.

"Rosca," he said, referring to me as he always did by my last name. "Tito is in trouble with the law."

His face struggled between anger and sadness, tinged with a crosscurrent of confusion. Tito was his pride and joy. His only son after four daughters. A twilight gift born to his wife at a time when he despaired of ever having a son, when their youngest daughter, Lola, was already ten years old and their oldest daughter twenty.

"He just finished his examinations at the state university. He was working this summer to save money for his second year when this terrible thing happened."

I could not in my wildest fantasies imagine young Vicente getting into any kind of trouble. He had always impressed me as a bright, polite young man who would inspire pride in any father. Even when he and old Vicente had quarreled about Tito going to college instead of working full-time, the old man had grudgingly come around to seeing the wisdom of it. But now. The law! I was stunned.

"Where is he?" I asked, imagining the nineteen-year-old in some filthy cell in the San Diego jail.

"I don't know." Then he looked over his shoulder toward the kitchen, as if to be certain no one was eavesdropping. "I think he went underground."

Underground! I had visions of drug-crazed revolutionary zealots. Bombs exploding in federal buildings. God knows what kind of madness.

"They're probably after him," he went on. Then he paused and stared at me as if trying to understand. "Tito always looked up to you and Lola. Of all the family it would be you he would try to contact. I want you to help me." Not help *Tito*, I thought, but help *me*.

I went to the cabinet for the bottle that I keep there for emergencies. I took a swallow to give me enough courage to ask the question. "What . . . did . . . he do?"

Señor Martínez stared limply at the glass in his hand. "You know," he said, "my father fought with Pancho Villa."

Jesus! I thought. If everyone who told me his father had fought with Pancho Villa was telling the truth, that army would have been big enough to conquer the world. Besides—what did this have to do with Tito?

"When my turn came," he continued, "I enlisted in the Marines at Camp Pendleton. Fought los Japonés in the Pacific." Finally he took a swallow of his drink and sat up stiffly as if at attention. "The men in our family have never shirked their duty!" He barked like the Marine corporal he had once been.

It slowly dawned on me what this was all about. It had been *the* topic all during summer school at Southwestern U. Registration for the draft. "No blood for Mideast oil!" the picket signs around the campus post office had shouted. "Boycott the Exxon army!"

"I should never have let him go to college," Señor Martínez said. "That's where he gets such crazy radical ideas. From those rich college boys whose parents can buy them out of all kinds of trouble."

"So he didn't register," I said.

"The FBI is probably after him right now. It's a federal crime you know. And the Canadians don't want draft dodgers either."

He took a deep swallow and polished off the rest of his drink in one gulp, putting the empty glass on the coffee table. There, his gesture seemed to say, now you know the worst.

Calmer now, he went on to tell me more. About the American Civil War; a greater percentage of Spanish-speaking men of New Mexico had joined the Union Army than the men from any other group in any other state in the Union. About the Rough Riders, including young Mexican-Americans, born on horseback, riding roughest of all over the Spanish in Cuba. About the War-to-End-All-Wars, where tough, skinny, brown-faced doughboys from farms in Texas, New Mexico, Arizona, Colorado, and California gave their all "Over There." About World War II, from the New Mexico National Guard captured at Bataan to the tough little Marines whom he was proud to fight alongside; man for man there were more decorations for bravery among Mexican-Americans than among any other group in this war. Then Korea, where his younger brother toughed it out in the infantry. Finally Vietnam, where kids like his nephew, Pablo, got it in some silent, dark jungle trying to save a small country from the Communists.

By now he had lost his calm. There were tears in his eyes, partly from the pride he felt in this tradition of valor in war. But partly for something else, I thought. I could almost hear his son's reply to his impassioned call to duty: "Yes, Papá. So we could come back, if we survived, to our jobs as busboys and ditch diggers; *that's* why I have to go to college. I don't want to go to the Middle East and fight and die for some oil company when you can't even afford to own a car. If the Russians invaded our country, I would defend it. If a robber broke into our house, I would fight him. If someone attacked you, I would save you. But this? No, papá."

But now Tito was gone. God knows where. None of his three sisters in San Diego had seen him. Nor any of his friends in the neighborhood or school or work.

I could hear preparations for dinner from the kitchen. Señor Martínez and I had another tragito while Lolita and Junior ate their dinner early, the sounds of their childish voices piercing through the banging of pots and pans.

When Lola called me Emiliano instead of by my nickname, Pata, I knew we were in for a lousy meal. Everything her father disliked must have been served. It had taken some kind of perverse gourmet expending a tremendous amount of energy to fix such rotten food. There was that nothing white bread that presses together into a doughy flat mass instead of the tortillas papá thrived on. There was a funny little salad with chopped garbage in it covered by a blob of imitation goo. There was no meat. No meat! Just all those sliced vegetables in a big bowl. Not ordinary vegetables like beans and potatoes and carrots, but funny, wiggly long things like wild grass . . . or worms. And quivering cubes of what must have been whale blubber.

Halfway through the meal, as Señor Martínez shuffled the food around on his plate like one of our kids resisting what was good for them, the doorbell rang.

"You'd better get that, Emiliano," Lola said, daring me to refuse by her tone of voice and dagger-throwing glance.

Who needs a fight? In a sense I was the lucky one because I could leave the table and that pot of mess-age. When I opened the door, a scraggly young man beamed a weak smile at me. "I hitchhiked from San Diego," Tito said.

Before I could move onto the steps and close the door behind me, he stumbled past me into the house. Tired as he was, he reacted instantly to seeing his father at the table. "You!" he shouted, then turned and bolted out the door.

Even tired he could run faster than I, so I hopped into the car and drove after him while Lola and Señor Martínez stood on the steps shouting words at me that I couldn't hear.

Two blocks later Tito finally climbed into the car after I bribed him with a promise of dinner at McDonald's. While his mouth was full I tried to talk some sense into him, but to no avail. H was just as stubborn as his father and sister. Finally, I drove him to the International House on campus where the housing manager, who owed me a favor, found him an empty bed.

"You should have *made* him come back with you," Lola nagged at me that night.

"He doesn't want to be under the same roof with his father." From her thoughtful silence I knew that she understood and probably felt the same way herself. When I explained to her what it was all about—her father had said nothing to her—it looked for a moment as if she would get out of bed, stomp to the guest room, and heave Señor Martínez out into the street.

The next day seemed like an endless two-way shuttle between our house and the I House. First me. Then Lola. If Señor Martínez had had a car and could drive, he would have followed each of us.

Our shuttle diplomacy finally wore them down. I could at last discern cracks in father's and son's immovable positions.

"Yes. Yes. I love my son."

"I love my father."

"I know. I know. Adults should be able to sit down and air their differences, no matter how wrong he is."

"Maybe tomorrow. Give me a break. But definitely not at mealtime. I can't eat while my stomach is churning."

The difficulty for me, as always, was in keeping my opinions to myself. Lola didn't have that problem. After all, they were her brother and father, so she felt free to say whatever she pleased.

"The plan is to get them to talk," I said to her. "If they can talk they can reach some kind of understanding."

"Papá has to be set straight," she said. "As usual, he's wrong, but he always insists it's someone else who messed things up."

"He doesn't want Tito to go to jail."

"That's Tito's choice!" Of course she was right; they were both right.

The summit meeting was set for the next afternoon. Since I had only one late morning lecture, I would pick up Tito, feed him a Big Mac or two, then bring him to the house. Lola would fix Señor Martínez some nice tortillas and chili, making up for that abominable dinner of the night before last. Well fed, with two chaperones mediating, we thought they could work something out.

When Tito and I walked into the house, my hope started to tremble and develop goose bumps. It was deathly silent and formal. Lola had that dangerous look on her face again. The macho, chauvinist jumping bean sat stiffly in his suit that looked like it had just been pressed—all shiny and sharply creased, unapproachable and potentially cutting, an inanimate warning of what lay behind Señor Martínez's stone face.

Tito and I sat across from the sofa and faced them. Or rather I faced them. Both Tito and Señor Martínez were looking off at an angle from each other, not daring to touch glances. I smiled, but no one acknowledged it so I gave it up. Then Lola broke the silence.

"What this needs is a woman's point-of-view," she began.

That's all Señor Martínez needed. The blast his eyes shot at her left her open-mouthed and silent as he interrupted. "I don't want you to go to jail!" He was looking at Lola, but he meant Tito.

Tito's response was barely audible, and I detected a trembling in his voice. "You'd rather I got killed on some Arabian desert," he said.

The stone face cracked. For a moment it looked as if Señor Martínez would burst into tears. He turned his puzzled face from Lola toward his son. "No," he said. "Is that what you think?" Then, when Tito did not answer, he said, "You're my only son, and damn it! Sons are supposed to obey their fathers!"

"El patrón, El Papa, and Dios," Tito said with a trace of bitterness.

But Lola could be denied no longer. "Papá, how old were you when you left Mexico for the U.S.?" She didn't expect an answer, so didn't give him time to reply. "Sixteen, wasn't it? And what did your father say?"

Thank God that smart-ass smile of hers was turned away from her father. She knew she had him, and he knew it too, but he didn't need her smirk to remind him of it.

He sighed. The look on his face showed that sometimes memories were best forgotten. When he shook his head but did not speak, Lola went on. She too had seen her father's reaction, and her voice lost its hard edge and became more sympathetic.

"He disowned you, didn't he? Grandpa disowned you. Called you a traitor to your own country. A deserter when things got tough."

"I did not intend to stay in Mexico and starve," he said. He looked around at us one by one as if he had to justify himself. "He eventually came to Los Estados Unidos himself. He and Mamá died in that house in San Diego."

"What did you think when Grandpa did that to you?"

No answer was necessary. "Can't you see, Papá?" Lola pleaded, meaning him and Tito. He could see.

Meanwhile Tito had been watching his father as if he had never seen him before. I guess only the older children had heard Papá's story of how he left Mexico.

"I don't intend to go to jail, Papá," Tito said, "I just have to take a stand along with thousands of others. In the past old men started wars in which young men died in order to preserve old men's comforts. It just has to stop. There's never been a war without a draft. Never a draft without registration. And this one is nothing but craziness by el patrón in Washington, D.C. If enough of us protest, maybe he'll get the message."

"They almost declared it unconstitutional," I said. "They may yet."

"Because they aren't signing women," Papá said in disgust. But from the look on Lola's face, I'd pick her over him in any war.

"If they come after me, I'll register," Tito said. "But in the meantime I have to take this stand."

There. It was out. They had had their talk in spite of their disagreements.

"He's nineteen," Lola said. "Old enough to run his own life."

Señor Martínez was all talked out. He slumped against the back of the sofa. Even the creases in his trousers seemed to have sagged. Tito looked at his sister, and his face brightened.

"Papá," Tito said. "I . . . I'd like to go home, if you want me to."

On Papá's puzzled face I imagined I could read the words: "My father fought with Pancho Villa." But it was no longer an accusation, only a simple statement of fact. Who knows what takes more courage—to fight or not to fight?

"There's a bus at four o'clock," Señor Martínez said.

Later I drove them in silence to the station. Though it felt awkward, it wasn't a bad silence. There are more important ways to speak than with words, and I could feel that sitting shoulder to shoulder beside me, father and son had reached some accord.

Papá still believed in el patrón, El Papa, and Dios. What I hoped they now saw was that Tito did too. Only in his case, conscience overrode el patrón, maybe even El Papa. In times past, popes too declared holy wars that violated conscience. For Tito, conscience was the same as Dios. And I saw in their uneasy truce that love overrode their differences.

I shook their hands as they boarded the bus, and watched the two similar faces, one old, one young, smile sadly at me through the window as the Greyhound pulled away.

When I got back home, Junior and Lolita were squabbling over what channel to watch on TV. I rolled my eyes in exasperation, ready to holler at them, but Lola spoke up first.

"I'm glad Papá got straightened out. The hardest thing for parents with their children is to let go."

Yeah, I started to say, but she stuck her head into the other room and told Junior and Lolita to stop quarreling or they were going to get it.

Ghost Talk

Ana Castillo

This is the city where it all happened/happens. The one movie directors love so much because the streets make for great chase scenes, cops in hot pursuit of the bad guys; the audience, full of popcorn and candied almonds, turns nauseated as the car rises up and makes a daring leap. Here is the street. i sense the approach to the little Cuban diner with the guanabana juice drinks in cans and those wicked sandwiches on toasted French bread, stuffed with ham and steak. There's the paleteria, right around the corner, next to the santeria shop. You can suck on your coconut popsicle while you decide which potion will be best suited to capture your lover's undying devotion, or drive away the competition.

i catch a glimpse of her profile in a store window. Her hair is cut shoulder length, the Indian braid buried somewhere in a bureau drawer. It is the cut of a woman well on her way to conservative middle age, some days it is lustrous and sexy. You have sexy hair, the hair stylist says, running a comb lovingly through it, then corrects herself as if women are not supposed to say such things to women. My mother said i looked like Greta Garbo and Juana said i should be in an Italian movie. Biased opinions.

Today i look like a ghost of Xmas past. i lived here before, with the braid and faded denims. All the walls are painted with ghosts, vestiges of the great movement, the onset of revolution, the uprising of the people.

i like the cafe, which must be a recent addition to the neighborhood. Great coffees of the world. You can sit in there alone and immerse yourself in a book, sip on an expensive cup of coffee for hours and no one will bother you. It's just you and your latest idol between the pages of the only book that matters in the world. The sun is super bright but it's brisk, ocean cool, and a slight shiver runs over your bare arms when you think of it.

Iraida remembers Habana. It was a small Paris, she tells me. There were people out at all hours of the day or night, and everyone was alive. She plays Afro-Cuban rhythms and educates me on the great cultural contributions Cubans have made to the world. She pecks her temple with a forefinger; we are intelligent people, she says. My father's idol is Pérez Prado, i tell her. She nods. Pérez Prado made his name in Mexico. The operetta. The record scratches some. The daughter of a slave woman and her white master falls in love with his son, her half-brother. She bears a child from him. He marries a white woman of the aristocracy and as the newly wedded couple leave the church, a black man, who is in love with the mulatta, stabs her lover. She finds refuge in the same convent where her mother had gone eighteen years before to give birth to her. Her mother and she pray to the Virgin for forgiveness.

Iraida believes black people deserve everything white people have, but she hasn't been able to shake off her personal prejudice. They still repulse her with their kinky hair and odd features.

i dab a little oil behind the ears to ward off the evils of envy. Envy is the root of all evil, not money, like white people say. My mother-in-law warns me against inciting envy. Don't tell anyone what you have and if they find out, say, it is God's blessing and you're humbly grateful.

i wonder if any of the artists are still around? The ones who published 1,000 copies of their poetry anthologies and ran off 500 silk-screen posters of the latest cause they joined. They may be teaching at Berkeley now, Stanford, or the University of Texas. Maybe they have lucrative jobs at major publishing houses or are still hiding in the same Victorian apartments with tall, bare windows and long corridors crowded with books, record albums, and other cultural paraphernalia, planning and waiting out all the present dictators. It won't be long, they say, sip expresso from cracked, stoneware cups, munch on pieces of stale toast.

Oh! Or maybe they are rolling up those delicious corn tortillas, wickedly fattening, smearing on avocado (it's not called guacamole if it's just avocado) and afterward rolling away like a bloody fat chince, a bedbug.

You nap, and when you awake, all the neon lights in Chinatown are blinking like a galaxy of stars. It's like NY. You find a little greasy-spoon place and ask the waiter for one thing but he doesn't speak a word of English so you're oh so happy with whatever he brings you, all strange and tasting of the stuff that grows at the bottom of the sea.

Loud blaring radios from low riders and hot young men hoping to get lucky tonight.

You are a ghost, like you were a ghost before because you were never here, but everywhere at once. *i wish i could talk like my eyes can see,* word you with what i smell, knock your socks off with aromas of a tiny metropolis tourists only catch glimpses of at the Wharf. A thousand LSD trips and middle-aged folks remembering Timothy Leary playing like the Pied Piper leading them all off to drown in the sea.

Somebody sewed up my mouth with Indian sealer thread. We are but we don't speak. We listen but we don't hear it, the thunder of buffalo hooves 'cross the plains. i hold my head up high. If i'm a drunkard, i don't know it. i like it, the way it burns swishing down my gut and widens a hole in my liver. The way it makes me smile and remember and forget when i don't want to remember and before i know it i'm talking and telling what maybe i should watch whom i'm telling it to but for the moment, who cares? Someone's smiling back and nodding and hearing, pretending to respect it. i'm my age and i ain't been around for nothing, but i ain't seen nothing and i ain't done nothing 'cause no matter how long a being lives, it's not long enough. But i'm glad i made it far enough to come back here.

i remember someone who used to live up that street, and a woman who painted murals who lived in a storefront with enough stuff to start her own museum. A museum of junk. She was all full of herself too, because she was a star in her own right. Now, who can remember her name? i don't. i do remember her contribution. And i'm thankful.

i'm not envious. Like my mother-in-law says, envy is evil. It eats up at you, like maggots, knocks out your eyes from the inside, nibbles away at your tongue and before you know it, no one wants to hear what you have to say because it's all worth that much: food for maggots. Listen: i went from looking like a Campesina to slick clothes, Panama hats and Italian shoes, to just being me again, a Campesina in disguise. i don't want anyone's envy. They can keep it.

i just want respect. That you earn. You put as much effort into it as making money, but kind of by doing all the complete opposite.

We are sitting in Iraida's kitchen. The old grandmother from upstairs knocks on the door for the third time that day. Did Iraida hear from her son yet? He left the day before and hasn't been heard from. Like a mother, I know what it is to worry about a child, she says. Iraida smiles. He just called. Gave no explanation but it didn't matter. He was alright. Iraida pours the old woman expresso in a tiny cup. You look Cuban, the old woman says. Iraida beams proudly. You look Cuban. Didn't I tell you? Where do you get looking Indian from? The old lady scrutinizes, but she does have a little of that Aztec look about her . . . After she gets past the questions regarding my marital status and i've pulled out a foto of my husband and me, the two women raising eyebrows and commenting on what a big, fine man he is to look at, she asks if i haven't had a family because i didn't want to or couldn't. Couldn't, i say, but my expression looks as if someone has just asked if i take one or two lumps of sugar in my coffee, and i smile politely, none for me, thanks. But as soon as i've let on that i would have a family if i could, both women raise their arms high in the air. Oh no! Each one talks simultaneously. Why do i want to ruin my life with children? All they do is make you suffer! You give your life to raising them for nothing! I've already lost one, says the old woman, he was all grown already too. He was still in Cuba and got sick. He died from a penicillin shot. The last time I saw him, my son was a cadaver.

One of Iraida's sons is manic-depressive.

This is all happening in memory, you see, back home, the windy city, Chi-town, where Latin people with open minds can congregate and share and talk as if we were all just passing through this country. Like it isn't so much a country as a large stretch of territory where one can work and survive and possibly do well enough to go back home to the real country, where palm trees sway the way they don't in Hollywood, and fish tastes like heaven smothered in sautéed onions, garlic, lime, and a variety of peppers. A country belongs to one exclusively. It is synonymous with home. One says, i am going back to "my" country. Bigoted North Americans who forget where their grandparents came from say, Why don't you go back to *your* country. i'd be very happy to, thank you, but *your* people have occupied it.

Anyway, one day Iraida and i work ourselves into a depression. She has placed two bottles of cheap wine before me and i have steadily drunk glass after glass until they are both gone and we have run the gamut on cultural topics from Russian literature to the recent mayoral primary race. We talk about friendship and we nod with wistful smiles. It is beautiful to capture the soul of another being, isn't it? i nod and add, particularly when it has been a special person. We are talking about friendship, that has its own tenets so we are not talking about romantic/love/sex capture of another soul but the true captivation of another's spirit, which happens between people of the same sex sometimes. We are both remembering such an experience, but she tells me that it is magic when it happens and magic cannot be contrived, so perhaps if one gives up that friendship, takes it for granted, does something typically egocentric to jeoparidze it, the magic vanishes.

We were snuggled last night watching the late, late movie, a western with Clint Eastwood. Clint has made an art of squinting. It hasn't been a bad winter but it was nippy since we keep the heat down. The gas rates going up 25 percent in one jump and all. The cat snuck under the covers.

He falls asleep just before the movie finishes and i can't stand not to know what happens in the end of anything, no matter how uninterested and bored i may have been until then, i just have to know. Did he give up being the toughest, baddest sheriff in the whole territory to settle down with the blond who ran the dry goods store or did he turn his badge in and ride off into the sunset, having been an incurable roamer from the start? i have to tell him how it ended in the morning as we heat up leftovers and squeeze oranges for breakfast. i make up a lie and say Clint was ambushed and shot up like Swiss cheese.

It's not how much you know but what you know, right? So i've read *Crime and Punishment,* am familiar with Beethoven's Fifth (who isn't?), and know that Nietzsche had some concerns about God's lack of tangibility in the human heart. So you put yourself in neutral and cruise all the way through what seems superficially like a very deep discussion.

i don't have a square back like Indians do, and my legs are curved, not birdlike. But i think people don't get past that. They focus on the narrow eyes, dark skin, the full lips and black straight hair. i don't tell anybody my father was white.

He was a foreman of the assembly line where my mother worked when she first came up North. He took her out to eat sometimes. A man twice her age, he already had grandchildren. When my mother got pregnant, he didn't have to fire her. She quit.

She told me he came to see her once after i was born. He gave me a chain with little pearls and a gold heart-shaped locket. i keep it in a tin box on the dresser. My husband's father sent him a photograph of himself on his first birthday. Jerk, he says, whenever his mother pulls it out.

My mother doesn't speak English, i tell everyone. No one believes it after thirty years. So one Saturday we are out shopping. There is a sale on potatoes at one market and another on chicken clear across town. Suddenly my mother is a bronzed statue. Her heavy-lidded eyes close to slivers and i turn to see what has immobilized her. He is very tall, although age has bent his body some and he walks slowly. A much younger woman, about my age, carrying a small child, chatters next to him. She is blond and the child is blond. He is bald so i can't tell what color his hair was. i begin to fantasize. Excuse me, sir, but i have reason to believe i am your daughter. He trembles a bit, looks at me as if i were a ghost, which i am; and the woman next to him gapes like a bird that's being strangled. i believe you owe my mother twenty-one years of child support. Make it out to her and her husband, minus four years, the first year after i was born and the three when i left home. My mother has a fryer in each hand, bits of melting ice drip on the floor. Are you sure, i ask her, and the way she ignores my question has answered it. i wait until the man and his granddaughter and great-grandchild are past the checkout counter and watch to see what car they get into in the parking lot. i memorize the license plate number.

So i'd had enough, the way young people always have had enough, impatient and too wise for their own good, so I left after high school. My husband and i went off to the city where it all happened/happens to become part of it.

For a time we are back there, though. He has a job and i'm feeling good about myself. We think maybe this is the place where we'll stay, until i see the man who was not so much my father as the jerk who pressured a young Mexican woman who didn't speak two words of English, rented a room in somebody's flat and couldn't, would never go home alone with a child, and then went on with his life, to his little bungalow in the white/Polish/Lithuanian part of town, with their immaculate front yards and one-car garages.

It was just like i pictured it. His wife had probably passed away by then, no vegetable garden or rose bushes in the back anymore. He was most likely retired, spent his days watching TV and baby-sitting. His station wagon was in the driveway. i rang the bell three times, then went around back and knocked on the kitchen door. When i came around front, he was at the door, looking around. He had that fear of old people who worry about strangers knocking on their doors. And when our eyes met he showed another kind of fear. Mexicans might be moving into the neighborhood.

But i showed him all my official papers and assured him that City Hall was an equal opportunity employer. i was working for the mayor's new department on the concerns of senior citizens. i only needed a few minutes of his time to ask a few questions.

He never smiled, but when i sat on the reupholstered couch across from his favorite chair, crossed my legs so that the skirt slipped up above the knee, i saw how his eyes licked my skin and i aroused an old familiar yearning. We were done in a few minutes, as i told him. When i put my important papers back into the attaché case, he got up and asked if i didn't want a cup of instant coffee or a Nehi orange drink, the kind that's always on sale. i said, fine, thank you, whatever's not too much trouble.

When he came back from the kitchen with a glass of orange soda with ice, i had the gun out and casually brought it up with an agile left hand pointing it at him. Sit down, Old Man, I said and smiled. He dropped the glass. Orange soda soaked into the gold carpeting. He looked around.

Maybe he was waiting for one of his grandchildren, or hoped one might pop up unexpectedly that moment, like they probably liked to do. He sat down at the edge of his chair. Make yourself comfortable, i said, uncomfortable myself with his uneasiness. i just want to talk with you. i only have a few more questions i'd like answered.

He shook so much i felt sorry for him. His big hand kept feeling for his heart. Maybe he thought it was going to jump out or stop without his knowing. Do you remember a woman, I asked, and told my mother's name. He shook his head. He was so upset he probably couldn't think clearly enough to remember. Sure you do, i said. You must. She looked a lot like me. I don't know any Mexican women, he said. No, none that you socialized with publicly, i smiled calmly. None that your good wife ever knew about. He was still trembling, but his eyes flinched so that i knew he knew what i was getting at. Maybe, though, he still didn't know which one of them i was talking about.

So i showed him the chain with the pearls and gold locket that now fit around my wrist. Miss, I don't know what this is about, but I am going to call the police . . . he said, his old body wanting to get up and get to the telephone despised me, because there was a time when he could have easily overpowered me, knocked the gun out of my hand, twisted my arm until i fell on my knees and begged him to forgive my audacity. i saw it all in the twitching of his eyes and the corners of his thin mouth, how he hated me, had started out with just tolerance of my presence in his house and now hated me, not because i was his daughter, or that i reminded him of a woman he had abused in another time in his life, but just because i was there, pointing a gun at him and he had heard so many similar stories of intruders slyly getting entrance into decent citizens' homes, killing them mercilessly, ransacking their houses, making off with the shoeboxes of crisp bills neatly stacked away.

My mother? Who was she, but some Mexican whore with almond-shaped eyes and a fine tush he liked to pat when no one was looking. So she got pregnant? That was her problem. His eyes darted from the gun to the telephone.

Don't call the police, Old Man, i said, feeling the same process of emotions, from feeling nothing to an intense hatred, but not enough to waste him, a hate that went from his little bungalow all up and down each one of those identical little houses throughout the entire neighborhood.

We got up and i got up. Since i didn't want to get close enough to where he might take the gun from me, i cocked it to stop him from picking up the phone. Then he gasped. Both his hands were over his chest and as he turned to see if i was going to shoot, i saw how his eyes bulged. Then he fell back, knocking over a small table with a huge, gaudy lamp in the shape of a geisha. It was useless. Either the man was faking it or really having a heart attack. i put the gun away and picked up my things. Do you want me to call the police, i asked. Do you want me to call a doctor? He just lay there on the gold carpeting right over the wet spot and gasped up at me. i left.

Two blocks down i pulled up at a gas station and called the emergency number to send an ambulance over to his house. Don't want that on my conscience, i said to myself, and went home.

He'll come after you and kill you, if he lived, my mother warned. He's a mean man. I don't know why you had to go over there in the first place; she pulls out a hanky from her apron pocket to blow her nose.

I never liked that place anyway. That's really why we decided to come back to this city. The one where everything happened/happens. The one movie directors love so much.

Willow Game

Denise Chávez

I was a child before there was a South. That was before the magic of the
East, the beckoning North, or the West's betrayal. For me there was simply Up the street, toward the spies' house, next to Old Man W's—or there
was Down, past the Marking-Off tree in the vacant lot that was the short-
cut between worlds. Down was the passageway to family, the definition
of small self as one of the whole, part of a past. Up was in the direction of
town, flowers.

My little sister and I would scavenge the neighborhood for flowers
that we would then lay at Our Lady's feet during those long May Day
processions of faith that we so loved. A white satin cloth would be spread
in front of the altar and we children would come up one by one and place
our moist expectations there, on that bridal sheet along with that bound-
less childish fervor saturated with the mystifying scent of flowers, the
vision of flowers, the flowers of our offerings. It was this alone, this bea-
tific sense of wonder that sent us roaming the street in search of new victims,
as our garden had long since been razed, emptied of all future hope.

On our block there were two flower places: Old Man W's, the Greek
who worked for the city for so many years and who lived with his daughter who was my older sister's friend, and the Strongs', a misnamed brother
and sister team who lived together in the largest, most sumptuous house
on the block, and who were secretly referred to by my sister and me as
"the spies." Mr. W always seemed eager to give us flowers; they were not
as lovely or as abundant as the Strongs' flowers, yet the asking lay calmly
with us at Old Man W's. A chill of dread would overtake both my sister
and me as we'd approach the Strongs' mansion. We would ring the doorbell and usually the sister would answer. She was a pale woman with a
braided halo of wispy white hair who always planted herself possessively
in the doorway, her little girl's legs in black laced shoes, holding back,
sectioning off, craning her inquiry to our shaken selves with a lispy, merci-
less "Yes?"

I always did the asking. In later years when the street became smaller, less foreign, and the spies had become, at the least, accepted, it was I who still asked questions, pleaded for flowers to Our Lady, heard the high piping voices of ecstatic children singing, "Bring flowers of the fairest, bring flowers of the rarest, from garden and woodland and hillside and dale . . ." The refrain floated past the walls of our torn-down church. It is the same song I sing to myself now when I am alone or afraid. "Our pure hearts are swelling, our glad voices telling, the praise of the loveliest Rose of the Dale . . ."

One always came Down . . .

Down consisted of all the houses past my midway vantage point, including the house across the street occupied by a couple and their three children, children whose names I have forgotten, children who became at a later date my charges, my babysitting responsibilities. This was the house where one day a used sanitary napkin was ritually burned—a warning to those future furtive random and unconcerned depositers of filth, or so this is what one read in Mr. Carter's eyes as he raked the offensive item to a pile of leaves and dramatically set fire to some nameless faceless woman's woes. I peered from the trinity of windows cut in our wooden front door and wondered what all the commotion was about and why everyone seemed so stoically removed, embarrassed or offended. Later I would mournfully peep from the cyclopian window at the Carter's and wonder why I was there and not across the street. In my mind I would float Down, past the Marking-Off tree with its pitted green fruit, past five or six houses, houses of strangers, "los desconocidos," as my Grandmother would say, "Y pues, quien los parió?" I would end up at my aunt's house, return, find myself looking at our house as it was, the porch light shining, the lilies' pale patterns a diadem crowning our house, there, at night.

The walk from the beginning to the end of the street took no longer than five to ten minutes, depending on the pace and purpose of the walker. The walk was short if I were a messenger to my aunts or if I were meeting our father, who had recently divorced us and now called sporadically to allow us to attend to him. The pace may have been the slow, leisurely summer saunter of ice cream or the swirling dust-filled scamper of spring. Our house was situated in the middle of the block and faced outward to a triangle of trees that became both backdrop and pivot points of this child's tale. The farthest tree, the Up tree, was the property of all the neighborhood children and was called the Apricot tree.

The Apricot tree lay in an empty lot near my cousin's house, the cousin who always got soap in her nose. Our mothers would alternate driving us and the Sanchez boys, one of whom my father nicknamed "Priscilla" because he was always with the girls, to school, the small Catholic school that was our genesis. My cousin Florence was always one of the most popular girls in school and while I worshipped her I was glad to have my nose and not hers. On entering Florence's home on those days when it was *her* mother's turn, I would inevitably find her bent over the bathroom basin, sneezing. She would yell out, half snottily, half-snortingly, "I have soap in my nose!"

Whether the Apricot tree belonged to Florence wasn't clear—the tree was the neighborhood's and, as such, the presence of this tree was as familiar as our own faces, or the faces of our relatives. And her fruit, often abundant, sometimes meager, was public domain. The tree lay alongside the irrigation ditch, her limbs draped luxuriously across those banks. The calm muddy water flowed down the ditch all the way from the Rio Grande to Main Street, to our small street where it was diverted into channelways that led into the neighborhood's backyards. The fertile muddy water deposited the future seeds of asparagus, weeds, and flowers, then settled into wavy tufted layers crossed by sticks and stones—hieroglyphic reminders of murky beginnings.

The Apricot tree was bound by the channelway that led to the Main Street ditch. We children drew power, along with the tree, from the penetrating grateful wetness. In return, the tree was resplendent with offerings— there were apricots and more, there were the chambers and tunnelways of dream, the sturdy compartments, the stages of our dramas, "I'm drowning! I'm drowning!" where we mock drowned and were saved at the last moment by a friendly hand; or "This is the ship and I am the captain!" where we vied for power, having previously transcended death. Much time was spent at the tree, alone or with others. All of us, Priscilla, Soap-in-Her-Nose, the two dark boys Up the street, my little sister and I, all of us loved the tree. Oftentimes we would find ourselves slipping off from one of those choreless, shoreless days, and with a high surprised "Oh!" we would greet each other's aloneness, there at the tree. The Apricot tree embraced us all selflessly.

On returning home one may have wandered alongside the ditch, behind the Wester's house, and near the other vacant lot which housed the second point of the triangle, the Marking-Off tree, the likes of which may have stood at the edge of the Garden of Eden. It was a dried-looking tree which struggled all the years of my growing up to hew a life of its own. The tree passed fruit every few years or so—as old men and women struggle to empty their ravaged bowels. The grey green balls that it brought forth we used as one uses an empty can, to kick and thrash. The tree was a reference point, offering no shade, but always meditation. It delineated the Up world from the Down. It marked off the nearest point to home, without being home; it was a landmark, and as such, occupied our thoughts, not in the way the Apricot tree did, but in a subtler, more profound way. Seeing the tree was like seeing the same viejito downtown for so long, with his bottle and his wife, and looking into his crusty white-rimmed eyes and thinking, "How much longer?" Tape appears on his neck, the voice box gargles a barking sound and the bruises seem deeper. There, at that place of recognition and acceptance, you will see that tree at the edge of my world—perhaps I am sitting on the front porch at twilight when the power is all about me and the great unrest twitters and swells like the erratic chords of small and large birds scaling their way home.

There to our left is the Willow tree, completing this trinity of trees. How to introduce you to her? I would take the light of unseen eyes and present the sister who lives in France or her husband who died when he was but thirty. I would show you the best of friends and tell you how clear, how dear. I would recall moments of their eternal charm, their look or stance, the intrinsic quality of their bloom. You would see inside an album a black and white photograph of a man with a white, ruddy face, in shirtsleeves, holding a plump, squinting child in front of a small tree, a tree too frail for the wild lashes, surely. On the next page an older girl passing a hand through windblown hair would look at you, you would feel her gentle beauty, love her form. Next to her a young girl stands, small eyes toward godfather, who stares at the photographer, shaded by a growing-stronger tree. Or then you would be at a birthday party, one of the guests, rimmed in zinnias, cousins surrounding, Soap-in-Her-Nose, the two dark ones (younger than in story time) and the others, miniaturized versions of their future selves. Two sisters, with their arms around each other's child-delicate necks, stand out—as the warps and the twinings of the willow background confuse the boys with their whips and the girls with their fans.

In this last photograph one sees two new faces, one shy boy huddled amongst the girls, the other removed from all contact, sunblinded, lost in leaves.

Next to us lived the Althertons: Rob, Sandy, Ricky and Randy. The history of the house next door was wrought with struggle. Before the Althertons moved in, the Cardozas lived there, with their smiling young boys, senseless boys, demon boys. It was Emmanuel (Mannie) who punched the hole in our plastic swimming pool and Jr. who made us cry. Toward the end of the Cardoza boys' reign, Mrs. C., a small breathless bug-eyed little woman, gave birth to a girl, Mr. C's tile business failed and the family moved to Chiva Town, vacating the house to the Althertons . . . an alternately histrionically dry and loquacious couple with two boys. Ricky, the elder, was a tall, tense boy who stalked the Altherton spaces with the natural grace of a wild animal, ready to spring, ears full of sound, eyes taut with anticipation. Randy, young Randy, was a plump boy-child with deep watery eyes who clung to Mrs. Altherton's lumpish self while lean and lanky Papa A. ranged the spacious lawn year round in swimming trunks in search of crab grass, weeds, any vestiges of irregularity. Sandy Altherton was a pigeon of a woman who clucked, "You don't say . . ." as simply as exhaling breath, and then would place her fleshy pink hands against her Appalachian apple doll's face and look out in wonder, "You don't say!"

Jack Spratt shall eat no fat, his wife shall eat no lean, and between them both, you see, they licked the platter clean . . .

The Altherton yard was very large, centered by a metal pole to which was attached the neighborhood's first tetherball. From our porch where my sister and I sat dressing dolls, we could hear the punch and whirr of balls, the crying and the calling out. Ricky would always win, sending Randy racing inside to Mrs. A's side, at which time, having dispatched his odious brother, Ricky would beat and thrash the golden ball around in some sort of crazed and victorious adolescent dance. Randy and Mrs. A. would emerge from the house and they would all confer for a time. Voices were never raised, were always hushed and calm. The two plump ones would then go off, hand in hand, leaving the lean to himself. Ricky would usually stomp away, down the neighborhood, flicking off a guiltless willow limb from our tree, de-leafing it in front of our watchful eyes, leaving behind his confused steps a trail of green unblinking eyes, the leaves of our tree. Every once in a while Randy would walk over to us, hover above our dolls or mud pies, hesitantly, with that babyish smile of his and ask us to come play ball. We two sisters would cross the barriers of Altherton and joyfully bang the tetherball around with Randy. He played low, was predictable, not like Ricky, who threw the ball vehemently high, confounding, always confounding. Ricky's games were over quickly, his blows firm, surprising, relentless. Ricky never played with my sister and me, to us he was godlike and removed, as our older sister, already sealed in some inexplicable anguish of which we children had no understanding. It was Randy who brought us in, called out to us, permitted us to play. And when he was not there to beckon us, it was his lingering generosity and gentleness that pushed us forward into the mysterious Altherton yard, allowing us to risk fear, fear of both Mr. Altherton with his perennial tan or Ricky with his senseless animal temper. Often we would find the yard free and would enjoy the tetherball without intrusion, other times we would see Ricky stalk by, or feel and hear the rustling approach of clippers, signifying Mr. Altherton's return. If we would sense the vaguest shadow of either spectre we would run, wildly, madly, safely home, to the world of our Willow where we would huddle and hide in the shelter of green labyrinth rooms, abstracting ourselves from the world of Ricky's torment or Mr. Altherton's anxious wanderings.

I have spoken least of all of the Willow tree, but in speaking of someone dead or gone—what words can reach far enough into the past to secure a vision of someone's smiling face or curious look—who can tame the restless past and show, as I have tried, black and white photographs of small children in front of a tree?

The changes of the Willow were imperceptible at first. Mr. W, the Greek, through an oversight in pronunciation, had always been Mr. V. The spies became individualized when Mr. Strong later became my substitute History teacher and caused a young student to faint, when she, who was afraid of the sight of blood, happened to look into the professor's nose and see unmistakeable flecks of red. The two dark boys grew up, became wealthy, and my cousin moved away. The irrigation ditch was eventually closed. Only the Willow remained . . . consoling, substantial. The days became shorter and divided the brothers while the sisters grew closer.

Ricky, now a rampaging, consumed adolescent continued his thoughtless forays, which included absently ripping off Willow limbs and discarding them on our sidewalk. "He's six years older than Randy," said my mother, that dark mother who hid in trees, "he hates his brother, he just never got over Randy's birth. You love your sister, don't you?" "Yes, mother . . ." I would say . . .

It was not long after Ricky's emerging manhood that the Willow began to ail, even as I watched it. I knew it was hurting. Then the tree began to look bare, the limbs were listless, in anguish, and there was no discernible reason. The solid green rooms of our child's play collapsed, the passageways became cavernous hallways, the rivers of grass dried and there was no shade, no darkened rooms of nighttimes within which to sleep idle seconds. The tree was dying. My mother became concerned. I don't know what my little sister thought, she was a year younger than I. She probably thought as I did, for at that time she held me close as model and heroine, enveloped me with her love, something Randy was never able to do for his older brother, that bewildered boy.

It wasn't until years later (although the knowledge was there, admitted, seen) that my mother told me that one day she had come outside to see Ricky standing on a ladder under our willow. He had a pair of scissors in his hands and was cutting whole branches off the tree and throwing them to the side. Mother said, "What are you doing, Ricky?" He replied, "I'm cutting the tree." "Do you realize that you're killing it," she responded calmly. It is here that the interpretation breaks down, where the photographs fade into grey wash, and I momentarily forget what Ricky's reply was, that day, so many years ago, as the limbs of our Willow fell about him, cascading tears, willow reminders, past the face of my mother, who stood solemnly and without horror.

Later, when there was no recourse but to cut down the tree, Regino Suárez, the neighborhood handyman, and his sons were called in.

Regino and his sons had difficulty with the tree, she struggled to come out of the earth and when her roots were ripped from the womb of dirt, there lay an enormous aching hole, like a tooth gone, the sides impressed with myriad twistings and turnings. The trunk was moved to the side of the house, where it remained until several years ago, when it was cut up for firewood, and even then, part of the stump was left. Throughout the rest of grade school, high school, and college—until I went away, returned, went away—the Willow stump remained underneath the window of my old room. Often I would look out and see it there, or on thoughtful walks, I would go outside near the Altherton's old house, now sealed by a tall concrete wall, and I would feel the aging hardness of the Willow's flesh.

That painful, furrowed space was left in the front yard where once the Willow had been. It filled my eyes, my sister's eyes, my mother's eyes. The wall of trees, backdrop of the traveling me, that triangle of trees— the Apricot tree, the Marking-Off tree, the Willow tree—was no longer.

One day Ricky disappeared and we were told he'd been sent to a home for sick boys.

As children we felt dull leaden aches that were voiceless cries and were incommunicable. The place they sprung from seemed so desolate and uninhabited and did not touch on anything tangible or transferable. To carry pain around as a child does, in that particular place, that wordless grey corridor, and to be unable to find the syllables with which to vent one's sorrow, one's horror . . . surely this is insufferable anguish, the most insufferable. Being unable to see, yet able, willing, yet unwilling . . . to comprehend. A child's sorrow is a place that cannot be visited by others.

Always the going back is solitary, and the little sisters, however much they love you, were never really very near, and the mothers, well, they stand as I said before, solemnly, without horror, removed from children by their understanding.

I am left with recollections of pain, of loss, with holes to be filled. Time, like trees, withstands the winters, bursts forth new leaves from the dried old sorrows—who knows when and why— and shelters us with the shade of later compassions, loves, although at the time the heart is seared so badly that the hope of all future flowerings are gone.

Much later, after the death of the Willow, I was walking to school when a young boy came up to me and punched me in the stomach. I doubled over, crawled back to Sister Elaine's room, unable to tell her of my recent attack, unprovoked, thoughtless, insane. What could I say to her? To my mother and father? What can I say to you? All has been told. The shreds of magic living, like the silken green ropes of the Willow's branches, dissolved about me, and I was beyond myself, a child no longer. I was filled with immense sadness, the burning of snow in a desert land of consistent warmth.

Today I walked outside and the same experience repeated itself; oh, not the same forms, but yes, the attack. I was the same child, you see, mouthing pacifications, incantations . . . "Bring flowers of the fairest, bring flowers of the rarest—It's okay—from garden and woodland and hillside and dale. Our pure hearts are swelling—It's all right—our glad voices telling— Please—the praise of the loveliest Rose of the Dale."

Jack Spratt could eat no fat, his wife could eat no lean, and between them both, you see, they licked the platter clean . . .

My mother planted a willow several years ago, so that if you sit on the porch and face left you will see it, thriving. It's not in the same spot as its predecessor, too far right, but of course, the leveling was never done, and how was Regino to know? The Apricot tree died, the Marking-Off tree is fruitless now, relieved from its round of senseless birthings. This willow tree is new, with its particular joys. It stands in the center of the block . . . between . . .

Rosa, la Flauta

Sergio Elizondo

El año pasado todavía tocaba la flauta. La estudié y la practiqué desde que tenía ocho años de edad, pero luego sucedieron esas cosas que me volaron la cabeza y ya no me interesa. Luego también era buena para correr, me gustaba correr los 400 metros; hasta me gané varios premios; me acuerdo que me sentía tan a gusto corriendo; pero también lo hacía para que mi hermana me viera y se animara y también lo hiciera para que le alcanzara el tiempo nomás para estudiar, estar en la casa, ir a la escuela, la iglesia y correr; me miraba y me miraba siempre y aunque yo no la podía ver me estaba mirando, pues porque yo iba pasando ocupada y no podía verla porque iba también corriendo, y yo bien sabía que ahí estaba con sus ojos cubiertos de brillo y porque nos queremos y es mi hermana.

Con un vestidito blanco, bien tieso en la falda porque mi mamá lo planchó con mucho almidón, me llegaba hasta la mera rodilla, ahí estaba en frente de todos con los labios entreabiertos, soplando aire suavemente detrás del agujerito de la flauta. Me la había aprendido de memoria y por eso podía tenerla horizontal, de ladito para tocarla y luego ver a la gente por encima. Ahí estaban todos: hasta mi abuelita y mi tatita vinieron de Los Lunas a ver y a oírme tocar ese aire de Mozart. Los podía ver a todos: hasta lo hice más despacio porque me sabía bien la pieza y para tener más tiempo para verlos, y bien que los veía. Me dijeron que en los recitales la gente se duerme, aquí no: yo no los dejé dormir porque los dominé con la vista, a todos y a uno por uno me les quedé viendo y con ambos ojos y líneas derechitas, bueno: casi derechitas me los tuve atentos a que oyeran mis sonidos y me vieran la cara, los ojos, los dedos sobre la flauta y que no se les ocurriera bajar la vista al filo de mi falda para que no me vieran las rodillas porque siempre se me ven más prietas que las otras partes de la piel. Si hubiera querido hubiera movido los dedos más rapido para qué dijeran: ¡Qué bien toca la flauta! ¡Y qué chiquita! Pues ahí me los tuve con las medias uvas de mis ojos que parecen ojos de gato.

Mi amá está bien sentadita haciendo un ángulo recto bien esquinado con sus muslos y la espina dorsal. En la boca, y en las esquinitas de la boca se le nota que está contenta y orgullosa de su hija, la famosa flautista: *¡Ay tan chula m'ija! ¡Qué talento!* He de verla en Avery Fisher Hall rodeada de más de cien maestros que la acompañan sinfónicamente. Y luego el Leonard diciéndoles con la varita de madera que todavía no, que se esperen hasta que yo quiera, y quiera y me dé la gana de pausar para que entre toda la orquesta filarmónica con esas ondas que hace cuando tocan. Luego me detengo un momento y con un ojo, nomás un ojo y la ceja izquierda le ordeno al Leonard que ya pueden entrar todos menos el do los tambores.

Mi amá tiene las piernas bien juntas. Dice que en un concierto así que una mujer decente no debe de cruzar las piernas, ni aquí ni en Persia porque es mala costumbre. Tiene las manos sobre su regazo, apenas tentando su bolso.

Mi apá se rasuró bien. Parece que le huelo el agua de colonia que se pone cuando se pone traje. Se le ve brillante la piel de la cara, así se pone cuando va donde hay gente. Está pensando en lo que va a hacer en el trabajo mañana. Aquí no me hace caso, dice que no entiende la música, pero cuando estamos en la casa y está en frente de la televisión y yo estoy encerrada en la cochera practicando, está pensando en mí y bien que le gusta oir la flauta. Pero ahorita no le hace caso a nadie; vino porque es el padre de la gran artista, esta gran concertante que se codea con los alemanes, los austríacos y los franceses.

La Patti me está observando cuidadosamente, ¡cómo me quiere mi hermanita! A ella sí que le gusta la música seria. No quiere que quede mal. Me dijo un día que cuando me oye tocar así que ella alarga las manos para que en ella caigan todas las notas de colores que estoy tocando y que no distraigan a la gente si caen al piso. Ella las ve de colores pero a mí me salen negras, nada más que de diferentes tamaños y, como que aunque no tienen cabeza ni pulmones, como que respiran. Pues no se me ha caído ninguna, la Patti las tiene todas y yo tengo las demás todavía en la cabeza porque no deben de salir todas de una vez, hay que contarlas.

Cuando quiero que las notas de la flauta salgan de madera fuerte y dura pienso en los ojos de mi hermana. Yo conozco algunas piezas para flauta del compositor austríaco que murió joven; no sé si cuando las compuso pensaba que las hacía para que fueran tocadas con flauta de madera o de metal, casi todas las que conozco las toco como si fueran de madera, pero esta noche he tocado de las dos: las de metal para la gente y las notas de madera para mi hermana. Lo mejor para ella.

Esta noche me siento feliz, todo está bien; soy todo lo que quiero ser. Una vez que practicaba, todos los de casa habían salido de casa y me dejaron sola, por eso me fui a mi cuarto a practicar en vez de hacerlo en la cochera. Fue diferente: sólo estábamos yo, mi respiración y las notas de ébano que hice; hice tantas que llené la recámara y ninguna de ellas se cayó al suelo. No las controlaba, las dejé que hicieran lo que quisieran y como que por complacerme se quedaron suspendidas en el ambiente, no volaban, ahí nomás estaban, aunque unas cuantas, chistosas quizás, se lucieron paseándose a diferentes velocidades por todo el cuarto pero sin molestar a las otras. Todas, menos las voladoras, eran esféricas, creí que querían decirme algo porque se me quedaban viendo y sonreían silenciosas. Yo tocaba muchas pero nada completo, era un potpourrí de aires alemanes y austríacos. Yo: de pié en el centro del cuadro, sentía mi cuerpo todo tibio, con los ojos cerrados a veces me dejé llevar por las cadencias que construía. Me sentía como que era la letra F con los dos brazos como que formaban curvas suaves que cambiaban con cada nota. Esta noche vuelvo a ser F pero ahora minúscula, mi cuerpo ha progresado, ahora lo siento como una f de color café claro; si me viera así la gente creería que estoy hecha de una substancia plástica suave pero yo sé bien que soy transparente. Se acerca el fin del programa, mis labios se preparan para un adagio; lo necesito para hacer una transición apropiada mientras vuelvo a como es la gente en la vida diaria para que no me lastime la salida y la entrada.

Una vez me llevaron a una función en la junior high. Era el primer año después del sexto, yo fuí la última de los cinco que pasamos al foro a hacer nuestros tonos. Desde que llegué me sentí como que estaba hecha de madera para la construcción de casas. Sentía que mi piel apretaba mi cuerpo, mis ojos se hicieron pequeñitos y casi negros, raro: porque son claros, tengo ojos de gato. Tenía los dedos mecánicos, aunque no de metal, estaban duros, tiesos y hacían un ruidito en las coyunturas como si necesitaran un poco de aceite. No me asusté porque yo ya dominaba bien la flauta, pero eso sí; el instrumento estaba completamente separado de mi ser. Esa vez me di cuenta que era posible construir con mis sonidos, podía fabricar muchas cosas, pero ahora que es diferente me doy cuenta que en aquel entonces algo faltaba, ahora sé lo que era. La gente me vió, me escuchó, pero nadie se dio cuenta que mis ondas no llegaban bien a ellos, sólo se acercaban, como que las notas no tenían fuerzas de llegar bien bien a ellos, no era el frío, era otra cosa. Mis padres y mi hermana estaban allí también, pero estaban sentados en la primera fila de las gradas del gimnasio y mis notas pasaban por encima de ellos. Esa noche fue únicamente de Telemann. Recuerdo que pensé en él cuando ejecutaba los aires y me dio vergüenza porque lo vi alejado, muy alejaldo de mi, las notas salían como si fueran astillas de madera. No conocía del Telemann más que su música, si hubiera conocido a la hermosa Alemania en aquel tiempo sospecho que nada se hubiera roto. Pero ahora él y yo nos queremos porque nos conocemos mejor.

Terminó el concierto. Aplaudieron. No me habían enseñado a hacer caravanas, sostuve la flauta de metal ante mi pecho y sonreí, pero mi sonrisa no fue para ellos sino para el campo vacío que vi ante mí en el futuro; ahí estaría yo alguin día; sonreí porque de allí a allá había tiempo para caber bien en ese espacio. Confieso que fue el único momento de calorcito que sentí. "Al menos aprendí algo," dije. Inocente criatura de mí, no me imaginaba que al terminar la última palmada que hizo con las manos la gente, en ese instante ya no fue aplauso sino que los vi a todos haciendo tortillas.

Al alejarme de mi lugar fue bastante difícil para mí regresar a donde estaba la gente, mi familia, el mundo ese, esa otra cosa que ahora veo que está ahí para los insensibles pero que existe para la gente suave. Juraría que mi cuerpo se resistía a "entrar" en eso. Buena lección, es instrucción que nadie me enseño, no la descubrí: me descubrió y pues las cosas no han sido iguales desde entonces.

Aquí, donde he vivido los quince años de mi vida llueve poco, es seco, la gente se acostumbra a eso. Pero esa noche no había estrellas allá arriba; llovía, era una de esas lluvias de invierno que duran varios días; si no hubiera sido por la lentitud de la lluvia, las pequeñas gotas que caían uniformes, no hubiera quedado bien mi mente cuando terminé lo de la flauta y tuve que alistarme para ese cambio. A veces quisiera que cada quien tuviera el poder de escoger la circunstancia en las transiciones. Pero no es así, esté una lista o no se tiene que pasar por eso.

Ya no me preguntan mis padres por qué no hago música, ni por qué no toco el radio de la música seria; creo que se dan cuenta pero no saben que la flexibilidad que tenía mi cuerpo y mi mente la perdí en los últimos dos años. No fue la sangre que ahora veo cada cuatro semanas, eso tenía que suceder, pero eso fue sencillamente una señal; luego vinieron esas otras cosas, el cosquilleo, la vez que dije que sí me animaba a fumar, la píldora colorada, lo que hicimos un muchacho y yo, y más: mi alejamiento de las balanzas de muchos platillos donde antes ponía todo mi ser. En dos años se cambió todo.

Los cuatrocientos metros ahora son sólo un cuatro con dos ceros de cola, la flauta es un tubo que finge ser de plata y está llena de aire que no se mueve; de mi boca salen sólo palabras, mis dedos sirven para nada, a menos que los cuente como diez apéndices que nomás cuelgan ái; los ojos no reflejan nada, no mandan nada pá juera, nomás dejan entrar cosas pá dentro. Un día reciente me puse los pantaloncillos con que antes corría, me los puse en lugar de pantaletas pero los sentía como que estaban hechos de madera con ángulos ásperos, no se moldeaban a mis caderas y muslos como que ya no querían correr conmigo, 'taban muertos: voy a tirarlos en el barril de la basura que está al lado de la pista y aunque ne vean en casa voy a coger la flauta con una mano y la voy a vender para comprar más para que se complete todo eso que debe haber cuando hay terminación donde se acabó algo. Ya no hay aires, mis labios callan.

Yellow Flowers

Carlos Nicolás Flores

The table is red.

Not a regular table, it consists of a round, flat piece of wood nailed over a barrel.

It is, moreover, surrounded by four other barrels, the same kind as the one upon which the top is nailed, to be used in the place of stools or chairs.

This arrangement—red table with three or four barrels—is duplicated several times in the two rooms that comprise the bar, creating a gaudy, flamboyant atmosphere. The minute you walk in the front door, the red strikes your eyes from every direction.

Such an arrangement is interesting, especially if you're a tourist, but, in my opinion, highly uncomfortable. Although the table itself is adequate, the barrels are awkward to sit on. After an hour or so of drinking, their metal rims begin cutting painfully into your buttocks.

This particular table—I mean, the one where Smith and I now sit—is located in the southwest corner of the second of the two rooms comprising the bar, the corner, in other words, created by a large, opaque window and the west wall of the bar converging at the point farthest from the stools and bar.

The rooms are approximately equal in size. They are connected by a wide archway in the partition separating them. The ceilings are high. The walls are covered with paper posters.

"Don't they ever change those posters?" Smith remarks.

"I don't know," I reply. "They've been there about four or five years."

"There's something I've never liked about this place."

"What?" I say, glancing about the room.

"Can't say exactly," he says. "Too much red. These barrels . . . it's a tourist bar. Maybe that's it."

"I like it. At least, it's different."

We fall silent and drink from our glasses.

You cannot see the stools, the bar, the waiters, or the people going in and out the front door in the next room. When the bar is full, as it is tonight, they are obscured by the heads and shoulders of the people occupying the table in the archway. This is not important, however, since nothing very interesting ever happens in that other room, the center of attraction being the low, wooden stage in the part of the bar where we sit. On Friday and Saturday nights there is usually dancing and singing on the stage, although I doubt seriously if there will be any tonight. Neither the guitar player nor the dark-haired girls with their castanets and noisy, ruffled dresses have arrived.

"I didn't think I'd ever come back to El Paso," says Smith, placing his glass on the table. "Thought I was through with it. But here I am. This place is still here. Hasn't changed much. You're right about that. I'm the one who's changed."

"Why'd you come back?" I ask.

"I . . . to settle a few things with my wife."

"Alone?"

"Yeah, I came alone. Bernice stayed in California."

"I didn't know that was your wife's name."

"That's my . . . ah, girl friend. I'm not living with my wife anymore. We separated about two years ago. Didn't you know?"

"Well, I'd heard some rumors. I never found out what happened. All I learned was that you'd quit your job and left town. That's all."

"I thought you knew. It seemed that everybody knew when I left."

"I heard some people talking about it in here one night. I never paid much attention. Didn't think it was any of my business."

"That's a surprise. Everyone was dying to find out all the details. As if anything really unusual had happened. It was ridiculous. Thinking about it embarrasses me."

He reaches for his glass and gulps the rest of the beer.

Noticing the waiter at the table in the archway, I raise my hand to wave, but his back is turned toward us.

I decide to wait.

The table in the archway is usually a favorite. Six people occupy it now—a heavy, Anglo-Saxon-looking man in a business suit; next to him, on the right, another man, also blond but slender and younger. The dark-skinned Mexican woman leaning on him is either his wife or lover; her black hair and swarthy face accent his diaphanous white complexion. Then, there is a woman I often see in this bar, although the closest I have come in contact with her is a courteous smile, a formal gesture, nothing more—

which is perhaps just as well, since I don't like the way she laughs or the calculated feminine ostentation with which she habitually displays her thin legs. The man with her must be her escort for the evening, certainly not her husband, probably the most recent of a number of middle-aged men I've seen in her company. Finally, between him and the first man I described, completing the circle of people, sits another woman in a sleek black dress, her face turned away, a long, silver bow draping down her back.

They are talking about something. I have no idea what it is. Their mouths move soundlessly. They may even be talking about something important; at times, the movement of their hands, the tilt of their heads, or the angle of their shoulders reveals their excitement. Yet, they are not, at least they don't seem to be, speaking about the same thing. At this distance, it's difficult to tell. It doesn't matter.

The waiter finally turns, I motion to him, he comes over, and we order another round.

"You know," Smith says, "I wish the hell we knew how to live before we even tried living. It would make things much easier in the long run, don't you think?"

"Yeah," I reply. "But who realizes that? Tell somebody he's living badly, tell him he's wasted his life, and he'll spit in your face."

"You can't blame him."

"No, I suppose not."

"It would've been so much easier staying with my wife. I could've avoided so many foolish things."

"Yes. But regret—especially, nostalgia—is stupid. You can't look back."

"Well, I'll tell you; it's been hard. This business of leaving a woman can be messy. I still don't know if it's been worth it. No, I can't say that. Only my wife doesn't . . ."

The wife?

I don't remember her well—at least, nothing more than such minor details as the way she combed her hair, swathed carelessly about her head like a rag; the Mexican sandals she customarily wore; a faded cotton dress; the thin, shrewd lips; and the eyes, the eyes—two flecks of steel. She had been an opera singer in New York where, as I understand it, she met Smith; then, for a time she gave private voice lessons here in El Paso. As a matter of fact, the last time I saw Smith, about three years ago, she was with him, and we had a few beers to drink in here. All I can remember from that afternoon is that we were all bored with each other. Many months after that the rumors of his running around with some young girl and his leaving for California began to spread. I never paid much attention to them, since the incident struck me as being just another petty scandal.

"Bernice doesn't like California," he begins again. "I don't either. L.A. is a dump. But I'd rather live where nobody knows us."

Bernice? I never spoke to her, never saw her, never knew her.

"I thought it'd be better if I came alone," he continues. "She's waiting for me to get back."

Bernice, his woman?

He goes on speaking. My attention begins to wander; his voice rises in pitch; my eyes glance about the room, settling momentarily on the heads of the people at the table in the archway, scanning the high walls, returning abruptly to the red table top and then to the movement of his lips.

Bernice? Yes, that's the woman he's talking about, the young girl waiting for him in California.

She's the one, he says, who has practically torn his life apart in the two and a half years they've been together. Or rather, he seems to be saying, it is the two women, the wife as well as the mistress, that are rending him asunder, splitting him down the middle, each one vengefully unwilling to settle for less than half of him. I don't understand the meaning of this, although the emotion is his voice seems to make sense. It must flatter his vanity immensely, knowing two women won't let go of him. Or is it he who won't let go?

Anyway, he explains he left the wife two years ago because he loved the other one, emphasizing he loves her as he's never loved anybody else and will marry her at all costs.

"But my wife," he hisses, "won't divorce me."

That's why, he says, he came to El Paso, even though he never expected to set foot in Texas after he'd left for California—namely, to settle the financial and legal aspects of this problem once and for all. He says he's through being pinned between the two; he says he knows what he must do. I don't quite understand the meaning of what he's telling me, although I'm sure it's of the utmost importance to him. My eyes have already strayed beyond his pinched face to the movement of faces and hands at the table in the archway.

Next to the middle-aged man sits a woman whom I've often seen in this bar, although the closest I have come in contact with her has been a courteous smile, a formal gesture, nothing more; in fact, I have seen all of these people in here before, except perhaps the woman in the black dress with the silver bow draped down her back. I cannot see her face.

This woman sits with her face averted, probably looking through the archway in the direction of the bar and the waiters in the next room or, if not in that direction, at either the darkhaired Mexican girl or the man sitting next to her. From where I sit, it is difficult to tell which way she is looking. Unable to see her face, much less the movement of her mouth, I cannot determine if she's even talking to the other people at the table. All I see is the silver bow stretching from her shoulders to her waist. Perhaps, she's new.

Smith: Smith and Bernice.

He says he didn't love his wife anymore; that he had lived with her long enough; that he left her two years ago because he was sick of his way of life, ruinously impotent and dispassionate; that he wanted to start again with this young woman, this girl, Bernice; that he wanted to have the children the first one (initially because they didn't want any, finally because she got a hysterectomy) had never given him in the thirteen or fifteen years they'd been married; that he wanted to destroy his old world, the old values that failed him ultimately; that he'd never realized how foolish he'd been with his life until he fell in love with this woman; that he had discovered a new world, a new way of life; that he felt young for the first time; that he felt passion; and that he knew a joy he'd never known before.

I politely agree, assuring him, "I know, I know. You're a man in love. I admire you for that. I don't envy your predicament but I admire you. You've suddenly realized you're not dead. You want to live. You are suffering. It's not easy. You risk everything when you love. I understand."

And what else can I tell him? That he's a forty-year-old adolescent? That if he's suffering he's suffering because he deserves it; that if his sanity is being ripped from him by the lacquered fingernails of two women it is because he hasn't acted, hasn't cut off the first one, the rejected and injured one, or if they, the two women, kill him as well as themselves, he deserves that too? No. I reassure him.

I reassure him, because I'm bored.

I've been watching the people at the table in the archway. Their mouths move soundlessly, mindlessly. The whole lot of them are smoking. The smoke rises from their midst, from an ashtray placed somewhere on the table, from cigarettes held lightly in their hands, or from their exhaling mouths. Rising through the space above their heads, the smoke twists and curls like tickertape. Uncurling, it stretches past the paper posters on the steep walls. The posters swarm with reds, blues, greens, and yellows, vivifying events long since dead, events that already took place in Spain:

bullfights, races, festivals, and so on. Although they haven't been changed in the years I've been coming here, I never cease to gaze at their flat reticence.

The woman in the black dress? Ah yes, she's still there. Her neck is long, her ears exquisitely chiseled. I cannot see her face. She may be looking in the direction of the bar, at one or two of the other people seated at the table, or at an object (a glass of beer or wine? a smoking cigarette? an empty coaster?) on the table.

Her silver bow is sleek as mother-of-pearl.

Smith now looks steadily at me, as if he expects me to resolve his dilemma with an epigram; he now glances away, gazing nervously at the posters on the walls, the muscles in his neck thickening, perhaps wondering why I've taken so little interest in what he's said.

Perhaps he now remembers the face of the woman—the young woman who loves him as he claims he's never been loved, waiting for him to return; or, if not that, then the face of the woman he must leave, her eyes frozen upon him through the days and nights passing; or, if not that, then perhaps both their faces in one anonymously pale face, judging him through remembrance, forgiving him in regret. I can't say. For they are his faces, his face is theirs, all three faces are one.

Smith now looks at me, his face tan and worn, not directly but obliquely as if his head were a boulder balanced precariously on his shoulders.

I look past him, past his shoulders, past the side of his face, at the woman, whose face I cannot see, sitting almost directly behind him in the distance. Still there, she sits immobile, elegant, looking in the direction of the bar, at one of the people seated at the table, or perhaps at some insignificant object—a glass of wine, a smoking cigarette, or an empty coaster.

I do not even know if she's worth looking at; she may very well be one of the many people that come and go through this bar, stopping long enough to drink a couple of beers and take in the atmosphere fabricated especially for them, their faces usually the vacant, wide-eyed faces of tourists, appearing and disappearing without leaving the slightest trace in your memory. Perhaps, it would be best if she never turned around, never moved from the position that favors her appearance so much, never exposed herself fully. I would never know the difference. All I would remember—all I would want to recall—would be the long, white neck, the ivory ears, and the silver bow.

Smoke laces into the air from their midst. It rises; it tangles. Then untangling, it rises again. It languishes past the greens, blues, reds, and yellows of things and events that took place a long time ago in another country to another people.

Quite unexpectedly the people at the table in the archway burst out laughing. I'm sure someone said something funny.

Smith just told me that Bernice had made three attempts on her life. When he first began speaking, it sounded implausible, slightly exaggerated in fact, even though his face bears the marks of strain and worry. If it weren't for the face, particularly the nervous twitch beneath his eye which I've just noticed, I probably wouldn't believe him. After all, how can any of us believe anything anybody has told us about his life?

He comments that what's happened to him is like an incident straight from a novel by Graham Greene, a comparison which no doubt evinces the glamor of these emotional matters, repeating that he has never suffered so much tension, grief, and rage, that he's neither been up against the wall as desperately nor has he had to come to terms with himself as now, and so on, and so on. I nod my head.

"Three times," he says. "Three times. First gas. Then pills. They didn't work. Probably just playing at first. But the third time. The third time it was the real thing. It's a miracle she's still alive. Simply a miracle. She wasn't even hurt. Thank God for that."

"She try shooting herself?" I ask.

"She drove off a cliff."

"A cliff?"

"The car was destroyed."

"And she wasn't hurt?"

"One or two bruises was all. But the car was destroyed. I don't understand it. It had to be a miracle. She should be dead today. The car was destroyed and she lived. I swear to God I don't know how it happened but it did."

Is Bernice dead?

No, he says, she lives.

The neck is long and graceful. The short black hair is tastefully set; the skin is white. The black velvet dress fits her well. The bow is as intensely silver as the moon on a clear night.

The face? The eyes? The nose and mouth? The legs? The stance and manner of walk? The propriety of motion and gesture? Of these, I can only guess.

"Three times! The third time she wasn't playing. How could I have doubted . . . not so much her or her love . . . as myself. How can I leave her now? Even if my wife refuses to give me the divorce, I can't leave her. I can't."

I cannot see her. She may be looking in the direction of the bar, at one or two of her companions, or at an object on the table. Could her face be as beautiful as her neck and ears?

"The funny thing about it is that she's not even beautiful," he continues. "I mean she doesn't suit the role. You'd think that after all that drama she'd at least be a beautiful heroine, you know, like in the movies. She's not. My wife was better looking when she was in her twenties."

Beauty?

"No," he goes on. "She's very plain, slender, almost skinny. Several inches taller than me in fact. My wife is more intelligent, too, but that doesn't matter any more than looks or money matters. At least, that's what you discover after you've been with them long enough. You look at them so much, you look at them in such different ways, when they're happy, when they're sick, when they're asleep, and then in the morning when they really look bad, that you forget that the face is too thin or too pale or the eyes too small.

"Then what happens—what seems ridiculous if you look at it objectively—is that you begin loving those defects as part of something greater that you love, not the soul, you don't even think about that, but something else, perhaps something in yourself that's not even in them. In the end it's not half as romantic as you'd like to think. It's pretty messy. Yet . . . yet when you know they're still there waiting for you, you go back to them."

"And your wife?" I ask.

"My wife? My wife is a boy. I married a boy when I married her."

"You never loved her?"

"Well . . . if you'd asked me that fourteen years ago, I probably would've said yes. But that was fourteen years ago. I was a different man. My wife was another woman. Unfortunately things and people change. A man can't help that."

"Nor a woman, I suppose."

"That's right. Nor a woman. But one has to live somehow. That's another thing you learn with time. You have to live somehow, no matter what happens. You do the best you can with what you have. I never learned that soon enough."

"How long did you say you've been with this girl?"

"Two years," he answers. "I know what you're thinking. You needn't say anything. It's two years too long for a man to decide to leave his wife once he decided he wants to leave her. I don't deny it. Well, I can't. But that's why I'm here. I've recovered from my foolishness. I intend to do something about it now."

He raises his glass of beer to his mouth.

Now she is leaning toward the man next to her, whispering or saying something, possibly excusing herself, for in the next instant, she stands up, her back still toward me, the face hidden, the sleek, silver bow gleaming. She is slender, well-formed. The black dress is tastefully chosen; it fits her well, complementing the head of black hair and white neck, accenting the curve from the waist to the hips.

The face remains hidden. She moves away from me, around the people at the table, moving well, neither awkwardly nor self-consciously but easily and naturally. Passing the jukebox, she disappears beyond the heads of the people at the table, beyond the smoke rising from their midst to the ceiling above.

"Bernice disappeared," Smith remarks, now gazing at the glass of beer before him, thinking perhaps that I'm still listening to him. "She disappeared when she found out my wife refused to give me the divorce. I couldn't find her. She wasn't at work. She wasn't in the apartment. I knew what'd happen. The same thing that'd happened twice already. Only this time it would be the real thing. I was going out of my mind. I was up against the wall. It was bad."

I, too, gaze at the glass of beer, gazing perhaps at the very same silver bubbles rising to the surface that Smith has been gazing at. They look like a string of pearls rising steadily, monotonously, through the yellow liquid.

Smith reaches for the glass and drinks from it.

I raise my eyes. The group of people at the table in the archway is incomplete. There are five of them now—the woman whose voice annoys me; the man accompanying her; the husky, blond man sitting by himself now; and the Mexican girl and her American husband or lover. I know these people; that is, I have seen them in here before. I know their faces almost as well as I know the posters papering the walls above their heads. I have seen these faces many times, exchanging a courteous smile, a formal gesture, or a polite word with them at one time or another, as I was about to pass the table where they might have been sitting, as I had stepped through the front door into the bar, momentarily catching their eyes, as I watched them come in and sit at a table, or as our eyes met accidentally across the room from where we sat. Nothing more, nothing less: a gesture, a smile, or a glance. No familiar words, no intimate handshakes or embraces, no friendly exclamations or welcomes.

Perhaps with the exception of the woman absent from their midst, I would say that I know the faces of all these people to the point of boredom. Yet, the woman seems different. I have never seen her in here before. But I can't say. She has held her face averted, looking in the direction of the bar, at one or two of her companions, or perhaps at some insignificant object on the table—a glass of wine, an empty coaster, etc.

But, for whatever it's worth, I will soon know. She will walk back to the table through the archway, around the people at the table, and sit down; I will see her full face—the eyes, the nose, the mouth, the lips—not just the details of her long neck and exquisite ears. She will undoubtedly glance in our direction. My eyes will meet hers; at that moment, I will know.

What was it Smith said? I believe he said something to the effect that his life was a complete waste, one enormous error. He explained how he had wanted to live one way and had been forced to live another; how at great cost to his sanity he had moved in one direction when he shouldn't have been moving at all; and how—I believe he said this as well—how he was desperately trying to make up for lost time at this late date in his life, at the age of forty-three or forty-four when most men know who they are and what they want. What else did he say? Oh, yes: he said he didn't know what would happen after tonight, what the outcome of this conflict would be, since it was even possible that his wife would slash his throat in his sleep tonight. But what is he doing with his wife tonight if the other one is waiting for him in California? I don't understand.

I believe I remarked, "Caught between Scylla and Charybdis."

The silver bubbles rise regularly to the surface of the beer in the thick, plump glass. The glass is frosted by the chill of the beer. Drops of condensed water occasionally scurry down the smooth roundness of the glass to the stem. The base of the glass rests on a moist cardboard coaster upon which is printed Budweiser in blue curlicue letters. Encompassing the dull brown of the coaster, the red tabletop gleams. The redness of this tabletop is duplicated several times by the other tables, giving the bar an artificially exciting, Spanish air.

Now, on one of these gleaming red tabletops rests an insignificant object—a glass of wine, a smoking cigarette, or perhaps an empty coaster—an insignificant object upon which the gaze of two feminine eyes might have rested, although it is possible that the object of this gaze might well have been one or two of the faces of the people at the table or the general view offered by the bar in the adjacent room. This scarcely matters. What matters is that this gaze was directed at something, at some specific object;

what matters is that this object was the reason a woman's face was averted and, consequently, the reason I have been unable to see the face of that woman.

"After I met Bernice," Smith continues, "nothing mattered. You understand?"

"I think so."

"Nothing but her. Even now, after all that's happened, I wish I could have those first days again, I wish I could see her face as I first saw her. The pretty, girlish smile, the naive laughter. I was so used to looking at my wife I'd forgotten what it was like to look at a really young face, even though at times I thought I was seeing my wife as I first saw her in this girl. But no. It wasn't so. This was another girl, another woman, young, not too pretty, as I said, not even very intelligent, thin and awkward."

He hesitates, taking a deep breath.

"I suppose I'd do the same thing all over again. There doesn't seem to be much else in this world worth anything, worth more than the face of a beloved. That's all that seems to make the pain bearable. Not just bearable but valuable, as if it were a credit to your love. Yes, that's it. The pain becomes as valuable as the pleasure. Absurd perhaps . . . but it makes sense to me."

"I agree," I remarked. "I know what you're talking about."

"At first, it was an affair," he says. "Nothing more than a common affair. They're all common affairs at first. Later you find out that they're never common. I guess if my relationship with my wife hadn't given out, the affair, I hate that stupid word but I'll use it anyway, wouldn't have been more than that, a liaison between a young woman and an older. . . . Christ! that sounds affected, *a young woman and an older man*, as if I were talking about two movie stars, eh? If I'd been satisfied. . . .

"But I wasn't. So here I am, long-suffering, romantic, maudlin, neurotic. At forty-four? These things happen to boys and very young men. To you, not me. It's worse than . . . than. . . .

"Anyway, I left her. I thought when I asked her for the divorce she wouldn't give me too much trouble. We didn't have any children or money. It would've been a mere formality. Well, the point is she wouldn't give me a divorce. And to make matters worse, she got sick. That happened seven months after I left. What could I do? I was against the wall. Against that damned wall. She didn't have any money, no relatives, hardly any friends to speak of; if she'd tried to work she couldn't because she was sick. So I sent her the money. I sent her half my paycheck for two years. Can you imagine that? I was hoping that by doing that she'd have time to get better and back on her feet. Maybe then she'd realize that I wasn't coming back no matter what happened.

"But no. Things didn't change. She stayed sick and I kept sending her the money. Half of my paycheck. That's a lot of money. Especially when you have another woman living with you. Anyway, when Bernice found out she wouldn't give me the divorce, she tried it the first time. Gas. But as I say, she was playing at it, because she told me herself she got up and shut the oven off after deciding it wasn't the way out. I sensed things would get worse but I didn't do anything about it."

"Excuse me," I begin. "There is one thing I don't understand."

His eyes focus directly on mine. He says, "Go ahead. What is it?"

"Perhaps I've not been listening carefully. Maybe it's not even any of my business. I don't know. It's just not clear in my mind why she's attempted to kill herself three times? I mean, if you love her as you say you do, why would she want to kill herself? Obviously, you're not going to leave her. I know it's none of my business. I was just a bit confused about that. Perhaps I've not been listening closely enough."

"No, no. That's perfectly all right. I know I've not been clear about all the details myself. Let me see now."

After the eyes rest momentarily on the glass of beer, he continues, "You see the root of the problem is that my wife still believes I love her. She thinks that because I've sent her money and because we're still not legally divorced I love her. She thinks that with time, after I've tired of Bernice or Bernice has tired of me, I'll return to her like some little boy. That's the last thing I'll do. Which is why I'm here."

The silver bubbles rise monotonously through the yellow liquid as he speaks.

"I told her I didn't love her anymore. I told her I was involved with another woman, that I was going to leave her, and that if I could I would marry the other one. I told her that was it: no more. I wanted no more of her. We were unhappy together. There was no reason why we couldn't get a divorce. But, as it turned out, it wasn't that easy. The woman would not let go. She refused to give me a divorce. She refused it in spite of the fact that I'd already quit my job, yes, in spite of the fact that I was already living with Bernice in California. That was a little over two years ago."

Even though he hasn't answered my question to my satisfaction, I now listen to him, watching the dark, haggard face speak, the eyes downcast and removed. No doubt, he is seeing the faces of those two women—two faces he has kissed and caressed in the darkness, two faces which now await him somewhere in the night beyond the walls of this bar, two faces (one young and fresh, the other one worn, withered), involuted upon each other through the memory of his kisses.

"My wife refused the divorce," he reiterates. "She refused to let go. Even though I told her I wasn't coming back, even though I was already sleeping with another woman. She absolutely refused to let go. So, as I said, she got sick—pneumonia, I think. Some lung infection, anyway. What could I do? I sent her the money and started thinking."

Their faces must come to him in his separation from them like ghosts.

"Maybe I was wrong," he relates. "Maybe it was I who was the selfish one; maybe I'd committed a mistake after all. Christ, you can't imagine how many doubts came to my mind. A million doubts and agonies. One night I said to Bernice that maybe it was wrong. Maybe it wouldn't work after all. I was forty-four years old; she was twenty. In ten years I'd be fifty-four years old; she'd be thirty. You know, the old arguments. What you least think about in the beginning, you end up paying for in the end. It never fails. Well, that did it. The next day I received an emergency call at work from my landlord. Bernice was raving mad. Hysterical, out of her mind. She'd just turned off the gas. I took the rest of the day off. I rushed to the apartment. I swore to her I'd never leave her. We made love, and it was over. As I said she was just playing."

The jukebox begins to play resonantly. I raise my eyes, glancing across the room to the jukebox, losing the thread of Smith's conversation with the rising pitch of the melody. Looking past the assortment of heads at the table in the archway, past the rising tangles of smoke, into the adjacent room, I see the silver bow. I had not anticipated this.

She leans over the jukebox. I still cannot see her face. Apparently, she's selected a song. She will turn at any second in this direction. She must walk back, through the archway, around the people, to her seat, to join her friends again.

The melody is instrumental. I have heard it many times before in this bar, from this very same jukebox. It is a Spanish melody to which I have wanted to dance many times; it is almost a classical piece of music.

Yet, how could she have known it was there, unless she's been in here before? A mischance, a mere coincidence? Perhaps she chose it at random? This is more likely, especially if she's never been in here before. Still . . . still there is another consideration; she may have recognized the title from another time and place. This too is a possibility.

Why shouldn't she play whatever she wishes? Why shouldn't she like it? People have been playing that very melody for as many years as I've been coming here. Should she be any different? Obviously not.

What matters is that the mystery of her presence—perhaps, somewhat exaggerated in my mind by now—will soon be resolved. I will see her; I will gaze upon the face I've been waiting to see all evening, for she must turn from the jukebox in this direction. She must walk back, through the archway, around the people, to her empty seat, to her friends.

She will select the last song; then, she will turn to walk back; then, she will come nearer, the features growing distinct—the eyes, the brow, the nose, the mouth, the chin, and so on. I will gaze directly at her, searching for a glimmer of recognition or warmth in the eyes, noting all the details of her face, judging if my expectations were correct.

Smith says something about Medea. His words come from beyond the resonance of the music. I cannot understand them fully. He may even think I'm paying attention to him: I'm not. I look past his ear, past his heavy shoulders, at the woman in black velvet still leaning over the jukebox.

That too seems odd. Why should she stop at the jukebox by herself? Why didn't she let her blond companion, or perhaps one of the other men at the table, or perhaps one of the waiters in the other room, play the music for her? If she had a lover or husband with her or even a familiar friend, why would she stop by the jukebox by herself? A whim? A caprice of feminine independence? I know that if I were her lover, friend, or husband, I would offer to play the music for her. I would instinctively know what she would want to hear; I would have obliged her.

Now the head turns. Now the whole body turns; now she moves obliquely towards us, the face extremely white, almost pale. But she moves in such a way that the heads of the people at the table in the archway obtrude. I only glimpse the face. She is too far away.

Now she is moving, now she is walking, now she is coming through the archway, now she is moving around the people seated at the table, now she is approaching. The motion is languorous. The head is held erectly. Now the face grows visible, now I see its features: finely penciled eyebrows, dark eyelashes, blue eyes, slight aquiline nose, full lips. Now she turns (but away from me this time) as she bends to sit down. I lose sight of the full face. I miss the profile, too, the motion of sitting down being too swift.

Nevertheless, the eyes were blue, the lips were full, the nose was slightly aquiline, the eyebrows and the eyelashes were well accented. No, I have not seen her before, either in this bar or anywhere else. I was correct. There was more to her than an elegant neck and exquisite ears viewed from a specific angle. No, I have never see such a woman in here before, not in the five years I have been coming here. I cannot say now—at least, not after such a brief glance—that she is beautiful. But she approaches it. Of this, I am certain. She approaches it.

Smith was saying something about Medea, something to the effect, I believe, that his wife is wreaking upon him the vengeance of a Medea, that she will not let him go out of pure vengeance, that the fire of the vengeance is the profound guilt he suffers, that . . . that: he went speaking about other things which really don't matter to me.

I have often wanted to dance this Spanish melody. Listening carefully, I have imagined myself striding gracefully across a polished dance floor, my ears full of the melody, my arms embracing a woman, perhaps a woman such as this one in black velvet. It would be a slow, rhythmic dance, requiring an entire solitary dance floor. The woman would have to understand the spirit of the melody. The very muscles in her thighs would have to feel the fullness, the solemn richness, of its movement; she would have to understand the complex movement of high heels across the sleekness of a dance floor. For, as simple as it sounds, such a melody would not be easy to dance.

Now her legs are crossed. They are no longer as they were before. But this is to be expected. Now she sits in a different position—the long white legs crossed, the black velvet hem pulled back over the thigh, the stockings sleek and smooth as plastic, the straps of her black high heels snug on the white flesh. In effect, the body is now turned away from the table, contrary to the position occupied formerly.

Now she faces the opaque window that joins the wall to form the corner where our table is situated. If she turned her face a few degrees to her right, looking past the head of the man next to her, her eyes would come in direct contact with mine. A few degrees to her right. But to do this she would have to want to look at me—I mean, that there would be no reason for turning her head those few degrees other than to look at me. This situation, however, is obvious only to me; it would not be obvious to anybody at her table, least of all to the man (either her husband, lover, or escort—I'm not certain) sitting next to her with his back towards me. It can't be obvious to her either—at least, not at this moment—because she still hasn't turned her head those few degrees and met my eyes. At this very moment, when thoughts and memories of another world, another man, are running through her mind, she doesn't know I exist; it is the farthest thing from her consciousness that I am watching her. At this very moment, as the smoke tangles from their midst, as the silver bubbles rise through Smith's beer, she does not know I am sitting at this table in this same room.

Now the music stops.

Now Smith speaks more distinctly.

And the music begins again: *Granada.*

Obviously, she likes Spanish music. Obviously.

Smith says his wife is a Medea. Didn't he say this already? I don't recall. Anyway, he says:

"I will not go back. I don't care what happens to her. I don't love her. If she never gives me a divorce, I will never go back. It's my fault she's still clinging to me, I felt sorry for her. I've sent half of my paycheck these last two years. Why? Because I felt sorry. Because I knew she was sick and would have a tough time working. Somehow, I felt that if I finally did leave something terrible would happen to her and I would be responsible for it. It was also my fault Bernice made those attempts on her life; I've faltered too much. I can't blame her. When I left my wife, I shouldn't have looked back. I should have just left. But I looked back. There she was—my wife. Miserable, pitiful. Sick. Lonely. Middle-aged. What could I do? Even now, even as I say I'll leave her for good, I know . . . well, I don't know. I don't know what'll happen."

"You staying with her?" I ask quietly.

"Yes," he replies, relaxing the muscles in his neck. "I'm staying at the house. That's all. I'm just staying there long enough to get things straight for her. Hospital bills. House payments. Some other things. And . . . I'll be telling her that's it. No more money, divorce or no divorce. No more visits to straighten her out. Nothing. Divorce or no divorce, that's it. I can't live like this anymore. It's either her or me. I've no choice."

"She won't try anything desperate will she?"

"I don't know. I don't know what'll happen after tomorrow."

I don't know either. I don't know if she'll turn her head those few degrees to meet my eyes, for it may simply never occur to her to do so. Yet, the possibility is there. Perhaps, I should rise and, walking past her to the jukebox or bathroom, catch her eyes. But the moment would be too brief, too quick—not enough time in which to linger in her eyes, nor enough time for her to realize that it was more than a casual glance. No, it would be best if she merely turned her head those few degrees. That would be best.

Smith finishes his beer.

Mine is still half full. I sip from it.

Smith raises his hand, signalling to one of the waiters in the next room.

She still has not turned her head. I believe she is talking to the blond, heavy set man.

Two beers are bought. The frosted, plump glasses are placed on two dry coasters. Bubbles scurry through the yellow liquid to the foamy surface.

Those few degrees . . .

Now Smith is speaking. Although I'm looking past him, I listen.

"The first two times," he says, "she was playing. Somehow she sensed it was a way to secure my love. She played at it first because she hadn't grown desperate. It wasn't until she felt the desperation in me that she felt it in herself. Anyway, they found her at the bottom of a cliff on the outskirts of town. The car was destroyed. She was unconscious but all right otherwise. Then I knew. I'd been playing too. I'd been playing at love. I'd lived with her those two years as if nothing would come of my indecision, as if my lack of commitment to either woman would never smack me in the face. Well, it did. It caught up with me. When I looked at her bruised face, her swollen eyes and mouth, when I saw what was left of the car . . ."

His face looks like a chunk of adobe. He's suffering. It's in the face, in the intense blankness of his eyes, in the momentary quiver at the corner of his mouth, in the film of sweat on his brow. The voice is unwavering, however. I detect no change in its tonelessness.

". . . I saw what an snivelling little coward I'd been. I saw too plainly what an utter fool I'd made of myself. That young girl had more guts than I ever did. She was willing to drive off a cliff. Can you imagine that? She was willing to do that, while I couldn't even say *no* to another woman. I hate myself for it. Sometimes, I hate myself so much that I think perhaps it'd be best if I took my life. But that would be as ridiculous as everything else that's happened."

I almost laugh. Instead, I rejoin his weak smile with a cynical one. After all, his predicament does seem somewhat preposterous—a man caught between the devil and the deep blue sea, as they say, between his past and his future, realizing that at forty he is a man, not a boy, and must abandon his wife for a younger woman with almost the same callow hesitancy a youngster leaves his mother for a wife. Maybe he is a fool. Who knows?

Will she look at all?

"Her eyes were swollen," says Smith. "When she looked up from that hospital bed, I. . . ."

It's a matter of a few degrees.

"She was hysterical," Smith continues. "I took her and kissed her, told her everything would be all right, that I'd come here to settle things once and for all."

The distance between eyes is. . . .

"That's why I made the trip all the way out here. I wanted to make an end of it."

The eyes.

"I even wish," Smith adds, "that I'd never seen her. I wish I'd never walked into that room where I first saw her. It would've been many times easier. I wish I'd never asked her out, had never kissed her, had never gone to bed with her. But at a moment like that, when you least suspect that . . . that your life will take a wild turn, when you least expect that anything can come of a moment, a look, a gesture, it happens. At least, that's the way it was with me. One day I walked into the office where she worked—the telephone company. That was it. It's sentimental, I know. It happens everyday. It's what bored housewives like to see in their soap operas. It's dull . . . unless it happens to you. But it does happen. That's what's important. It actually happens."

She has not looked. Immobile, abstracted, she remains seated in the same relaxed position she assumed when she sat down, looking vaguely at the man next to her, who seems to be explaining something with an excess of energy.

Now her gaze moves away from the man's face, past and beyond his head, not at me (although I now see her full face) but at the posters on the walls, languorously interested, it seems, in their faded colors and forgotten events; while the man continues moving his hands even more zealously in his explanation, perhaps unaware of her casual indifference.

I watch the movement of her eyes carefully. The face is serene, lucid—the lips, nose, eyes, brow, and cheeks converging in a moment of grace. I must admit I have not seen a woman like this in here before; in fact, I can't remember exactly the last time I saw such a woman. It has been years.

Now the face moves, the eyes descending in a flash of blue. I gaze directly into the blueness, experiencing a violent flow of blood in my gut. The eyes focus. Her look is blank, expressionless, steady in my gaze. Neither casual nor suggestive, the exchange of glances lingers.

Suddenly, it is broken by the outstretched hand of an old Mexican woman selling corsages.

Where did the pink and yellow flowers, the stooped shoulders in a shawl, come from? Did she come in the front door?

The blond man takes a corsage and reaches into his pocket.

Pink and yellow flowers? Damn them.

The eyes are gone.

The man smiles; he says something which, of course, I cannot understand from where I sit. She too smiles but does not say anything. At least, I don't think she says anything, since her face is tilted downwards—although she might have said something like, "Thank you. How sweet of you," or "What beautiful flowers!" Her long, white fingers work gracefully among the yellow flowers, pinning the corsage on the dress. Leaning back the man smiles again, apparently very delighted with his gesture.

But she seems to be having trouble with the corsage. Perhaps, her long fingernails make it awkward for her to handle the small pin; perhaps, she's never done this before and feels self-conscious—I doubt it. The man attempts to help her by holding the corsage with his fingers; this courtesy doesn't seem to work. He removes his hand.

She leans forward, scanning the floor. The man also looks and is about to crouch down when she brushes him on the shoulder, laughing. She's dropped the pin. Now, she places the corsage on the table. Has she abandoned the idea of pinning the corsage? The man sits back, also laughing but less enthusiastically. The yellow flowers remain on the red table, and the old Mexican woman is gone.

I see the clear blue of her eyes even though she is no longer looking in my direction. I see them looking at me, steady and unperturbed, the details of her face individually distinct; I see the blank expressionless gaze. Perhaps, she will look again. But no. How can she? Her thoughts will no doubt be preoccupied with the attention the other man has bestowed on her.

Still, she must know, she must sense—after all, she's a woman—that the intensity of my gaze has not abated. No, I imagine that for the time being—at least, until the interest raised by the corsage has subsided—she dare not betray a glance in my direction.

Smith is getting high. It's just as well, since I haven't been paying him any attention. His tone has changed slightly; he's grown more lachrymose about the matters he's been relating. What was it he said? He said he felt I understood, that he knew I'd suffered and would sympathize with his predicament.

I say nothing. What can I say?

"It seems," he says, "that my whole life is on the line, that this is where I find out what kind of a man I am. If I'm a man. Yes, I thought I would go on loving her, I thought I would go on kissing her and making love to her, without my life falling apart on me, without paying in the end. Here's to love."

The hand raises the fat glass momentarily, then swings it to his mouth.

I take a deep swallow from my own.

Perhaps, he's talked most of it out of his system. The face has relaxed, the eyelids have grown heavy, the mouth is less tense, the film of sweat has evaporated. Perhaps, he has spoken enough, the beer taking its effect.

"Tell me, do you think it's worth it? Do you think in the end it'll make any difference?"

"Probably not," I reply.

"No. That's right. It won't. It won't make a goddamn bit of difference. But the point is that it's happening, that I'm in it, that I just can't walk off, I just can't walk out and forget about it, as if I'd never see her."

He falls silent with this last statement.

I walk to the jukebox, rising from my seat without precisely knowing where I'm going, arriving at the jukebox without remembering which song I had thought to play, standing there momentarily, the white glare from the jukebox in my face, searching for the title of the song, then the selection number, at last placing the dime in the slot, pushing the red buttons, and turning.

Before I reach the table, the music resounds loudly at my back.

I sit down.

The eyes meet again—the moment I slip into my seat, raising my eyes to hers—meeting, as it were, in blank, empty space, somewhere between the two tables.

I gaze directly into that blueness, focusing upon two points of cobalt blue.

The pitch of the music rises and falls sonorously beyond the tables, echoing throughout the two rooms. It is the melody—the same melody, the Spanish melody—she played: classical, subdued, mournful.

The eyes linger.

The melody resonates through the empty space where the eyes met.

The blood flows wildly.

Smith asks, "What's that you played?"

"A Spanish dance," I mutter.

Now the eyes, the melody, and the blood swirl into each other in a pool of sensations, losing their identity, their inherent difference.

The faces, shoulders, arms, and backs of the other people at the table remain in static, blurred relief.

Suddenly, as if it were a pretty white blossom swept into that empty space between us, hanging there lightly in mid-air, a smile breaks from her lips, her white teeth dazzling.

I'm embarrassed; I hadn't anticipated this.

The music swells in volume.

And now we are moving. . . .

Lost in the radiance of the sudden smile, the eyes merge.

And now we are moving, moving through that empty space between the tables where our eyes met and beyond, moving across a floor so highly polished that our reflections speed swiftly beneath us. . . .

Smith says something.

. . . moving without actually being conscious of our legs moving out of our surroundings, whirling, holding firmly to each other in one perfect motion, the dance floor carrying us beyond this common bar, beyond this garish imitation of another world, into that other world of high, papered walls, another world, another country, where men and women celebrate festivals, cheer screaming racers, and *olé* the violence of thin, elegant men. Yes, we dance with the severity, the discretion, of bullfighters, moving through that empty space between the tables, where our eyes met.

Moving, until Smith interrupts again.

"Want to go to another bar?"

"No," I reply curtly.

The eyes are lost now, the mouth gone, the face averted.

"Well, how much longer do you expect to stay here?"

"Let me finish this one."

The jukebox stops playing; laughter and chatter of people fill the rooms.

"Anything wrong?" he asks.

"No. Nothing. Just thinking about what you told me."

"Hmm. Well, forget it. It's not that important. Things will work out somehow. They have to."

"I hope so. For your sake. It's no good being miserable."

"Drink up."

The blond, well-dressed man motions with his hand in the direction of the bar. The waiter, short and olive-skinned, comes. The man reaches in his pocket and gives him several bills from his billfold; the waiter bows, uttering what is a "Thank you" or "Gracias," then leaves. The man looks at the woman sitting next to him, then at the others, exchanges a few words with somebody, turning once more to look at the woman who may or may not return his look.

The young man and his darkhaired Mexican wife rise from their seats.

The couple across from them—the woman whose laugh annoys me and the man accompanying her—follow suit.

Is she leaving so soon?

"Drink up and let's go," says Smith. "I feel like getting drunk tonight."

"In a few minutes," I reply.

Finally, she too rises from her seat, taking a small, black purse from the table. The man stands up beside her, his back towards me, saying something to the young man, chuckling.

They begin to file out through the archway, into the next room, and out the front door.

Why is she leaving so soon? Is that all?—a few glances, a smile, so very little?

I look for the eyes again—nothing.

She walks around the table, the well-dressed man behind her.

She stops, waiting momentarily for the woman before her to move on through the archway.

The head turns casually, as if she were taking one last look at the posters in the room.

The blueness flickers; the eyes meet briefly—that's all.

She passes through the archway, the man in her wake.

"Come on," insists Smith, "drink up. Let's go. I want to get to the Jester Club before they close. I'm sick of this beer. We need some mixed drinks."

"All right, all right. I'm coming."

I quaff the last of my beer, replacing the chubby glass on its moist coaster.

I'm slightly groggy; the effect of the beer glows through me. I didn't realize I'd drunk so much in such a short time.

She's gone.

It was pleasant—the eyes, the mouth, the hands. . . .

Smith goes on ahead of me.

My buttocks are numb from the bite of the rim of the barrel—this bar is charming, but it can be most uncomfortable.

I walk past the round table where she sat.

Smith is already in the other room paying the waiter.

I now move around the table, my feet treading the steps she took across the tile floor.

I glance at the edge of the table where she sat.

What? They're still there? How is this possible? She must have forgotten them. But how could she? How could she have forgotten so easily? Yet, there they are—pale, yellow, abandoned.

Without another thought, I pick them up immediately between my fingers, breathing their fresh aroma. Delightful.

I walk through the archway to the front door where Smith is waiting.

Waving our arms and hands, saying "Buenas noches, buenas noches, hasta mañana!" we step into the warm night.

We pause in the red and blue glow of a neon sign with a flamenco dancer caricatured on one end, announcing THE BAR MADRID.

Smith looks in my face, then at my hand, then in my face.

"What's that you have?" he asks obliquely.

"A gift."

"Where'd you get them?"

"A beautiful lady gave them to me," I answer.

Beyond the luminescence of the neon sign, the night is black.

"Where?"

"In there."

"You mean you found them."

"No. A beautiful lady . . . well, what's the difference? They smell beautiful—that's what's important. Here, smell."

I raise the yellow flowers to his face which he turns away, saying, "Come on. We're wasting time. We've the whole night to drink."

I laugh, taking a deep whiff from the flowers.

Slack, weary from the beer, we cross the deserted street.

The pavement, the buildings, the sky, and the night are black.

We walk into an alley, headed in the direction of the Jester Club at the opposite end of the block.

From the bar I hear the muffled sound of the jukebox playing another song.

The Wedding

Lionel G. García

The wife brought the old man into the kitchen, holding him up by the arm, and steadied him as she reached for a chair. Having placed the chair behind him, she pushed him down gently. He quivered and shook as he slowly lowered himself into the chair. She took his hat off and threw it on the chair next to him.

"Be careful with my hat," he said in Spanish. "It cost a pretty penny."

"I don't see why he needs a hat," the wife said to me, completely ignoring him, "he never goes anywhere. Never even goes outside the house. Why the hat? I'll never know."

He remained silent, looking out the window. He was old and could hardly walk.

"Get me some coffee," he said, rapping on the table with a little authority. "And some crackers," he added.

She took her time heating the coffee, and this seemed to irritate him. Finally, after much waiting and nervous anticipation on his part, she brought the coffee and a cracker and placed them before him on the table. There was an air of defiance on her part, and I couldn't help but think that it was odd behavior after such a long marriage. I thought that by now she would have forgiven him for any pain that he had caused her.

The cup rattled as he picked it up from the saucer. His hands shook as he brought the cup to his lips. After sucking mostly air, he said, "This coffee is too hot," and he placed the cup back with difficulty.

"He always complains," the wife said. "The coffee is too hot! The coffee is too cold!" She was standing behind a small counter that separated the kitchen from the dining table.

He ignored her and looked at me with more intensity than I had seen during the day that I had been there. His one good eye (the right one had a cataract) seemed to penetrate me, and after a while it seemed to water excessively. Little did I know at the time that he was trying to size me up. He wanted to be sure I could appreciate his story.

"I must tell you what happened to me in 1900, when I was ten years old."

The wife stood up straight and went over to the sink. "He's going to tell the wedding story again. I'll bet my life he's going to do it." She looked at me and raised her hand and pointed to her temple with her index finger and made a circle in the air. "He's a little crazy from old age," she said out loud.

"The story concerns a wedding that I attended at a ranch near my childhood home. It was a typical ranch wedding. We, the children, were having a good time riding horses, throwing rocks at birds, and doing all the things children that age do. But I'm ahead of the story." He took a drink from the cup, spilling a good deal. "The coffee is much better now. At least I can drink it."

He took a small piece of cracker and placed it gently in his mouth, as if he were taking communion. He followed with another sip of coffee and then he chewed slowly.

"In those days people were very mean," he said. It amused me that he made that statement. After all, it didn't seem to be logically connected to what we were talking about. "I don't know why, but they were. We don't see meanness like that very often anymore. Oh yes, one could say that our neighbor here on my right is not good, is lazy, but he is not mean."

"Don't talk about the neighbors. Don't you know any better?"

"He's always been a bad neighbor, very lazy and a scoundrel. But that's not important. I know he's lazy and a thief. Didn't he steal my rake?" he asked me. I didn't know.

"Your rake is in the garage underneath all the pile of garbage that you never cleaned in forty years of living in this house. Don't accuse the neighbors of anything. You're the one who is lazy and a scoundrel."

"The neighbor to my left is just as bad. He beats his wife until the poor woman comes running to us for help. But what can I do at my age? I'm ninety-two years old. I'll be ninety-three in eight months. If I were younger I would show him that to hit a woman is a sin against the natural order, besides it's against the law."

His wife was now sitting in a wooden chair across the counter. She was rolling up her sleeves. "You certainly did a lot of hitting when you were young, and I have the scars to prove it."

He looked past the woman as if she were not there. "To hit a woman the way he hits her is against all the laws of man. But what can you do? They say she goes out on him. At night I sometimes see a car go by. I may be wrong. But I do notice that the car slows down in front of the house, and it always passes by when the husband is not around. What do you make of that?"

"He hit me many times when he came home drunk," she said to me. "But what could I do? I had children to think of. If it hadn't been for them I would have left him years ago. Now the children are grown, don't like him, and don't come to visit him. I'm stuck here with him, not able to see my children. I'm not sure they appreciate what I did for them. It was hard, very hard. And then he would take after the children and almost kill them with blows. He would be so drunk that he wouldn't remember, but I'll tell you this, the children never forgot, and they never forgave. Right now he could die, right where he sits, and they wouldn't care. This is the legacy that he has left behind. What is cruel for me is that in his old age he has forgotten what he did and he's not paying for it. He feels no remorse. How can he? He doesn't know what day it is."

I had an uneasy feeling. I didn't want to become involved. The woman wanted desperately for me to agree with her. The old man was ignoring her.

He continued.

"One night she came in running and had blood all over her clothes. The other neighbor, of course, couldn't care less. When I asked him about it, he said it wasn't any of his business, that he was having trouble with his wife also. To think that this is where we wound up living, among these savages. But they aren't as mean as the people I was telling you about. Do you want some more coffee?"

I replied that I had enough.

"If you need some more just ask," he said. "Just as if you were in your own home."

"There were three brothers, mean as wolves, and they delighted in creating trouble wherever they went. Never was a person at peace when they were around. Let me tell you that they one time killed a young calf in front of his owner and asked him if he was going to fight about it. The poor man said no. Who would fight someone like that, and especially when there were three." He pointed three raised fingers at me.

"The week before the wedding they had had an argument with the bride's father . . . nothing serious by anyone's standards. The old man happened to be drinking a beer at a tavern and he said something about another man, an acquaintance of his, an innocent remark in any case, except that the brothers were there and they took exception to the man's remark. They claimed the man being talked about was their uncle. Can you imagine that? They probably didn't even know the man. The man apologized and left, or tried to leave, I should say. They accosted him, tore off his shirt, and slapped him around. The man begged to be left alone and they released him, warning him to be careful how he spoke from now on."

He cocked his eye at me again and held it open until a tear rolled down his face. He wiped the tear with a crooked brown finger as he continued to study me. He took the rest of the cracker and placed it on his tongue. He chewed for a while and then swallowed the cracker with some coffee.

"In any case there was bad blood between the two parties. The man's sons, upon learning what had happened, were angry and had to be restrained from going after the three brothers.

"I remember as if it were yesterday, that the wedding was on a hot August Sunday. We were in the middle of the dog days of summer, the so-called canicula, when even the wind burns your face—the type of weather we had when we blazed the road from San Diego to Freer. It was so hot then that the snakes would hide under the hollow roots of the older trees. All we had to do was go to the old tree and throw gasoline at the trunk and the snakes would roll out in a tangled mess, some so angry that they would strike at each other and would fight to the death locked around each other. We would take a shovel or a grubbing hoe or an ax and kill them. But the more we killed the more there seemed to be. It was like the tale that has no ending."

With a shaky hand he took a handkerchief from his shirt pocket and wiped drool from the corner of his mouth.

"The wedding was beautiful. All morning long people had arrived—on horseback, and wagons, and even one old car. Who brought the car?"

The woman was caught by surprise. She seemed to wake up at the question. "There were no cars in 1900. You've got your stories mixed up. The first car we saw was in 1913–1914, somewhere around there." She returned to her thoughts.

She was not interested in the old man; she had been with him so long that she didn't care for him or his conversation. The most I could say about her was that at least she didn't constantly interrupt the old man while he spoke, only occasionally.

"The wedding itself was at about eleven o'clock that morning. After the ceremony we ate barbecue. The father of the bride, Antonio was his name, Antonio Briones, had killed a calf and his friends had barbecued it in earthen pits all night long. Needless to say, they had been drinking all night long. This is not good, for men to drink all that much."

"Look who's talking now," she said. She looked at me and made a motion like a man drinking beer and pointed at him. She laughed. "They used to call him 'hollow leg' because he drank so much. How quickly this man forgets. I cannot believe this."

He completely ignored her. "Let me tell you why it is wrong for a man to drink a lot. After a while he abandons his family, his wife, his children, everything dear to his heart."

She got up and left. "I can't take anymore of this," she said. She walked out of the kitchen and through a door to the side of the stove. It hadn't occurred to me that there was a room behind the kitchen, but apparently there was one, for this is where she went.

"You understand that we as children were not allowed in the wedding ceremonies. We were observers and we were fed last. We took our plates to the woods to eat. We could hear the laughter of the celebrants as they ate and drank. We were happy also, but not for long. From the woods we could see three men riding across the corn field toward the house, trampling the corn as they came. You understand that to injure a man's crop is to insult him gravely. At that time we didn't know who they were. They were, in fact, the three brothers, the trouble makers, and we were to remember them for the rest of our lives.

"Remember that this happened some seventy-five years ago and I have difficulty remembering names. The father's name was Antonio Briones and he had two sons, Adolfo and Octavio. Two of the men that had been drinking all night were the brothers Juan García and Julian García. The trouble makers, the mean brothers were Juvencio, and. . . ." He couldn't remember.

"Eusebio and Carlos," came the voice from the other room.

"Eusebio and Carlos," the man repeated as if he had thought of the names himself. "And their last name?"

"González," she replied. "And quit bothering me. I'm in the middle of my rosary."

"Juvencio González rode to the table where the wedding party was eating. His two brothers remained behind by the house. I could see him ride almost to the table, almost touching it, and the startled people looked up at him. Antonio Briones, the father, jumped up immediately when he saw the man on horseback.

" 'What do you fellows want? Why do you trample my crop?' The wind was blowing in my direction and I could hear their voices as if I were standing behind them. 'I thought that I had passed the word that I didn't want you at the wedding.'

" 'That's the word we received,' Juvencio replied. 'And it sticks in our craw that anyone would insult us, my brothers and me, in this way. After all, we did you no real harm.'

" 'I have already forgotten that,' Antonio said. 'And as for my sons, they have also. You were not invited and I'm asking you in a friendly way to leave.'

"By that time the men in the wedding party were standing up. The bride was being led quickly away. The women were almost carrying her to the house. The groom, Pablo García, stood. I could see very plainly for I was directly behind a mesquite tree and hiding my body from everyone. Pablo walked to where the conversation was going on. Upon seeing Pablo approach their brother, Juvencio, the other two rode up on their horses. It was then three against two.

"Antonio's sons, Adolfo and Octavio, had been in the house and when they saw what was going on, they reached for their rifles and came out running.

" 'There will be no violence,' Antonio shouted to his sons. 'This is a day for celebration and joy. Let us not destroy it!'

"I can hear the man say those words right now as if I were still hiding behind the tree. The other children that I was with had scattered, and I could see them hiding much the same as I.

"From here on, my mind becomes very vague, as if I had seen this in a dream. The reality did not strike me until I was a young man.

"I had been looking around at my friends when suddenly I heard a shot. By the time I looked up, and it was almost instantaneously, all I could see was a puff of smoke rising from the barrel of a pistol held by one of the terrible brothers. My first instinct was to look to see who had fallen? No one! Then I realized he had shot into the air. Juvencio, the oldest of the mean ones, dismounted. He had a smallish bay horse, smallish but fine looking. He pushed the father backward and I could see the old man trying to resist. Again he was pushed back, and I could see the men coming closer.

" 'Let them fight!' shouted Eusebio, the younger of the malos. He knew it was not a fair fight. 'Leave them alone and I mean it,' he said. He had a menacing look to him as he spoke to the men. 'Anyone interferes and he has me to deal with!'

"Mean Juvencio struck the father on the head and the poor man fell to his knees. Blood started flowing from the top of his head. He had been hit with some type of instrument. Immediately I saw that it was a long-barreled pistol, the same type that the Rangers used in the old days. God help you if you are ever hit on the head with a pistol such as that one. The barrel was thicker than my thumb." He showed his thumb, a worn-out wrinkled digit, brown with age. "The sons, seeing their father bleeding, could not restrain themselves. Who would? Your father is bleeding profoundly and on the ground, his enemy standing over him ready to shoot. They opened fire. The confusion was great, as you can imagine. Juvencio fell dead, but not before firing several shots into poor Antonio, the father of the bride. He also died immediately. Now everything becomes a blur to me, for the action was so fierce, so intense, that I could not follow it. There were too many things going on at one time. The women were crying and screaming in the house. They could see exactly what was going on, but they were powerless. But it seems to me that Pablo García, the groom, was the next to fall. There was no cause to kill him. He fell by the side of his father-in-law. The two surviving mean brothers, Eusebio and Carlos, were shooting at everyone, and Adolfo and Octavio were shooting at them. The women had broken through the door and were running toward the scene. The brothers, Juan and Julio García, were unarmed and did not have a chance. Both fell as they tried to intervene.

"The thing is that Adolfo and Octavio, the old man's sons, apparently were enraged when they witnessed the father being attacked. Who wouldn't? Wouldn't you have done the same?

"After it was over, and it was over quickly, although at that time it seemed an eternity, there were eight men killed. Most children never experience the violent death of one single person in their life-time, but here I was, on that day I had seen the death of eight men. Let me tell you who they were: Antonio Briones, the father of the bride and one of his sons, Adolfo. Octavio survived the onslaught and had a very prolonged recuperation. He was maimed for life. Pablo García, dead. He was the groom. Killed defending his father-in-law's honor. That's three. The three brothers who would cause no more problems. That's six. And the brothers Juan and Julio García who had been drinking all night.

"The aftermath was horrible, even more horrible than the shooting itself. The women were on the men as soon as the shooting stopped. They were screaming and crying and could not contain their grief. They were running from body to body screaming. The bride's dress, which had been white and beautiful shortly before, was now splattered with blood. She tried to hold her husband's head on her lap, but she jumped up and ran toward her father, torn between the two men. The bride's mother, Antonio's wife, was in a rage and she picked up a revolver that belonged to God knows who and began firing at Juvencio, her husband's killer, even though he was already dead.

"You can imagine what an episode like that does to a child. I have lived with that memory for most of my life."

He was silent for a while as he looked at me with that crooked eye. He took one last piece of cracker and a drink of coffee. Then he reached over and picked up his hat by the crown. He placed it straight on his head and I noticed how large his ears were.

"Are you through?" came the voice from the room.

"Yes," he answered.

She came out, grabbed him by the arm and led him away. He tried to say something, but she told him to hush. "You've talked enough already."

"Wait a minute," he said, forcefully removing her hand from his arm. "I have more to say."

"No, you don't," the woman replied. "You're going to bed."

"Leave me alone!" he shouted. "Can't you see that I need to say one more thing? God damn it, why must you bother me so?"

He braced himself with his hand on the counter and swayed gently back and forth. "When I was a child," he said, and a tear came down his face, "my father would take us to a small lake near where I was born. And on the surface of the lake you could see the salt as it collected and floated to the shore. We would go there and pack salt and in the winter we would kill the ducks that had migrated from God knows where. We would take the dead birds and wash the lice off them in the salt water, skin them, feathers and all, and clean them to take home. My father loved the tails. He ate them raw. He would chew the tail off the ducks just like one chews the end off a loaf of bread. My brothers and I, we would laugh and feel like vomiting, but mostly we would laugh. No one knew why the lake was salty, but you could float almost anything in it. We bathed in it during the summer, but we were never allowed to go to the deep end. Someone had told my father that it was very deep. Later on in my older years when I was operated on in my head for a tumor I dreamed after the operation, that we were cutting large slabs of salt and loading them on mule drawn wagons, and it seemed the dream went on forever, the salt went on forever. But," he said turning toward the woman and extending his arm to her, "those were the good days when I was like new."

I could hear her scolding him in the back room as she put him to bed.

"Do you need to go to the toilet?" she asked.

"No," came the meek childish reply.

"Tomorrow maybe I can tell him about the snakes," he said.

"Shut up and go to sleep," she said. "You've already talked enough for two days."

Para Siempre, Maga

Juan Felipe Herrera

Sí Maga. Ya se que no quieres que te visite en la librería.
Dices que sólo llego para observarte como un astrónomo literario o que te rodeo como hombre-nube; que me acerco léntamente y me quedo fríamente suspendido frente a ti.

Me lo has dicho varias veces.
Me acusas de existir en un tipo de anti-disfraz que es un velo a la vez. No. No con la indumentaria de esos detectivillos de la agencia aquí en Tijuana o de vendedor de lotería, ni como uno de esos profesorsillos cucarachos que beben su lágrima de cafe en el Hotel Nelson. Mi disfraz es diferente. ¿Verdad?

Soy el fino actor de salones literarios, como este. ¿No? No utilizo máscaras ni maquillaje. Nada de ligas o resistol. Solamente gestos: momentos transparentes que nadie puede leer, solo tú. Soy aquel hombre elegante y bien educado que al entrar a este paraíso de sílabas fúnebres levanta un ancho libro de *Seix Barral* o de *Joaquín Mortiz* y frunce la frente y analiza cada ese, qu y zeta y al preciso instante—sin perturbar ni una ceja-se hecha un jaa ja jaaa ja ja jaaaa.

Este es el drama que siempre estreno en esta sala en los sábados por la noche. Todo lo preparo minuciosamente para disfrazar mi única intención: verte. Estudiarte. Verte más.

Mentiras.
Tú eres la actriz, Maga. Te ríes porque llego y te cuento de mis pequeñas tragedias como cuando era chamaco en San Diego y vine a Tijuana solamente para electrificarme en el *Cinema* en medio de la película *La Momia Azteca* porque toqué los metálicos sillones sudando; mis tíos me habían forzado vestir un pinchi traje de lana. Te ríes artificialmente.

En otra ocasión entré corriendo y te grité que los güachos habían detenido al Meño de San Ysidro porque andaba distribuyendo folletos sobre los derechos de los de *Cartolandia,* esos pobres que vivían en casas de cartón debajo del puente viejo que ahora han convertido en *Río-Tijuana.* Te mostré su foto en el periódico. Abriste la boca en horror.

¿A poco crées que todo lo que te digo es un teatrito que invento para poder oír a los escuincles de la Alba Roja comprar su librillo de primaria o el aplauso dental de los rucones que al acariciar las últimas del *Esto* estallan con nuevas apuestas de soccer?

Vango a tu salon de raros abecedarios porque no existe en ninguna otra parte de esta ciudad un asilo de imágenes tan claras. Sí Maga, no tienes que pronunciar ni una vocal. Créeme.

¿Ves a esa chavalona afuera, como a 15 metros de aquí, allí afuerita del Cine Roble? No necesitas asomarte, la puedes divisar bien de donde estas. Casi cada noche durante la última semana ha llegado. Se queda erquida. Nadie se da cuenta. Viste faldas floreadas o pantalones de mesclilla a la moda. Su pelo es brillante, negro como una hoja de acero. Tendrá unos años menos que yo, como 28 o 29. Mira como se acerca al cartelón y a los anuncios en la ventana. ¿La ves Maga? Nadie ha notado como se va acercando. Paulatinamente.

Doña Aurelia sigue vendiendo sus conos de pepitas. Ferni el bolero, lo de siempre: correteando a los gavachos para cobrarles bonito. Ni el cirujano, el Doctor Quiñones, ha notado algo—el que tiene su clínica a media cuadra de "Tortas el Turco". Nadie. Mira como se va acercando al afiche de Rigo Tovar.

Rigo, eres mío.
Totalmente mío. No importa a donde viajes o que nunca regreses te quiero y sé que siempre llevarás mi imagen contigo, siempre.

¿La conoces Maga?
Te la señalo porque es una mujer perfecta. Carga una X sobre el pecho.

A las siete de la noche baja de la *Colonia del Rubí* o del *Kilómetro 24* o de *La Cacho* levantando su crucifijo secreto, su doble cicatriz hacia la estampa del Señor Rigo Tovar bajo la dorada luz de la taquillera sacerdotisa para murmurarle su lealtad, sus mandas y sus ocultas soledades a su amante nocturno. Y frente a esta parroquia de ambulantes de neón mostrará sus heridas gemelas y nadie tornará los ojos y nadie la escuchará rezar.

Te lo repito Maga, este es el extasis de la perfección: mantenernos perfectos en nuestras incompletas búsquedas.

Usted señor, no se preocupe. Ya se que a veces le tomo demasiado tiempo a Maga. Es una señorita muy formal. ¿verdad? Siempre esta aquí a su lado. Yo vine como siempre, a visitar y charlar con ella. Nomas mírela, que hermosura, parece un ohra de arte. ¿No crée señor?

Ya se que no quiere que los moleste. Pero, mire, la librería estaba vacía y quise acompañarlos. No se apure. ¿Quién esta hablando del Meño? Lo que pasó voló. Siga sentado.

Al contrario, busco unos libros que cargaba el Centro Cultural de la Raza en San Diego. De vez en cuando usted los ordena. Busco la última obra de Omar Salinas, creo que se llama *Darkness Under the Trees* y un libro de Evangelina Vigil, poeta Chicana de Texas. ¿Me los puede buscar? Y me voy, de volada.

¿No les molesta este cigarro, verdad? Esta mañana cuando manejaba de San Diego divisaba la alambrera que corre a través el oriente al poniente de la frontera. Vi un vapor de pesadillas. Oí las uñas de mil pájaros rasguñando los nudos de púas, pepenando algo; quizás las aromas de las sombras que cruzan sin papeles—sin disfraz—las que tienen años de construir piñatas, expertas en la contabilidad de lavaplatos, maestras de lavabaños. Punzan grietas. Y a cualquier momento explotan y vacían su honda bilis de siglos y quedan tiezas al lado de algun matorral con el beso final de la migra. Y al curso de los años las púas de la *línea* van alzando sus banderitas: pequeñas estampas de piel o de camiseta o de blusa como recuerdos de los olvidados sepúlcros de aquellas oscuras figuras de sed. Y de repente caen los pájaros para celebrar estas razgadas migagas de extraño pan.

Ya sé que estoy repitiendo lo que todos ya saben. No me lo tienen que advertir. ¿Es hora de cerrar, verdad? Tiene a su esposa esperándolo y Maga tiene que acostarse en el cuarto aquí atrás mientras encuentra un apartamento. Páseme el cenicero por favor.

¿Apunta a estas hojas que tengo enrolladas en mi saco? ¿Le interesan? No. No son poemas. Son garabatos que de lejos aparecen como rayas y a una distancia extrema se asemejan a párrafos. ¿Qué no va a cerrar? Mire como están saliendo del primer estreno de Rigo Tovar. Bueno, investigue usted mismo, A Maga le gustan mis garabatos. Aquí estan. A ver póngase sus lentes, vea.

¿Qué le parecen señor? Aquí esta uno cortito.

No eres buen poeta, Esteves. Estos "garabatos", como dices ni son garabatos. Son instantes concretos de tus profundas debilidades, pero, no escuchas. Nunca te diste cuenta. Vienes aquí a medio dia y te quedas hasta media noche. Tormentas al señor y a mi. Me regalas estos poemillas. Alarmas a los pobres clientes con tu confetti de fantasía y wiri-wiri.

Tú mismo has inventado tu X. ¿Qué te importan los ilegales? ¿Qué sabes tú de los polleros y su gula? ¿Acaso conoces a las putas y sus escenarios de esclavitud? Lo pretendes, como en tu poema *El Blue-Fox/1966,* que hace poco se publicó por aquí.

Te burlas, te imaginas, pero nunca te das cuenta de lo que realmente sucede. ¿A ver, como se llama esa mujer frente a la ventanilla de Rigo Tovar? Ilusiones tuyas. No le está suplicando nada. Imbécil. Se esta untando lipstick o *Maybelline.* Usa la ventana como espejo. Allí espera a sus amantes. ¿Y qué?

Vienes de San Diego con tu ristra Chicana; bola de pochos altaneros. Y compran libros de Miguel León-Portilla, Garibay y Octavio Paz. Los compran como compran el pan de *La Tapatía.* Idólatras. ¿A poco crées que a Don Octavio Paz le importa a lo que le llamas "El movimiento chicano"? Fanfarronadas.

Tú y tus tales chicanos—hasta con X se la hechan, *Xicanos*—caen como santos paracaídistas y dan sus conferencias y presentan sus paneles *para el Pueblo.* ¿A ver pues, cuál pueblo fue a escucharlos? solamente esas liguillas de macisitos adolecentes. Babosadas.

¿Sabes qué, ustedes nunca realmente salen de la librería, verdad? ¿Qué hicieron con la poesía Náhuatl de Garibay? ¿Quién aprendió a leer maya para organizar a los obreros? Sí, la cosa es más compleja. Todo se entiende,

Naturalmente. Estoy de acuerdo, no ha sido una farsa total. De ésas ya tenemos suficientes. Ha sido un drama barato, Esteves.

A lo más han logrado un teatrito de limosna como esos chavos que andan vestidos de acólitos mamones con su peinado francesito imitando a los de "Menudo". Qué nice.

¿Esto es lo que me has querido decir con tus "garabatos", con el cuento de tu trajesito de lana? Pobrecito. Estas agonías nos causan risa. Jaa ja jaaa.

¿Vés al señor, a poco ha levantado una ceja desde que llegaste? Cuando entraste esta tarde, ¿quién meneó una méndiga pestaña? ¿Yo? No gastes saliva Esteves. No queremos ver tus fotos del Meño que recortaste del *Alarma* hace años, ni las pinturas de tus artistas *Xicanos* que vienen al Mercado Hidalgo y le compran flores plásticas a las indias y al mes o dos regresan con una exhibición sobre la "Realidad Indígena".

Nadie seriamente lee tus "garabatos".

Esteves, ya no nos visites. El señor está anciano y yo no estoy para circo. Lárgate.

Buenas noches, señor. ¿Ha visto a mi esposo, Steve? Habíamos quedado de encontrarnos acá afuera del *Roble* cerca de la figura de Rigo Tovar. Ya tengo tiempo esperándolo y nada. No aparece. Se que pasa por aquí seguido. Stevie. ¿Qué tienes? ¿Qué se te olvidó que a las 9:00 frente al cartelón? ¿Oyes? Estevan. ¿Pues, qué te sucede? ¿Acaso no reconoces? Estevansito.

Estevansito, ven aquí. Ya pues. No tienes que gastar tanto tiempo aquí. ¿Que tanto le ves a Maga para ignorar unos cuantos momentos conmigo? Andale, ven. ¿Me oyes? Mira m'ijo, ya tienes bastantes horas mirando esa foto en la portada de ese libro que siempre recojes cuando venimos a Tijuana. Le murmuras. Le suplicas. Le acaricias. Estavansito.

Te lo compro pues, ok? Vamos a la playa en vez de al cine, a caminar. ¿Qué te parece? No me gusta verte encerrado en este subterráneo de papel. ¿Qué tanto le ves a Magdalena Murillo, esa actriz española que hace años salía en las películas con Joaquín Cordero? Nunca se supo más de ella. Tu mismo lo has dicho.

¿Qué está tartamudeando ese viejo, Maga? Parece que esta soñando en estereo otra vez. Ya hubiera cerrado hace horas. Viejo codo. Nomás se desvela para ver si puede chuparse otro centavo de algun fulano que por mala suerte se tropiece por estos rumbos. Ni hizo el esfuerzo de buscarme los libros.

Si, Maga, vine a verte a ti, y para decirte que es hora de irnos. Vámonos. Solamente tú y yo. Los dos. Es tarde.

Ya la cúpula del cielo está deslizando su abanico de negro incienso y brisa y el cuarzo en las metálicas entrañas de los jardines empieza a pulsar su luz espesa. Ha llegado nuestro momento.

En poco tiempo las sombras de todos comenzarán ha despertar el fluido eléctrico que corre a travez de esta gran sala al lado de la costa Pacífica. Te enseñaré las transparentes multitudes marchando hacia sus cajas sagradas de perfectos deseos y perfectas memorias. Te mostraré donde guardan sus bultos antiguos almacenados en las lomas de *La Obrera* o al lado de alguna lijada cruz blanca en la carretera o en las húmedas sustancias de un puño de arena trigueña forjado por el mar.

Ven querida.

Al fin estaremos juntos. Ven amor. Quedaremos escritos en la cumbre de algun precipicio que nadie divisará; uno sobre el otro, como una X mayúscula sobre la tierra del Sur. Brillante. Para siempre.

Para siempre, Maga.

The Circuit

Francisco Jiménez

It was that time of year again. Ito, the strawberry sharecropper, did not smile. It was natural. The peak of the strawberry season was over and the last few days the workers, most of them braceros, were not picking as many boxes as they had during the months of June and July.

As the last days of August disappeared, so did the number of braceros. Sunday, only one—the best picker—came to work. I liked him. Sometimes we talked during our half-hour lunch break. That is how I found out he was from Jalisco, the same state in Mexico my family was from. That Sunday was the last time I saw him.

When the sun had tired and sunk behind the mountains, Ito signaled us that is was time to go home. "Ya esora," he yelled in his broken Spanish. Those were the words I waited for twelve hours a day, every day, seven days a week, week after week. And the thought of not hearing them again saddened me.

As we drove home Papá did not say a word. With both hands on the wheel, he stared at the dirt road. My older brother, Roberto, was also silent. He leaned his head back and closed his eyes. Once in a while he cleared from his throat the dust that blew in from outside.

Yes, it was that time of year. When I opened the front door to the shack, I stopped. Everything we owned was neatly packed in cardboard boxes. Suddenly I felt even more the weight of hours, days, weeks, and months of work. I sat down on a box. The thought of having to move to Fresno and knowing what was in store for me there brought tears to my eyes.

That night I could not sleep. I lay in bed thinking about how much I hated this move.

A little before five o'clock in the morning, Papá woke everyone up. A few minutes later, the yelling and screaming of my little brothers and sisters, for whom the move was a great adventure, broke the silence of dawn. Shortly, the barking of the dogs accompanied them.

106

While we packed the breakfast dishes, Papá went outside to start the "Carcanchita." That was the name Papá gave his old '38 black Plymouth. He bought it in a used-car lot in Santa Rosa in the winter of 1949. Papá was very proud of his little jalopy. He had a right to be proud of it. He spent a lot of time looking at other cars before buying this one. When he finally chose the "Carcanchita," he checked it thoroughly before driving it out of the car lot. He examined every inch of the car. He listened to the motor, tilting his head from side to side like a parrot, trying to detect any noises that spelled car trouble. After being satisfied with the looks and sounds of the car, Papá then insisted on knowing who the original owner was. He never did find out from the car salesman, but he bought the car anyway. Papá figured the original owner must have been an important man because behind the rear seat of the car he found a blue necktie.

Papá parked the car out in front and left the motor running. "Listo," he yelled. Without saying a word, Roberto and I began to carry the boxes out to the car. Roberto carried the two big boxes and I carried the two smaller ones. Papá then threw the mattress on top of the car roof and tied it with ropes to the front and rear bumpers.

Everything was packed except Mamá's pot. It was an old large galvanized pot she had picked up at an army surplus store in Santa María the year I was born. The pot had many dents and nicks, and the more dents and nicks it acquired the more Mamá liked it. "Mi olla," she used to say proudly.

I held the front door open as Mamá carefully carried out her pot by both handles, making sure not to spill the cooked beans. When she got to the car, Papá reached out to help her with it. Roberto opened the rear car door and Papá gently placed it on the floor behind the front seat. All of us then climbed in. Papá sighed, wiped the sweat off his forehead with his sleeve, and said wearily: "Es todo."

As we drove away, I felt a lump in my throat. I turned around and looked at our little shack for the last time.

At sunset we drove into a labor camp near Fresno. Since Papá did not speak English, Mamá asked the camp foreman if he needed any more workers. "We don't need no more," said the foreman, scratching his head. "Check with Sullivan down the road. Can't miss him. He lives in a big white house with a fence around it."

When we got there, Mamá walked up to the house. She went through a white gate, past a row of rose bushes, up the stairs to the front door. She rang the doorbell. The porch light went on and a tall husky man came out. They exchanged a few words. After the man went in, Mamá clasped her hands and hurried back to the car. "We have work! Mr. Sullivan said we can stay there the whole season," she said, gasping and pointing to an old garage near the stables.

The garage was worn out by the years. It had no windows. The walls, eaten by termites, strained to support the roof full of holes. The dirt floor, populated by earth worms, looked like a gray road map.

That night, by the light of a kerosene lamp, we unpacked and cleaned our new home. Roberto swept away the loose dirt, leaving the hard ground. Papá plugged the holes in the walls with old newspapers and tin can tops. Mamá fed my little brothers and sisters. Papá and Roberto then brought in the mattress and placed it on the far corner of the garage. "Mamá, you and the little ones sleep on the mattress. Roberto, Panchito, and I will sleep outside under the trees," Papá said.

Early next morning Mr. Sullivan showed us where his crop was, and after breakfast, Papá, Roberto, and I headed for the vineyard to pick.

Around nine o'clock the temperature had risen to almost one hundred degrees. I was completely soaked in sweat and my mouth felt as if I had been chewing on a handkerchief. I walked over to the end of the row, picked up the jug of water we had brought, and began drinking. "Don't drink too much; you'll get sick," Roberto shouted. No sooner had he said that than I felt sick to my stomach. I dropped to my knees and let the jug roll off my hands. I remained motionless with my eyes glued on the hot sandy ground. All I could hear was the drone of insects. Slowly I began to recover. I poured water over my face and neck and watched the dirty water run down my arms to the ground.

I still felt a little dizzy when we took a break to eat lunch. It was past two o'clock and we sat underneath a large walnut tree that was on the side of the road. While we ate, Papá jotted down the number of boxes we had picked. Roberto drew designs on the ground with a stick. Suddenly I noticed Papá's face turn pale as he looked down the road. "Here comes the school bus," he whispered loudly in alarm. Instinctively, Roberto and I ran and hid in the vineyards. We did not want to get in trouble for not going to school. The neatly dressed boys about my age got off. They carried books under their arms. After they crossed the street, the bus drove away. Roberto and I came out from hiding and joined Papá. "Tienen que tener cuidado," he warned us.

After lunch we went back to work. The sun kept beating down. The buzzing insects, the wet sweat, and the hot dry dust made the afternoon seem to last forever. Finally the mountains around the valley reached out and swallowed the sun. Within an hour it was too dark to continue picking.

The vines blanketed the grapes, making it difficult to see the bunches. "Vámonos," said Papá, signaling to us that it was time to quit work. Papá then took out a pencil and began to figure out how much we had earned our first day. He wrote down numbers, crossed some out, wrote down some more. "Quince," he murmured.

When we arrived home, we took a cold shower underneath a waterhose. We then sat down to eat dinner around some wooden crates that served as a table. Mamá had cooked a special meal for us. We had rice and tortillas with "carne con chile," my favorite dish.

The next morning I could hardly move. My body ached all over. I felt little control over my arms and legs. This feeling went on every morning for days until my muscles finally got used to the work.

It was Monday, the first week of November. The grape season was over and I could now go to school. I woke up early that morning and lay in bed, looking at the stars and savoring the thought of not going to work and of starting sixth grade for the first time that year. Since I could not sleep, I decided to get up and join Papá and Roberto at breakfast. I sat at the table across from Roberto, but I kept my head down. I did not want to look up and face him. I knew he was sad. He was not going to school today. He was not going tomorrow, or next week, or next month. He would not go until the cotton season was over, and that was sometime in February. I rubbed my hands together and watched the dry, acid stained skin fall to the floor in little rolls.

When Papá and Roberto left for work, I felt relief. I walked to the top of a small grade next to the shack and watched the "Carcanchita" disappear in the distance in a cloud of dust.

Two hours later, around eight o'clock, I stood by the side of the road waiting for school bus number twenty. When it arrived I climbed in. Everyone was busy either talking or yelling. I sat in an empty seat in the back.

When the bus stopped in front of the school, I felt very nervous. I looked out the bus window and saw boys and girls carrying books under their arms. I put my hands in my pant pockets and walked to the principal's office. When I entered I heard a woman's voice say: "May I help you?" I was startled. I had not heard English for months. For a few seconds I remained speechless. I looked at the lady who waited for an answer. My first instinct was to answer her in Spanish, but I held back. Finally, after struggling for English words, I managed to tell her that I wanted to enroll in the sixth grade. After answering many questions, I was led to the classroom.

Mr. Lema, the sixth grade teacher, greeted me and assigned me a desk.

He then introduced me to the class. I was so nervous and scared at that moment when everyone's eyes were on me that I wished I were with Papá and Roberto picking cotton. After taking roll, Mr. Lema gave the class the assignment for the first hour. "The first thing we have to do this morning is finish reading the story we began yesterday," he said enthusiastically. He walked up to me, handed me an English book, and asked me to read. "We are on page 125," he said politely. When I heard this, I felt my blood rush to my head; I felt dizzy. "Would you like to read?" he asked hesitantly. I opened the book to page 125. My mouth was dry. My eyes began to water. I could not begin. "You can read later," Mr. Lema said understandingly.

For the rest of the reading period I kept getting angrier and angrier with myself. I should have read, I thought to myself.

During recess I went into the restroom and opened my English book to page 125. I began to read in a low voice, pretending I was in class. There were many words I did not know. I closed the book and headed back to the classroom.

Mr. Lema was sitting at his desk correcting papers. When I entered he looked up at me and smiled. I felt better. I walked up to him and asked if he could help me with the new words. "Gladly," he said.

The rest of the month I spent my lunch hours working on English with Mr. Lema, my best friend at school.

One Friday during lunch hour Mr. Lema asked me to take a walk with him to the music room. "Do you like music?" he asked me as we entered the building.

"Yes, I like corridos," I answered. He then picked up a trumpet, blew on it and handed it to me. The sound gave me goose bumps. I knew that sound. I had heard it in many corridos. "How would you like to learn how to play it?" he asked. He must have read my face because before I could answer, he added: "I'll teach you how to play it during our lunch hours."

That day I could hardly wait to get home to tell Papá and Mamá the great news. As I got off the bus, my little brothers and sisters ran up to meet me. They were yelling and screaming. I thought they were happy to see me, but when I opened the door to our shack, I saw that everything we owned was neatly packed in cardboard boxes.

Florinto

E. A. Mares

He would arrive like the approach of a sudden storm coming in from the west. First there was the din of the iron-rimmed wheels as they scraped and thumped on the pebbles, rocks, and hard-packed dirt of New York Avenue, as the dirt road leading into Old Town was somewhat pretentiously called. Then came the clatter of hooves mingling with the groaning wheels, the rattling old boards of the wagon, the creaky harness and the crack of a whip in the clean blue air of a late summer day. Out of this clamor would come the joyous and piercing shout of Florinto—Heyaaahhh! Heyaaahhh!—as he encouraged Relámpago, his old long-suffering, and reluctant donkey tugging at the harness to make the effort to pull the claptrap cart just a little further on, un poco más allá, más allá.

For us, the children of Old Town, nothing in our experience quite compared with the arrival of Florinto.

"¡Aquí viene Florintoooh! Here he comes! Here he comes!"

"Heyaaahhh! Heyaaahhh! Relámpago! ¡Andaleeeh!"

"Pablo, throw a rock at him. Watch what'll happen!"

"I will, but you better not tell on me when school starts. Sister Caritas will really give it to us."

"Híjola, he stopped the cart! Run, run, he'll catch us for sure!"

This general uproar caused by the sudden appearance of Florinto in our midst was the moment of highest drama in our days which were not without other adventures, especially toward the end of summer when we knew we would have to crowd our good times into the short space remaining before grade school started once again.

I was one of the youngest and smallest members of the Old Town "gang," as we called ourselves. Despite my age and size, I was always ready to plunge into the mysterious world that Old Town was for every member of the gang. On many a summer afternoon, I sneaked out the bedroom window of my home during nap time, rounded up the other boys, and launched a commando raid on the forest of magical fruit, the

111

cherry orchard, which belonged to Mr. Alarid, my parents' landlord. I was among the daring few who slipped through the broken door panel and crept up the stairs of the "haunted house" at the corner of Old Town Plaza. It was a deserted adobe building filled with junk and abandoned furniture covered with sheets which the layered dust of many years of neglect had turned the color of weathered parchment. For us it was gothic and forbidding because an old woman had lived and died there. Some said she had murdered her children and no one would ever go near her and that was why the building was locked up. If you listened carefully, you could hear her crying and howling in the wind which came whistling through the cracked vigas and the broken windows. The moaning sound would wither all but the stoutest hearts. I was also one of the altar boys who raided the priest's wine cupboard behind the altar of San Felipe Church and drank deeply of that sacred beverage. Not even the hours of dawn which turned the statues of every medieval saint lurking in the dark corners of the sacristy into exterminating angels deterred us from those frequent and delicious raids on the wine. But there was something about Florinto which made me hesitate and retreat from the aggressive and cruel teasing with which the gang taunted him.

It was certainly not fear of Sister Caritas which prevented me from tormenting Florinto. My knuckles still hurt when I remember how she would rap us because of our misdeeds. She would stand me in line with the other rowdy children of San Felipe School, hands extended palms down, and then strike us one by one with a wooden ruler. Sometimes the ruler would break into flying splinters as it crashed down on the backs of our hands. Nor was it only respect for the opinion which my parents and all the grownups had of Florinto which made me pause and reflect about teasing him. They thought him to be an "inocente," one who was capable of no evil and who, indeed, was especially protected by God. Rather it was the burning depth of his eyes which fascinated me, made me wonder if he saw something which I could someday understand.

I even felt ashamed of myself for participating in and enjoying the mild practical jokes which the altar boys played on Florinto. There was the Sunday morning, for example, when my friend Pablo who was serving Mass with me lured Florinto into creating a disturbance in Church. "Florinto, si pegas un gritito, if you shout or make a little noise during Mass, I'll give you a nickel," Pablo said to him before the service began. Right after Father Nuñez finished his sermon, Florinto made a noise from between his tobacco stained teeth which sounded something like an owl— "whoo whoo, whoo whoo." No one dared laugh out loud, especially those parishioners who were caught in the dark glances and frowns of the women in black dresses and black shawls, the grandmothers and widows and elderly aunts of Old Town, but many blushed and coughed nervously in their effort to feign a composure which had, in fact, been shattered. Florinto looked at the gathered faithful with mischievous eyes and a wide and proud smile, much as a young child who has just performed a very successful stunt or prank. Father Nuñez, a strict Jesuit fresh from Spain, glared at Pablo and me. He know who the culprits were. The very next day, Monday morning, Sister Caritas administered the inevitable justice to us. Our hands, as well as our behinds, were very sore for a little while.

I'll never forget the day Florinto's mother died. It was the same day the carnival came to celebrate the Old Town fiesta. My grandmother, my mother, and my many aunts took me, an unwilling hostage, to the velorio, the wake which was held for the departed. Florinto lived with his mother and his elderly sister in an ancient adobe house, really a converted stable, on the Rancho Seco Road, a mere wagon rut winding off New York Avenue. Florinto's mother died in the morning. When we arrived, early in the evening, she was laid out in black and holding a black rosary with a silver cross in her hands. We viewed the body and prayed the rosary led by Juana la Rezadora, the veiled and saintly woman who said the rosary and mourned at all the Old Town funerals.

Then we filed into the kitchen for the ritual meal. The long table was filled with huge kettles of posole, steaming dishes of tamales, and plates of empanaditas fresh from the oven. Every neighbor had contributed something and everyone was there, except Florinto. Much later, just before midnight, he returned from the carnival.

"Florinto, shame on you!" His sister scolded him. "Your mother's body is still warm and you are out celebrating at the carnival. Have you no shame?"

"¿Pues que mal hice?" he asked in a just and resonant voice. He said that he had been celebrating because his mother was now in heaven and he knew that only her body was here and that all good friends and vecinos of Old Town would be praying for her soul. He said that was why God had sent the carnival, to celebrate this occasion with joy. "No hice mal." No one, of course, was able to answer Florinto.

At Christmas time Florinto would go from house to house. "On' 'ta mis crismes?" he would ask. It was the middle of the Great Depression and everyone in Old Town was poor, but no one turned Florinto away empty handed, even if the gift was only a couple of oranges, or an old piece of clothing. Once, for Christmas Midnight Mass, Florinto showed up wearing in great splendor the pale blue pin-striped Palm Beach suit my father had given him much earlier in the year. The next day, Relámpago was seen to be sporting Mr. Duran's one-time favorite sombrero.

During the rest of the year, Florinto supported himself by collecting old clothes, rags, and the garbage once a week from all the homes in Old Town. Some people paid him fifty cents, others only a quarter. He would go from house to house in his cart pulled along by Relámpago. It was on these occasions that we children experienced the most welcome and exhilarating moment of the entire week.

"¡Aquí viene Florinto!"

First we heard a far-off tremor in the air, the beginning, so it seemed, of a small earthquake. Then the very curtains of heaven were rent in half by the thunderous cry: "Heyaaahhh! Heyaaahhh!" At that moment, in the screeching uproar of metal wheels on the graveled road, Relámpago would heave into sight with his head raised high and proud.

"Let's chase Florinto!"

"Get some rocks!"

"Throw the rocks and run because he'll get you."

"Yeah, Florinto is fast! You've gotta watch him!"

"¡A la chingada!"

There in the middle of all the dust and noise stood Florinto in his cart looking as I imagined a Biblical prophet to look. His white and untamed hair formed a riot of light about his head. His body was ramrod straight and his eyes were filled with a secret and fiery knowledge. He held the reins firmly in his gnarled fist while high above his head he whirled his right arm like a sling shot as he prepared to fling small stones at us. Miraculously, no one was ever hit by Florinto's stones, which shot past our ears with a menacing whiz.

I would hang back from the gang at these times and hide myself behind a convenient elm tree, or behind Mr. Alarid's garage door. From some such vantage point I would watch the attack and subsequent panic and rout in the wake of Florinto's counteroffensive.

On one of those memorable days, I was so transfixed by the drama that I forgot to run away. Florinto stopped in front of me. The other boys had scattered into alleys and over backyard fences and he knew there was no sense continuing the chase. He knew that I had not participated in the attack on him but that I had witnessed it. He said nothing to me. He stood there. We stared at each other. What I clearly remember now, all these many years later, was the intensity of that moment beneath the blazing summer sky. His eyes seemed youthful in an otherwise old and deeply wrinkled face, and as always there was the hint of mild humor in his expression.

We stood there in a moment of time that had no beginning and no end. His eyes held me and as I looked into them I had the sensation that the whole history of my family was unfolding in that gaze. I saw my father and my father's father before him, and an infinite regression of lives and passions and histories which had led to this moment. They were all there: the Mares brothers who drove cattle north from Guadalajara deep in Mexico across the Jornada del Muerto and then on to Santa Fe and Taos; the Martínez clan which settled in Abiquiu and pushed branches of the family into the valleys of the Chama and up into the high country of the Sangre de Cristos; the Gutierrez and Garcias who helped found Old Albuquerque and built the San Felipe Church as a testament to their great need to span the distance from earth to heaven; the Devines, those restless Irishmen who were dreamers, soldiers, adventurers, poets and musicians. I saw the generations of sons and daughters of the Mares and Martínez families who had endured everything and survived, even the wars and depressions which had led to the loss of their land and sent them hurtling south again, down the tracks of the Santa Fe Railroad, south to Albuquerque, to Old Town, to marry with the Irish Devines. I knew what it was to be a *coyote,* a half-breed who was to live forever on the fringes of the swirling cultures to which I was heir. I could not, at that time, have found the words to express this effect which Florinto had on me. It had come from the dream time, only for a moment, and then had returned to the dream time. Florinto never uttered one word. He only smiled. Then he turned abruptly, walked back to his cart, climbed on board, and gave rein to Relámpago. Florinto never looked back as the cart went rumbling down the road, down New York Avenue.

Another summer had come and gone, and then another and another, and after that I lost track of them. World War II had ended and a trickle of tourists, soon to become a flood, came to Albuquerque to visit Old Town. About that time, the city decided to pave New York Avenue and change its name to Lomas Boulevard, which had a more authentic, native ring. A long dead tongue of asphalt now ran from Old Town clear up into the Heights at the other end of town. The Anglos who lived in the Heights began to travel down the new road into Old Town in ever large numbers. They would come in their shiny cars and wearing their beautiful new clothes. They would walk around the plaza, take pictures, visit the San Felipe Church, and go to one of the restaurants on the plaza where they would enjoy "authentic Spanish food," which was really Indian and New Mexican food prepared with a very mild chile sauce. They came, most of all, to recreate in their minds a fantasy of the "Spanish way of life," to confirm what they had seen in countless Western movies, complete with real Indians who sat around the plaza selling the jewelry they had made. The merchants of the city moved quickly to take advantage of the tide of money which poured into Old Town. The Spanish-speaking familes which had lived there for centuries were shunted aside, forced by new zoning laws and by economic pressure to move to the poorer neighborhoods near the Rio Grande. Florinto's crumbling home on the Rancho Seco Road fell victim to a bulldozer and he and his very old sister found an even more delapidated shed near the river bank, with a tiny corral for Relámpago.

Old Town had a smart prosperous appearance now but it was no longer the same community. I tried to hold on to the vision Florinto had shared with me for one moment so many years ago. But as I struggled with my own adolescence that vision began to blur in the face of the changes which were taking place in myself and in the surroundings where I lived. One by one the elders of the community died and with them went their songs and their stories and much of the Spanish language. Their sons and daughters packed up and left in ever-increasing number for California where life was supposed to be fast and there were more and better jobs to be had. The yearly fiesta was still celebrated but it became more organized and formal and much more commercial. The carnival was still fun but there were more fights and stabbings then ever before. I enjoyed the brashness, the new excitement in myself and in the plaza, but there was a part of me which I did not understand then that longed for the stories told by the viejitos, for the ballads and corridos played on a cherished guitar or a violin in the cool evening in the plaza, for at least one song to rekindle the fire at the very center of the bowl of life rimmed by mountains to the east and volcanos in the west and reflected in the infinite and immense sky above, for one more triumphant cry from Florinto.

Our gang was beginning to scatter but there were still enough of us left in Old Town to gather in the city park nearby, or loiter around the drug stores and filling stations, or the plaza itself, where we could watch the tourists and flirt with the pretty girls who would walk by. One day, late in the afternoon and toward the end of summer, we sat listlessly on the worn-out tires in the empty lot behind Hedges' filling station. We cracked gross adolescent jokes and watched the endless traffic go by on Lomas Boulevard.

"This new road is sure going to be the end of Florinto," I said.

"Yeah, Ernesto, as the newsreel says at the movies, 'time marches on,' hah hah." No one thought Pablo's humor was very funny.

"Pablo, where are you going to school this fall?"

"I dunno, Fidel. I guess Albuquerque High. How about you?"

"I guess Saint Mary's. I dunno. What are you going to be, Frankie, when you grow up?"

"I am grown up, cabrón."

"You now what I mean, Frankie jodido. Are you going to school or what?"

"I dunno."

"Well," Ramon said, "we have to go to school until we're eighteen. Then I'm cutting out for the coast, man."

"Yeah, well that's okay," Abel said. "I don't care what I do or where I go just so long as those nice-looking women are waiting for me there." He already considered himself a Don Juan.

"I haven't seen Florinto in a long time," I said.

"Nah, neither have I," said Pablo. "He's getting pretty old though."

"I bet Relámpago is getting stiff legged by now."

"Don't worry about Florinto so much, Ernesto. His time has come and gone," Frankie said.

"But summer used to be more fun when we could chase him. Híjola. Do you remember when—"

"Yeah, but those days are done for," Frankie interrupted me. "Besides, he'd get killed on Lomas now."

For me the idea of a world without Florinto was unthinkable but I said nothing. A car honked somewhere off in the distance. There was the shrill sound of brakes, then silence, and once again the common rumble of traffic. We had already smoked a few cigarettes and we had passed around the terrible sweet wine, Orchard Delight Tokay, that Frankie had bought at the Palms Bar with his phoney I.D. card. David, "El Sonso" as we called him, was bored and spoke to no one because no one wanted to butt heads with him. He had a forehead with the bone structure of Neanderthal Man. He was not the toughest kid in the gang but no one in Old Town could stand up to him in a head butting contest. I could take only one or two head-on butts with him and the searing pain would make me give up. It was late and twilight was beginning to drift toward night. We were about to part, head for our separate homes and call it a day when suddenly we heard a murmur far down Lomas Boulevard. The murmur turned into a ripple and then quickly built up to a raucous tumult of sound. Just another great big Mack truck, we thought, probably Navajo Freight.

"Heyaaahhh! Heyaaahhh! ¡Ándale Relámpago! Heyaaahhh!" We were so stunned that we didn't move. Instead of the Mack truck, there came Florinto hauling a load of clanging trash cans and empty paint buckets which he had picked up at some construction job. Our astonishment lasted but a second. "Florinto, Florinto, Florintooo!" the battle cry went up. The older boys, aware of their growing strength, only skimmed small stones at him, but everyone joined in the chase.

Everyone except me. Once again I stood back and looked steadily at what was happening. Florinto, older now but in great form, stood straight in his cart and held his own. Relámpago, a true veteran, never lost his stride or even wiggled an ear to acknowledge the hail of small stones.

"Heyaaahhh! ¡Relámpago! ¡Malcriados! ¡Diablitos! ¡No saben lo que hacen!" he shouted in a still vibrant voice. His right arm flailed the air in the grand old manner and he let fly a truly fearsome stone which shot right though our midst without harming anyone.

Passing cars swerved and honked furiously. Red-faced drivers shook their fists in impotent rage at Florinto. Nothing touched his composure. He ignored the blaring cars as if they were fragments of a passing nightmare. He had something more serious on his mind and would not be distracted. He had set his course on a destination un poco más allá, further on down the road, around the distant curve into the dream time where the carnival whirled and the good times rolled forever. He cracked the whip above Relámpago's head and pushed on towards the realm of song and the burning bush at the center of life. Florinto went clattering off into the night. He had cast the final stone, the mirror stone of memory, against death and oblivion and it had found its mark.

Small Arms Fire

Robert L. Perea

It had been a week since the convoys of GI's, ARVN's, and supplies had passed the base of Dragon Mountain heading west into Cambodia. All of us on top of the mountain, which included Renfro, myself, and the twenty soldiers of the Army of the Republic of Vietnam who protected our radio-relay station, had stood in amazement watching the miles of trucks, Armored Personnel Carriers, and assorted larger track vehicles rumble down the road from Pleiku and turn west toward the Cambodian border. From base camp reports we knew some of the fighting in Cambodia had been ferocious, with the ARVN's especially taking heavy casualties. For some reason, not much of the fighting was being reported in the *Stars and Stripes*. All the publicity seemed to be focused on the invasion of the Parrot's Beak area much farther south.

Back on top of the mountain in our ten-by-ten wooden hootch we called home, I relaxed on one of our two bunks while Renfro worked the radios. Short and thin, with stringy blond hair, Renfro had only recently joined me on the mountain from our base camp on Engineer Hill. We would both be spending a couple more months on the mountain. At first I didn't think we'd work out. A short, blond ex-hippie and a tall, black-haired Mexican-Sioux. But after two weeks we realized we had a hell of a lot in common. To us, there was a heaven. It was on earth. It meant being civilians again back in the "world." We both hated Vietnam. We both hated the war. We both hated the fuckin' Army. In short, we were draftees.

"Hey Rodríguez," Renfro said putting down the hand-mike from one of our two radios, "sounds like a chopper over head."

"It's Major Beeber," I answered after sticking my head out the front door of the hootch. Major Beeber would land on Dragon Mountain almost daily on his way from Cambodia to Engineer Hill. We heard the motor of the helicopter shut down and in a few minutes Major Beeber and his pilot, a Warrant Officer Ogilvie, walked in. The Major's strict military air and manner always made Renfro and me nervous.

119

"Morning, sir," Renfro and I said in unison.

"As you were," Beeber said taking off his hat, his red hair neatly in place and cut very short. After the usual "how are things going" and taking what he wanted from our supply of C-rations and cigarettes, Major Beeber wandered outside. His pilot stayed to finish a cup of C-ration coffee.

"I'd better hurry up and drink this," Ogilvie said. "We got an important mission to fly," he added chuckling to himself.

"What's the joke?" asked Renfro.

"The Major," said Ogilvie.

"The Major's the joke?" asked Renfro.

"The Major's trying to qualify for some kinda combat flying medal," answered the pilot sipping on the coffee.

"I thought you had to fly so many missions supporting combat troops to get any kind of flying medal?"

"And," added Renfro, " 'sides what Rodríguez says, you also gotta be flying something like a Huey with door-gunners or some kinda fire power. All you n' the Major's got is a small scout-type chopper. The only way you could kill somebody with that thing is land on top of them and even then you'd probably only hurt 'em." Renfro laughed hard at his own joke.

"Well, I guess I can level with you two," said Ogilvie, peeking out the door of the hootch. "We fly over some of the fire fights taking place across the border in Cambodia. The Major pulls out a pistol and fires a couple rounds into the trees and we dee-dee mow. Technically, in our log, that qualifies as flying a combat mission in support of ground troops. We been doing it for a week or so now and with today's trip the Major'll have his precious little medal."

"Why's he want the medal so bad?"

"All he ever talks about," Oglivie said, "is getting promoted to lieutenant colonel, so I suppose he figures a medal will help him get the promotion."

"Doesn't your chopper take any ground fire?"

"You kiddin'," answered Oglivie, "We fly over so fast I don't think the gooks even see us. Well, I'd better go," Oglivie said standing up and finishing his coffee.

After he left I spent the next few hours on the radios. Renfro sat out back smoking pot he'd bought at the bottom of the mountain from the vendors who hawked things to passing convoys. Just then Renfro came in the back of the hootch.

"There's a cloud of grey smoke on the dirt road that heads to Cambodia," Renfro said pointing out back. "I think I heard an explosion."

I went outside to see. We could also see a cloud of dust moving up the side of the mountain along the winding road. The cloud of dust turned out to be made by a three-wheeled scooter, so common in 'Nam, coming up the mountain road at full speed. We could see it as it reached the top of the mountain on the other side. Renfro and I ran to the front of the hootch. The scooter came to a screeching halt in front of us, leaving us choking in thick dust. When the dust cleared, we saw the young Vietnamese girl we'd named Wendy sitting in the driver's seat of the scooter. Wendy was probably sixteen or seventeen. She reminded me of a high school cheerleader, always talking and always smiling. The war and the needs of GI's had turned her into a pimp. She was proud of having never gone to bed with a GI, although she'd brought many Madam K's to Dragon Mountain for the benefit of passing convoys. She had on occasion brought a few up to our hootch.

"Very bad thing happen," Wendy said anxiously pointing to the cloud of grey smoke at the bottom of the mountain. Almost immediately she started crying and shaking and we couldn't understand her English. Renfro ran and got Sergeant Lee, the only ARVN on the mountain who spoke English. We learned from Sergeant Lee that apparently a truck full of ARVN soldiers had run over a land mine.

"Very bad, beaucoup blood all over," Wendy said after Sergeant Lee finished. Then she broke down crying again. Sergeant Lee put his arm around her and said something to her in Vietnamese that seemed to calm her down.

"Look, Renfro. You get on the radios and get a medevac chopper. Sergeant Lee and I will take Wendy's scooter and try to help the soldiers with the first aid stuff we've got in the hootch."

"Better take a Prick Twenty-five with you," said Renfro referring to the PRC-25 battery operated radios we used as spares in the hootch. "And take some smoke grenades so a medevac can spot your location from the air."

"Roger."

We loaded up the scooter with the first aid supplies and took off down the mountain at full speed, nearly turning over a couple of times on the winding mountain road. We reached the truck, but things looked very wrong. The truck looked like it had been heading toward Dragon Mountain and Pleiku from Cambodia when it had run over the mine. Then I figured out why. These weren't soldiers heading for combat, they were coming from combat. There were at least twenty of them scattered over the highway with wounds a land mine couldn't have made.

It was the most grizzly sight I'd ever seen in my life. One soldier was lying against the tire of the overturned truck with his face shattered. He didn't have a chin. His jaw bone was almost completely separated from his face, attached only by a strand of skin. His face was a mass of blood and I could tell he was still alive because he was moaning. Another soldier had apparently stepped on a mine while in Cambodia. His leg was missing below the knee. A dirty makeshift, blood soaked bandage covered it. When he saw us, he tried to stand on his good leg, but fell down screaming in pain as he landed on his stump. At least half a dozen soldiers had bad head wounds with dirty makeshift bandages covering their wounds. The screaming and groaning made my body shiver. The sight of one soldier's intestines neatly piled in front of him made me gag, but I managed not to throw up.

Wendy was in the back of the scooter and refused to look up, her head buried in her lap. The only thing that kept me from falling apart was Sergeant Lee. He looked very calm and sure of himself. I guess he'd seen sights worse than this since he'd been in the infantry before being assigned to Dragon Mountain. I set up the Prick Twenty-five and called Renfro on the mountain.

"Relay-One, this is Rodríguez at the bottom of the mountain, over,"

"This is Relay-One, over," answered Renfro

"Did you make contact with a medevac? We got some serious cases down here, over."

"Roger, all of 'em say they don't even have enough choppers to bring in all the wounded from Cambodia. But the Major's chopper is due in from Cambodia any minute. We'll get him to dust off the wounded," answered Renfro.

"We'll do what we can in the meantime, over."

"Roger, out."

Sergeant Lee had the medical supplies ready. He'd also somehow gotten Wendy to get out of the scooter and help. The three of us moved from soldier to soldier.

"This one dead," Sergeant Lee said as he checked the pulse and heartbeat of the soldier with the shattered jaw. As I looked at his chinless face, I felt an almost sense of relief to see he was no longer suffering. We moved to another soldier whose foot was blown off. He also had a nasty gash on his forehead. Blood was caked half an inch thick on his face from the gash. Wendy and I cleaned his head wound while Sergeant Lee put a tourniquet on his leg to keep him from bleeding to death. We could see he was in great pain. I tried hard not to think about that and let it bother me. I knew it would only slow me down.

We went from body to body, doing as much as we could with our limited supplies. Our main task was one of stopping a lot of bleeding by applying pressure on wounds or putting tourniquets on the most serious bleeding wounds. At least four soldiers had big "T's" printed in blood on their foreheads so the medics would know. Otherwise if left on too long, the lack of circulation will cause the limb to die. The one medical supply we could have used the most was morphine.

Finally, we separated the soldiers into the wounded, the seriously wounded and the dead. A stench was already starting to come from the one dead soldier. I had to control the urge to throw up more than once.

"Look!" yelled Sergeant Lee pointing to the sky. Major Beeber's helicopter was hovering over Dragon Mountain like some insect hovering over a huge beast. It landed. I ran for the radio.

"Relay-One, Relay-One, this is Rodríguez, over."

"This is Relay-One," answered Renfro. "Be back ASAP." Major Beeber will be able to save some lives, I thought. In a few minutes Renfro was calling back saying the Major would not help out.

"Why the fuck not!" I repeated to Renfro.

"Says he's got an important meeting ASAP with the general," answered Renfro. "Says he ain't gonna shitcan going to an important meeting on account of a buncha wounded gooks. He says we got everything under control and to be patient 'til a medevac is available. He says the gooks can wait, but the general won't, over."

"Well then, all you can do is get a medevac and call us when you do, over," I said as I saw the Major's chopper begin its take-off from Dragon Mountain.

"Roger, out," said Renfro.

Just then I heard M-16 rounds go off. I whirled around. Sergeant Lee, who must have overheard my conversation on the radio, had gotten ahold of my M-16 from the scooter and was firing at Dragon Mountain. Major Beeber's helicopter was still hovering above it, getting ready to head back to Engineer Hill. The M-16 rounds were falling very short of the mountain.

"Him numba' ten thousan'. Numba' fuckin' ten thousan'." Sergeant Lee mumbled pulling out the empty clip and throwing it down. "I see him again, I crocodile him for sure."

But it looked like there might be no need for Sergeant Lee to crocodile Major Beeber. We watched the helicopter start to head south. Then what looked like a big gust of wind from nowhere blew the helicopter to one side. It straightened up, then stopped. I held my breath. Some sort of engine trouble maybe, I thought. Whatever it was, the huge blades came to a complete stop in mid-air, and the helicopter came crashing down into the side of Dragon Mountain. We saw it go up in flames. Sergeant Lee, Wendy and I looked at each other stunned.

I heard Renfro back on the radio. He'd contacted a medevac chopper. Using our smoke grenades we directed it to our position for a dust off. It took three trips to medevac all the ARVN's to a hospital. Unfortunately, one ARVN had already bled to death. He, the soldier with the shattered jaw, and the soldier with his intestines on the ground were our three casualties.

Tired, covered with blood, and smelling of death, but feeling good because we'd been able to help some of the ARVN's, Sergeant Lee, Wendy, and I along with Renfro spent the rest of the day on top of the mountain, drinking warm beer and smoking pot in our hootch.

A week later Renfro and I were in company headquarters on Engineer Hill picking up our mail.

"Stars 'n Stripes" just came in," said the company clerk, handing each of us a newspaper. "There's a story on Major Beeber on page five," he added.

> North of Pleiku, Republic of South Vietnam, Viet Cong snipers, in a barrage of small arms fire, shot down a U.S. Army helicopter carrying Major Otis M. Beeber and the pilot, Warrant Officer Timothy Ogilvie. U.S. Command said both were reported killed in the crash. The helicopter had just returned from a mission and was shot down attempting to rescue an American and a group of ARVN soldiers who were pinned down by hostile sniper fire. The U.S. Command also said both officers will be awarded Distinguished Flying Crosses posthumously for their heroic actions.

La Boda

Alberto Alvaro Ríos

Tonio farted a fart that cut a rent through that room like something it might have taken the Colorado River thousands of years to do.

"Where's the TV thing, the TV Guide?" demanded Arturo.

"Ay, viejo. It's right on the floor where you left it," answered Lilia. They had both heard Tonio, Tonio the littlest, the most sensitive, the biggest problem to reward them after such good lives they had both led.

"Where is he?"

"In the kitchen."

"Ay, m'ija, not with the food again."

"I can't keep him in his room, viejo." They had been all through that, and the embarrassment too of the visit to the doctor and what happened in the waiting room. No, it was too much. And no answers.

"He's going to fart at the wedding; you know he's going to fart at the wedding, Lilia."

"Stop cussing in front of me. You keep saying that, stop it." She never would get used to the word. She didn't even have a word of her own for it. It simply happened and didn't deserve a name. It was terrible,and their own son, ay no! "The doctor said it would stop, anyway."

"In time, m'ija, in time. But not in time for la boda, the wedding."

Lilia clicked her tongue. Tonio farted again.

"Let it be Ray, please, I already told him."

"But what about Jaime, Delia? What will Mario say?"

"Jaime's married, Mamá. So what do we do about his wife? Are we supposed to leave her out? Now they can both be in it." Delia looked at the list in front of her. It would all work out perfectly, now. If Jaime agreed— Mario would convince him and she would convince Mario—and if Jaime's parents Arturo and Lilia would say yes, too, that they would also be in the wedding, then it would be perfect. The invitations could be printed. Arturo and Lilia would say yes; of course they would say yes. And the Casino was already scheduled for the reception.

"Okay, okay, Madre Santa! But are you sure you want little Jorge to be the ring bearer?"

"Yes, he is going to look so cute."

"Ha, he's not your brother, what do you know? Wait and see, if you *can* see him. Maybe he will leave his mud at home? Do you think?"

"Ma-ma!"

"De-li-a," she mimicked.

It was a good lunch. It must have been because he farted. Loud.

"Otro pedo?" yelled his father from the living room. "At least get out of the kitchen, Tonio, por favor!" He was not asking nicely but it didn't matter to Tonio. Not any more, not when he finally realized. Farting was a power, "pedo power" his brother Jaime called it, and it was a very worthwhile thing to do. It meant that he had eaten good food, that he didn't have to go to first grade, that he had a room of his own which no one else in the whole town, probably, could brag about. It meant "I am special," and Tonio was proud, sort of. Red-faced but proud. And he had gotten used to the smell.

Of course, only his little cousin Jorge from next door would play with him, and he *had* to play with Tonio because no one would play with him, either. He was always dirty. Dirty so that there was always mud on him somewhere, any time of the day, no matter how many baths they gave him. He was too young to go to school and so he and Tonio fell naturally together. Tonio was the leader, though. Farting is much more impressive. Jorge didn't care about the smell. He always said he didn't smell anything. In fact, it made him laugh, and Tonio appreciated this. It was not a mean laugh, like sometimes with other people, it was a real laugh. Sometimes Tonio was asked to take a bath with Jorge because it was the only way Jorge would take one without a life or death struggle. It was the opinion of Jorge that Tonio's farting under water was incomparable. That was, in fact, the opinion of everyone.

"I'm sorry, Jaime, I chickened out." Mario shrugged his shoulders. "I promised Delia her cousin Ray could be best man, and I promised her mother even more so. But listen, now you and Anna can be padrinos. Take your pick, padrinos of anything you want."

"It's okay, don't worry. It's better this way, especially for you, later, you know? I mean *much* later. Take my word for it." They both laughed. "Ray's the guy in the Navy, right?"

"Yeah, he's coming in special. Delia's real excited."

"Did you ever meet him?"

"Yes, once, but I know him perfectly the way Delia talks about him."

"Maybe he'll come with us to Paco's for your party. Does he drink?"

"He's in the Navy, asshole."

"So, another wedding, Delia and Mario now, and they want us to be padrinos."

"Of course they do, vieja, we give presents."

"Arturo!"

"So, it's wedding season again. La boda lives. Same as baseball season, have you ever noticed? And everyone wants to be in the World Series of weddings, that's why they want us to be padrinos, even if it's just padrinos in charge of toilet paper for the wedding. Ever since that boda where we gave the big silver punch bowl. Boy, if only they knew we had gotten it free and had to give it because we couldn't afford to buy anything. And if only we could tell everyone, then we wouldn't have to keep worrying about how we have to keep giving just a little more each time. And this time your sister's daughter. Money." Arturo shook his head.

"Stop it, it's a wedding."

"It's money."

"Arturo . . ."

"And did you forget about Tonio? You know what he's going to do, you know it."

"Ay, don't say it, I know, I know. But it's okay, Jorge will be there; we won't be the only ones with problems. They have to take him, and not only because it's his brother getting married but because Delia wants him to be ring bearer. What a day it's going to be!" She clicked her tongue.

"Maybe we can think of some way . . ."

"I already accepted, Arturo. I had to, after all."

"Had to, humph."

"And Raymundo will be there; he's going to be best man."

"What about Jaime? I thought he and Mario were . . ."

"Well, Delia wanted to include Anna, so they are going to be padrinos, too."

"The World Series."

"So your brother is getting married, Jorge."

"Yes." Jorge was not at all cheerful.

"And I heard you are going to carry the rings."

"Yes."

"So what's wrong, are you nervous?"

"No."

Tonio looked at him, then started to run toward the arroyo. "Come on," he yelled, "let's go."

Jorge followed after him, then tripped.

"Come on, Jorge, stop yelling; it doesn't hurt that much. And they'll hear you. You don't want that, do you?" They weren't supposed to go to the arroyo.

"No, but it does hurt, I don't care what you say."

They headed straight for "their place." It was where two mesquite trees hung over the arroyo from opposite banks so that, after the two boys had cleared off all the little branches, there was a natural bridge across the water when there *was* water. Sometimes sewage ran through and so their parents didn't want them down there, but in summer the two boys knew better; there would only be rain water from up in the mountains and it wasn't the season, yet, for flash floods. Plenty of reason, then, for a club, for the "Aztecs of America." And besides, they had a secret.

It was a gun. With two bullets. So what if it was rusty. And old. And it hadn't worked even though they had tried. They would get it to work. But they had to wait for a special occasion, and that's why they had it on that little shelf. A specially carved little shelf, with two smaller shelves, one each for the bullets. They covered it with a blanket that sparkled which Jorge had kept from under the last Christmas tree. All this in a small cave carved into the bank of the arroyo, specially, with a door made of the mesquite branches from the two big trees bundled and tied together. The cave was almost right on the spot where they found the gun. And both of them wanted to use the gun a lot, so they decided that neither would use it after the first couple of attempts. It was too special, too neat, a secret.

"What do you mean, why marry?"

"Hey, it's okay, you know? Everyone's growing up," said Ray.

"Not that much," said Mario.

"How will you feel, Delia, leaving flowers for the Virgin? How will you be honoring *that?*"

"Don't be silly," answered Delia, "I'll be leaving flowers because I'm sorry for her." All three laughed.

"Hey, you're tough, prima, but not that tough. I'm in the Navy, after all." Ray opened his mouth and pointed: "Look, an anchor tattooed to the back of my throat. *That's tough. "* More laughter.

"I didn't know you could get tattoos in San Diego," said Mario. Ray moved his lips and moved his head left and right, mimicking Mario.

"Ay, Ray, the Navy hasn't changed you!"

"Are you kidding? I joined the Navy so the world could see *me!*"

"Booo. That's really old, Ray."

"Old as the hills on grandma's chest!"

"First time I heard that I laughed so hard I fell off my dinosaur," Mario smiled.

"Cute, but ugly. I'm the one in the Navy so I can get away with this; you can't." Everyone laughed.

"Ay, Ray," sighed Delia.

"No, *I* Ray, *You* Delia."

Mario grimaced. "Me sick."

Lilia read the invitation, looking for their name first. "Here it is, Arturo. Look how big this will be, everyone will be there."

"Everyone. What a time to be out robbing." He looked at the outside of the invitation, a picture of a bride and groom with her veil covering their faces as they kissed in the woods. "A new creation, two of us. Like the dawning of a new day. Shee-it."

"ARTURO!"

He opened the invitation and skimmed: Mr. and Mrs. and Mr. and Mrs. invite the honour of your presence . . . "Presents, Lilia, presents, I told you!" at the marriage of their daughter, son, and cordially invite you and your family to a religious ceremony on . . . at St. John's Catholic Church at . . . Best Man: Raymundo; Padrinos de Lazo: Jaime and Anna; Padrinos de Ramo: Arturo and Lilia; Ring Bearer: Jorge . . . Reception at El Casino Ballroom . . . 9:00 p.m. Please Present Invitation. Or present, thought Arturo. "I guess I'll have to rent a tuxedo, too."

"Arturo, of course, and I'll have to make a dress."

"There's no money, Lilia."

"Oh, shush. There is if we don't go to any more weddings, or at least, if we don't give any more presents or be padrinos."

"Oh, sure. Have the World Series first, then work backward and since we already know who won, we won't have to go."

"¡Cállate, Arturo! Oh, and you know what? Delia says there will be no rehearsal."

"No rehearsal?" Lilia shook her head no. "Of course not, they already know how," Arturo winked.

"Ay, ¡que horrible! Don't even say such a thing. She's wearing white."

"And the presents won't hurt," said her mother. Delia shook her head.

"Ay, Mamá. You're making this all so big, even though you *know.*"

Her mother lowered her head as if to keep on reading. "Everyone should have a wedding."

"Every parent you mean."

"Ay, Delia."

"Oh, Mamá, I don't mean it I guess. I'm kind of having fun. I just don't want to make it more than it is."

"And what about your father, anyway? Would you care to explain this to him?"

"Stop it, we've already been through all this. I wouldn't hurt my daddy for anything."

"Ay, hija."

"Oh, it's all okay."

"Okay? You having that Raymundo for best man. Humph!"

"Well, I should have something, after all. You know *you* practically accepted this proposal for me. I wasn't even sure I wanted to get married."

"Delia!"

"Oh Mamá, I'm not a child. You were so glad that Mario proposed. '*Un hombre no compra la vaca cuando esta agarrando le leche gratis,* ' that's what you said to me, a man won't buy the cow when he's getting the milk free. What relief there was on your face! It was *almost* worth a wedding just to see that look."

"¡Eres imposible!" Her mother shook her head.

"Well, everyone's okay, you've seen the family. Jorge still breathes mud. Oh, and did you know about little Tonio, my cousin next door?"

"No, what about him?" asked Ray.

"Well," Delia smiled.

Ray asked with his hands.

"He farts."

"He farts? He, oh, he farts! That is fantastic! Oh this is great! A built-in whoopee cushion."

"Ray . . ."

"When did this start?"

"I don't know, a while back, and there doesn't seem to be anything they can do."

"Oh, thank you God, thank you, you *do* exist! Oh, wait till church, ohboyohboyohboy!"

"That's terrible, Ray."

"Oh Delia, don't be silly. This could be the best wedding I've ever been to! Oh, no one's going to believe it, it's going to be too good."

"But poor Tonio, Ray. He's just a little guy and everyone laughs at him. They've had to keep him out of school."

"Boy, does he know how to operate. I should take him back into the Navy with me."

"Ray . . ."

"Oh, Delia, I'll be good. Don't worry, prima." Ray laughed some more.

"And my brother Jaime and Anna are going to be padrinos of something. Ha, Jaime only ever makes fun of me." Tonio shrugged his shoulders.

"Yes," answered Jorge. Neither knew what a padrino was.

"Jorge, what is wrong with you?" They were sitting in the little cave. They would sit there until Tonio farted, then they had to move out into the air because it was too strong even for them.

"Well, Mario's getting married and . . ."

"And what?" asked Tonio.

"I have no present, nothing to give him."

"Dummy, kids don't have to give presents." Tonio shook his head.

"I know that, Tonio, I know. But I want to."

"Oh."

"My parents are giving him, and Delia too, a bunch of stuff."

"My parents are giving them some forks and spoons and that kind of stuff. And some money, I think. They're something in the wedding so I guess they have to." Jorge was something in the wedding, too. And Tonio was, almost, because everyone in his family was.

"Yeah, they're something, I don't know what. But see, everyone is giving something."

"I'm not," said Tonio, but thought that maybe he should, too. He hadn't thought about it. Maybe this was some magic, something grown-up, something people didn't laugh at. "Cheer up, Jorge, we'll think of something."

"Well, I already thought of something," Jorge said, avoiding Tonio's eyes.

"Oh? What?"

Jorge looked up at the gun.

"But we can't do that, I mean, I mean come on, it's ours, yours and mine, come on . . ." Tonio farted.

"Ray, this is Jaime, Delia's cousin."

"Hey, brother," said Ray. Jaime gave him a Raza handshake. "All right!"

"He set up the party at Paco's."

"Hey, Jaime, good deal. Can I give you some bread?" Ray started to take out some money from somewhere in the pant leg of his uniform.

"No, no," Jaime waved him to stop. "You brought enough beer with you there." He pointed to the barrel in the back of Mario's pickup. "There's going to be plenty of stuff. Are you sure you people from the Navy can handle it?"

"Is the Pope Catholic?" They laughed. "Oh, I'm sorry," he said, looking at Jaime.

"We told him about Tonio," said Mario.

"Don't be silly," he waved them off to say it was nothing.

"Vámonos!" yelled Ray, running to the pickup and pulling a can of beer from behind the barrel. "To the bachelor," he said, raising the can of beer then pouring it all over Mario.

Jorge ran back with the tape. Tonio was waiting for him. They added the finishing touches.

It was beautiful. Wrapped up in the sparkling Christmas paper that was almost like cotton and was only a little smudged, either because it had been protecting the gun from the dirt or because of Jorge.

"Maybe he won't want it and he'll give it back."

"Oh stop it, Jorge. Who wouldn't want it? Wouldn't you like to get it as a present?"

"Yeah. But now we have something, both of us. A wedding present. What about these?"

"Oh, bring them here." They wrapped each of the bullets.

Tonio had farted right away in the car so he and his parents were a little late getting to the church where everyone was set to start. "I'm sorry, we had to get out and open all the windows and wait," said Arturo to Lilia's sister. She smiled and looked down, embarrassed like Lilia.

Delia came over. "A picture, que hermosa," said Lilia. Her sister came over and took her by the arm. "Lilia . . ." "Ay, your daughter is so pretty," "It's true, Lilia, and I'm so happy. Lilia, I talked to the priest. He said that Tonio could go up into the chorus balcony with the singer, Mrs. Garcia, so that if he did anything the music would probably drown it out. Mrs. Garcia said it was okay." She lifted her eyebrows to see if Lilia would agree. "Of course. Thank you."

Ray and Mario were off to the side of the church and Arturo walked over and told them everything was ready. Ray gave him an "okay" sign with his fingers. They walked into the church. It was fairly crowded as far as the average number of people who actually go to the church part of the wedding. This was a good sign in predicting how many people would come to the reception. You take the number of people in church and multiply by 11.

"Stop it, Mamá, you're so nervous. Look at daddy, he's okay," said Delia. "What does he know? Tonio is taken care of. Everything is ready, now. Are you?" The music started. Ray would get his chance to meet the maid of honor, now. With no rehearsal it seemed as if no one knew anyone else. Delia decided it was better this way, not so mushy.

Arturo and Lilia walked in first, they were the padrinos de ramo and so they carried the extra flowers that Delia would leave for the Virgin. Jaime and Anna were the padrinos de lazo and so they carried the lazo, the big double-rosary. Then the maid of honor. Then the little flower girl tossing petals onto the carpet and Jorge carrying the rings and walking with one muddy shoe, looking from side to side, smiling. He had a secret. Then Delia, with her mother on the left and her father on her right. It had to be that way, said Delia, the new way. She wanted her mother to walk down the aisle with her, too.

When Delia reached the altar, Mario took her hand and they kneeled in front of the priest. Ray turned and smiled at the people in church. On the soles of Mario's shoes, in black shoe polish, were painted the words "Good" and "bye!"

The priest began to speak, while from up in the balcony Mrs. Garcia sang first lowly then loudly depending on the priest's speeches, and everybody whispered how good she was, how perfect. The first "Ave Maria" almost got applause. Arturo whispered to Lilia that at least Jaime didn't have to pay for Mrs. Garcia and the priest like he might have had to. It was not so bad that he wasn't best man. It was cheaper.

Jaime and Anna got up with the lazo and went over to the kneeling couple, putting it over their heads and around their shoulders, then stepped back. Delia and Mario stood up and took each other as man and wife, Delia frowning almost horribly as the priest said "wife." Maybe a rehearsal wouldn't have been so bad. Ray winked. Jaime and Anna then took the lazo off and went back to sit down. Then communion; first Delia and Mario walking up to the altar, then the priest giving communion to the rest of the wedding party, then everyone else. And Mrs. Garcia sang. Jorge wiggled in his seat; this was all too long. "Go in peace," said the priest and it was almost over. Arturo and Lilia took the flowers for the Virgin, the ramo, and gave them to Delia. Mrs. Garcia started the full length "Ave Maria" as Delia went over to the left side of the altar to contemplate her final pure moments with the Virgin Mary, leaving the flowers as a farewell offering. Mrs. Garcia took a breath.

Pppphhhtt! Pht!

It was a fatal breath. Everyone bit his tongue. Delia smiled at the Virgin. Ray started to laugh but Mario kicked him. Arturo looked at Lilia and started to say something but she nodded her head no. Delia's mother fanned herself as her father patted his wife on the back as if to say it's okay. Why me, she breathed. Jorge stood up on the pew and looked back at the balcony. La boda was ended, and it was time to go.

The bride and groom stood by the exit and shook hands and received the abrazo from everyone. They reminded the guests to come to the reception and everyone said they would, of course, don't be silly, how does it feel. They giggled. A lot of pictures. The fancy ones had already been taken during the wedding by a professional photographer who would be taking more at the reception. He asked if they wanted a picture of the boy in the balcony.

It was all too much, thought Tonio. He had heard Ray laugh and he had a plain view of everyone else in that church. Even the priest. And now, here at the reception, all the same faces, and more who surely knew by now. Jorge sat with him instead of at the wedding party table, near the presents. They had a secret.

It was all too funny, said Ray to Mario. Can you believe what timing? Where was Candid Camera when you needed them. A fart, no, the King of Farts right there in church, right at the quietest second. Perfect. But no, said Ray, don't worry, I understand, the poor kid. Hey, he asked, pass the cerveza. Mario agreed. Poor kid.

It was all too, too, I don't know, it's like cussing, I don't know, it's embarrassing, said Lilia to Arturo in a whisper. Arturo answered with a shrug and said that he couldn't believe that his tuxedo went out for $25 a shot. They *should* be shot. It was ridiculous. Did you hear, he wondered, what they would be serving for food?

They had all marched in time to the wedding music played by Love Unlimited, Mr. Chávez's band, as they entered the reception room, El Casino. This was the home of all weddings, it had swallowed hundreds and everyone was comfortable here. It was all okay, now, thought Delia.

It was nothing so terrible and how poor Tonito must feel. At least there was plenty of music, noise here. Good.

Why me, asked Delia's mother. All evening.

Otra cerveza, yelled Ray.

After the first waltz, everyone danced: cumbias, *El Jarabe Tapatillo*, "modern." Two kids did a new dance, hitting hips and everyone stared. They were only teenagers, can you imagine? Don't be silly, Mamá! Who would invent a thing like that? Otra cerveza! Then came the mariachis.

Mariachi Santa Cruz came to give the serenata to the bride as Love Unlimited watched. Then the Dollar Dance, and everyone lined up except Ray who almost had to be held up. That stupid guy, said Tonio. Yeah, said Jorge. They were more interested in the silver-flecked package on the presents table.

He used a ten-dollar bill, Lilia, said Arturo. I only used a five. *Ay,* that Ray, said Lilia's sister who overheard. And Tonio was being very good here at the reception, not a sound. Look how much money they have on them now, Lilia, said Arturo, what a honeymoon they will have with that. Boy, what we could do with that money. Shush, said Lilia. Delia and Mario were full of other people's kisses. Yuk, said Tonio. Yuk, said Jorge. Ray was yelling for another beer. No one would give it to him.

What do you mean? Ya, cálmate, Ray, come on, said Jaime. So? Come on, Ray, don't be like that, said Mario. Ray winked at Delia. The Mariachis were leaving and Love Unlimited was setting up again.

"Come on, Jorge, it's time," said Tonio. They didn't have any dollars, so they had to come up with something just as good. Bullets. They each had one in their pockets. These would be their dollars, their dance.

Everyone watched them. It was the first time either one had gotten out of his seat tonight. And they were, after all, celebrities. Sort of. Ray saw them. He stopped shouting for beer. He put his hands on his hips. He shouted something different.

"Well, lookit who's coming." He pointed. "It's little mudder and farter!"

It was too funny, and the timing as too perfect. The room took one big breath and laughed and one big laugh and didn't stop.

Tonio ran for the presents' table, for the silver-flecked package. Jorge looked at Mario and pulled out his bullet. "It's a gun. For you. And this bullet, too. They were the only things we had to give you."

"A gun," yelled Mario, "wait, Tonio!"

Ray stood there looking, nothing was sinking in.

"Why me," said Delia's mother.

Tonio grabbed the packet and ripped it open. He stopped for just a second and wiped the water from his eyes and noise from his ears. He loaded the bullet into the gun. It had never worked. It had to work now. He didn't know if the bullet was in the right place. He ran back toward Mario and Jorge and Ray. And Ray.

"Tonio, hey, what's that, man? said Mario stepping in between Tonio and Ray. "Looks like a wedding present. Is it?"

"Yes," said Tonio. He stood there. Everyone stood there.

"Hey, a gun, wow!"

Tonio stood there.

"Oh, and hey, it's a blank gun—why didn't you tell me? And Jorge says there are two bullets; well, I guess they're blanks, no? Thank you guys."

Ray fell to the floor drunk.

"What did you guys do," asked Mario looking at the rust on the gun—*it was a gun*—"find this stuff?" He went over and got the gun. He tousled Tonio's hair. He tousled Jorge's hair. He looked at the engaged safety. Jesus.

Tonio looked at Jorge. Who looked back at Tonio. Not even a real gun?

Jorge farted. The room, the world stopped. Jorge?

"Why me, why me?"

The Scholarship Jacket

Marta Salinas

The small Texas school that I attended carried out a tradition every year during the eighth grade graduation; a beautiful gold and green jacket, the school colors, was awarded to the class valedictorian, the student who had maintained the highest grades for eight years. The scholarship jacket had a big gold S on the left front side and the winner's name was written in gold letters on the pocket.

My oldest sister Rosie had won the jacket a few years back and I fully expected to win also. I was fourteen and in the eighth grade. I had been a straight A student since the first grade, and the last year I had looked forward to owning that jacket. My father was a farm laborer who couldn't earn enough money to feed eight children, so when I was six I was given to my grandparents to raise. We couldn't participate in sports at school because there were registration fees, uniform costs, and trips out of town; so even though we were quite agile and athletic, there would never be a sports school jacket for us. This one, the scholarship jacket, was our only chance.

In May, close to graduation, spring fever struck, and no one paid any attention in class; instead we stared out the windows and at each other, wanting to speed up the last few weeks of school. I despaired every time I looked in the mirror. Pencil thin, not a curve anywhere, I was called "Beanpole" and "String Bean" and I knew that's what I looked like. A flat chest, no hips, and a brain, that's what I had. That really isn't much for a fourteen-year-old to work with, I thought, as I absentmindedly wandered from my history class to the gym. Another hour of sweating in basketball and displaying my toothpick legs was coming up. Then I remembered my P.E. shorts were still in a bag under my desk where I'd forgotten them. I had to walk all the way back and get them. Coach Thompson was a real bear if anyone wasn't dressed for P.E. She had said I was a good forward and once she even tried to talk Grandma into letting me join the team. Grandma, of course, said no.

I was almost back at my classroom's door when I heard angry voices and arguing. I stopped. I didn't mean to eavesdrop; I just hesitated, not knowing what to do. I needed those shorts and I was going to be late, but I didn't want to interrupt an argument between my teachers. I recognized the voices: Mr. Schmidt, my history teacher, and Mr. Boone, my math teacher. They seemed to be arguing about me. I couldn't believe it. I still remember the shock that rooted me flat against the wall as if I were trying to blend in with the graffiti written there.

"I refuse to do it! I don't care who her father is, her grades don't even begin to compare to Martha's. I won't lie or falsify records. Martha has a straight A plus average and you know it." That was Mr. Schmidt and he sounded very angry. Mr. Boone's voice sounded calm and quiet.

"Look, Joann's father is not only on the Board, he owns the only store in town; we could say it was a close tie and—"

The pounding in my ears drowned out the rest of the words, only a word here and there filtered through. ". . . Martha is Mexican. . . . resign. . . . won't do it. . . ." Mr. Schmidt came rushing out, and luckily for me went down the opposite way toward the auditorium, so he didn't see me. Shaking, I waited a few minutes and then went in and grabbed my bag and fled from the room. Mr. Boone looked up when I came in but didn't say anything. To this day I don't remember if I got in trouble in P.E. for being late or how I made it through the rest of the afternoon. I went home very sad and cried into my pillow that night so grandmother wouldn't hear me. It seemed a cruel coincidence that I had overheard that conversation.

The next day when the principal called me into his office, I knew what it would be about. He looked uncomfortable and unhappy. I decided I wasn't going to make it any easier for him so I looked him straight in the eye. He looked away and fidgeted with the papers on his desk.

"Martha," he said, "there's been a change in policy this year regarding the scholarship jacket. As you know, it has always been free." He cleared his throat and continued. "This year the Board decided to charge fifteen dollars—which still won't cover the complete cost of the jacket."

I stared at him in shock and a small sound of dismay escaped my throat. I hadn't expected this. He still avoided looking in my eyes.

"So if you are unable to pay the fifteen dollars for the jacket, it will be given to the next one in line."

Standing with all the dignity I could muster, I said, "I'll speak to my grandfather about it, sir, and let you know tomorrow." I cried on the walk home from the bus stop. The dirt road was a quarter of a mile from the highway, so by the time I got home, my eyes were red and puffy.

"Where's Grandpa?" I asked Grandma, looking down at the floor so she wouldn't ask me why I'd been crying. She was sewing on a quilt and didn't look up.

"I think he's out back working in the bean field."

I went outside and looked out at the fields. There he was. I could see him walking between the rows, his body bent over the little plants, hoe in hand. I walked slowly out to him, trying to think how I could best ask him for the money. There was a cool breeze blowing and a sweet smell of mesquite in the air, but I didn't appreciate it. I kicked at a dirt clod. I wanted that jacket so much. It was more than just being a valedictorian and giving a little thank you speech for the jacket on graduation night. It represented eight years of hard work and expectation. I knew I had to be honest with Grandpa; it was my only chance. He saw me and looked up.

He waited for me to speak. I cleared my throat nervously and clasped my hands behind my back so he wouldn't see them shaking. "Grandpa, I have a big favor to ask you," I said in Spanish, the only language he knew. He still waited silently. I tried again. "Grandpa, this year the principal said the scholarship jacket is not going to be free. It's going to cost fifteen dollars and I have to take the money in tomorrow, otherwise it'll be given to someone else." The last words came out in an eager rush. Grandpa straightened up tiredly and leaned his chin on the hoe handle. He looked out over the field that was filled with the tiny green bean plants. I waited, desperately hoping he'd say I could have the money.

He turned to me and asked quietly, "What does a scholarship jacket mean?"

I answered quickly; maybe there was a chance. "It means you've earned it by having the highest grades for eight years and that's why they're giving it to you." Too late I realized the significance of my words. Grandpa knew that I understood it was not a matter of money. It wasn't that. He went back to hoeing the weeds that sprang up between the delicate little bean plants. It was a time consuming job; sometimes the small shoots were right next to each other. Finally he spoke again.

"Then if you pay for it, Marta, it's not a scholarship jacket, is it? Tell your principal I will not pay the fifteen dollars."

I walked back to the house and locked myself in the bathroom for a long time. I was angry with grandfather even though I knew he was right, and I was angry with the Board, whoever they were. Why did they have to change the rules just when it was my turn to win the jacket?

It was a very sad and withdrawn girl who dragged into the principal's office the next day. This time he did look me in the eyes.

"What did your grandfather say?"

I sat very straight in my chair.

"He said to tell you he won't pay the fifteen dollars."

The principal muttered something I couldn't understand under his breath, and walked over to the window. He stood looking out at something outside. He looked bigger than usual when he stood up; he was a tall gaunt man with gray hair, and I watched the back of his head while I waited for him to speak.

"Why?" he finally asked. "Your grandfather has the money. Doesn't he own a small bean farm?"

I looked at him, forcing my eyes to stay dry. "He said if I had to pay for it, then it wouldn't be a scholarship jacket," I said and stood up to leave. "I guess you'll just have to give it to Joann." I hadn't meant to say that; it had just slipped out. I was almost to the door when he stopped me.

"Martha—wait."

I turned and looked at him, waiting. What did he want now? I could feel my heart pounding. Something bitter and vile tasting was coming up in my mouth; I was afraid I was going to be sick. I didn't need any sympathy speeches. He sighed loudly and went back to his big desk. He looked at me, biting his lip, as if thinking.

"Okay, damn it. We'll make an exception in your case. I'll tell the Board, you'll get your jacket."

I could hardly believe it. I spoke in a trembling rush. "Oh, thank you sir!" Suddenly I felt great. I didn't know about adrenalin in those days, but I knew something was pumping through me, making me feel as tall as the sky. I wanted to yell, jump, run the mile, do something. I ran out so I could cry in the hall where there was no one to see me. At the end of the day, Mr. Schmidt winked at me and said, "I hear you're getting a scholarship jacket this year."

His face looked as happy and innocent as a baby's, but I knew better. Without answering I gave him a quick hug and ran to the bus. I cried on the walk home again, but this time because I was so happy. I couldn't wait to tell Grandpa and ran straight to the field. I joined him in the row where he was working and without saying anything I crouched down and started pulling up the weeds with my hands. Grandpa worked alongside me for a few minutes, but he didn't ask what had happened. After I had a little pile of weeds between the rows, I stood up and faced him.

"The principal said he's making an exception for me, Grandpa, and I'm getting the jacket after all. That's after I told him what you said."

Grandpa didn't say anything, he just gave me a pat on the shoulder and a smile. He pulled out the crumpled red handkerchief that he always carried in his back pocket and wiped the sweat off his forehead.

"Better go see if your grandmother needs any help with supper."

I gave him a big grin. He didn't fool me. I skipped and ran back to the house whistling some silly tune.

The Migrant

Mario Suarez

It was still dark when the food truck arrived at Williams Farms, Camp Three, causing the dogs in the vicinity to start a round of barking. The driver maneuvered the truck onto a clearing between two rows of shacks and parked. He turned off the motor and lights, honked a couple of times, and then got out to remove the sides of the truck to display his merchandise and wait for customers.

Very slowly the women of the camp emerged from their shacks, many in house coats, some already in work clothes, to buy the overripe fruit, vegetables, and assorted cans as well as the fading baloney, cheese, and day-old bread. Teofilo Vargas, who had been lying awake most of the night, fully dressed, on some boards which served as his bed, walked out of his shack, took his place among the customers, and bought a loaf of bread and some slices of baloney, his ration for the day. He treated himself to a large cup of coffee and then walked back to his shack.

Seated on a wooden crate, Teofilo slowly drank his coffee. Meanwhile, the barking of dogs gradually became distant, isolated. In the slowly receding darkness the cries of demanding infants and the shouts of waking children began to compete with radios suddenly turned on at full blast. Momentarily Teofilo thought of his own children. Teofilo swallowed hard and closed his eyes with the determination of one who would shut out his past, present, and future. At dawn, his food supply carefully put away, Teofilo padlocked his shack and walked to a nearby ravine and eased himself. Then, with the sun coming over the horizon, he slowly walked to the fields to get a sack in order to start up and down the rows of cotton.

The first hours went by quickly. To begin with, the sun was not, as yet, oppressive. A pleasantly cool breeze was blowing, perhaps announcing the end of the summer. Because it was Saturday and many of the local pickers were not brought out from Clayton, the fields were not crowded. In addition, the cotton was easy to pick. At the rate he was going, Teofilo estimated that he would pick no less than 400 pounds during the day. He

142

only hoped the picking would last into the afternoon since the ranchers always called it a day if they saw there were not enough hands to make the picking worthwhile. Then he would go to Clayton and send the money he had earned during the week to his wife. It was not much, but he knew Natalia would put it to good use. Perhaps he might treat himself to a meal in town.

At noon, however, the cotton picking was called off. The notice ran by word of mouth through the fields. "Se acabó." "No más pisca." Gradually the fields emptied as the pickers worked their way toward the scales. There the bags were weighed and emptied. The pickers were paid off. The tired men and women, through for the rest of the week, shook the dust from their clothes. The locals got into their cars and drove toward the highway. The migrants returned to their shacks, Teofilo Vargas among them. This week he had not earned as much as he had hoped, but he had worked while the picking was available. That was the important thing. In camp Teofilo bought a bottle of soda and walked toward his shack to eat a baloney sandwich.

Some time later, the lunch pause over, the men came out of their shacks to raise the hoods of their cars and trucks in order to work on dirty, neglected, often abused motors. Salesmen, their cars and station wagons full of blankets, T shirts, slips, socks, silk stockings, and general merchandise were making the rounds. The women came out to hang clothes in the hot sun. Still other migrants, their children hastily scrubbed and dressed, emerged from stuffy shacks and piled into cars and trucks in order to drive to Clayton. Teofilo knew that if he was going to buy a money order to send his family, he also had to go. But, he didn't want to get to town too early. Town, on Saturday, meant places to spend your money. Town meant cheap restaurants and cheap clothes at high prices. It meant enticements to have your picture taken by sidewalk photographers. It also meant enticements to buy dark glasses, watches, rings. More than that, town meant bars for drinking and dancing, leading to whoring and gambling. And the next day, the Sunday hangover. Teofilo, for the moment resting in the scant shade of the wood and tar paper shack, intended to hold on to his hard earned money and spend as little of it as possible. There were rumors that the cotton picking machines were on their way to Williams Farms. When they got there, it meant that he, along with many others, would have to move on.

But then, Teofilo mused, his entire life had consisted of moving on. With his parents Teofilo had moved from the Texas valley to Oklahoma, the Dakotas, Kansas, Illinois, and Michigan to the cotton, beet, carrot, and berry fields. He had slept on the flat, hard boards of the family truck, in tents, shacks, barracks-like housing and under the stars. He had survived sand storms, dust storms, rain storms, and heat waves. At last, when his parents, exhausted and worn, finally bought a house with the GI insurance paid them when his brother was killed at Bastogne, they settled down. Teofilo might have settled down with them, but the lack of opportunities and the postwar let-down forced him to the fields again, to Oklahoma, Kansas, the Dakotas, wherever. And he always returned to the valley not much better off than when he left. At twenty-two Teofilo decided to change his luck and, with some friends, he struck out for California, from where everybody returned to Texas rich. In order to avoid the low wages in the Imperial Valley, Teofilo and his friends went North. In the Central Valley Teofilo and his friends moved from crop to crop, worked from dawn to dusk, ate unevenly, and slept in barns, cars, shacks, and bus stations. For all their trouble, California's riches eluded them.

Then came Natalia, a city girl Teofilo met at a Sunday matinee when the old car he and two companions were driving back to Texas broke down near Central City in Arizona. Natalia, whose family had left the migrant trails during the early 40s, found Teofilo handsome and unpretentious. She told him she would be at the matinee again the following Sunday.

Teofilo, in turn, was in love. In order to see Natalia again, he decided not to go on to Texas. The next day he bid his friends goodbye and rented a room in downtown Central City. For the next few weeks, as his chance meeting of Natalia flowered into a courtship, Teofilo picked cotton in the nearby fields. And in February, Natalia's love assured, Teofilo departed for California.

Very carefully Teofilo sought to avoid the mistakes of the previous year when, in a vain effort to outguess the weather and the contractors, he crossed and recrossed the state. This time his travels took him directly to Ventura, then Salinas, and ultimately Delano. In the orange groves, lettuce fields, and grape vineyards he worked like a man driven. By being careful with his expenses and reducing his pleasures to an occasional movie, he mailed every possible dollar to Natalia for safekeeping. He returned to Central City in mid-September to march Natalia to the altar in a rented tuxedo, to ride around town in a decorated car, and to dance at the home of his new in-laws at the reception. The fields of California, for the time being, were relegated to the back of his mind. Teofilo still picked cotton during the first months of his marriage, but now he arrived at the cotton fields with an ample lunch, and after picking the quota he set for himself, he boarded the bus back to town and went home for a shower and a hot supper. Teofilo's life underwent other changes. At Natalia's insistence he got dental check-ups and bi-weekly haircuts, along with a new wardrobe for evenings and Sundays. But the most dramatic change came when three months after their marriage, a doctor informed Natalia that she was pregnant. Teofilo was jubilant. "One thing for sure," said Teofilo, planning ahead. "My son is going to school. He will never be a farm worker."

"What if we have a girl?" asked Natalia.

"All the more she will go to school," said Teofilo. "No daughter of mine will even go close to the fields."

When the cotton season came to an end, rather than take the bus to California, Teofilo, through the intercession of his father-in-law, got a job at the ice plant. His job consisted of swinging ice chutes on to the railroad cars as they passed through Arizona on the way to eastern markets. The work, though hard at first, soon became routine. The pay, though not much, was steady. The fields of California receded farther and farther into Teofilo's memory.

And, far away from the blazing sun in distant fields, the uncertainties of the elements, the hasty rush between crops to find ranches taken over by braceros and "illegals", plus the allied discomforts and indignities suffered by farm workers, Teofilo prospered. He bought a new car, not one of the battered hulks the used car lots sold to desperate field hands. He started buying, on time, a lot on which to build a house. And months later, when Natalia gave birth to a daughter later christened Adriana, Teofilo paid the doctor and the hospital fee on the spot.

Meanwhile Teofilo's manners, namely his tendency to use a tortilla as a fork and his often careless use of the wash basin, began to improve. When he forgot and noticed Natalia gazing at him, Teofilo replied: "O.K. O.K. So once a farm worker, always a farm worker."

"Many of us are ex-farm workers," Natalia reminded him.

Late in the afternoon Teofilo was awakened when someone started banging on the door of his shack. Teofilo got up and opened the door. It turned out to be the camp gorilla, dressed in a brown pin-striped suit, patent leather shoes, and smelling like a barber shop. He was collecting the agreed on dollar-a-day rent. "You owe me for today and you might as well pay me for tomorrow," said the gorilla. "I won't be back until Monday." Teofilo reached into his pocket and paid the gorilla two dollars. When the gorilla walked out, Teofilo, aware that it was getting late and that he must get to Clayton in order to buy a money order, changed his pants and put on a clean shirt. Then he padlocked the door of his shack and walked out of camp.

Luck, somehow, was with Teofilo. As he walked up the road toward the highway, a family in a pick-up stopped. Teofilo ran up. "Van a Clayton?" he asked. They gave him the sign to jump in back. Some fifteen minutes later Teofilo was dropped off in Clayton and he set about the crowded main street to look for the store where, he had been told, money orders were sold. Asking directions, he located it. At the store, not only did Teofilo buy the money order but also a stamped envelope which he addressed at a wall counter. On walking out of the store, Teofilo dropped the envelope into the first mail box he saw. As he walked away from it, he breathed easier.

Afterwards, while he might have followed the crowds shopping in the many stores, eating in restaurants, lining up outside the movie theaters, or walking into one of the noisy cantinas, Teofilo's only stop was at a market where he bought a can of beans, a small can of sausages, and two oranges. With the bread and baloney he had in his shack, Teofilo had enough food to last him through Monday. Teofilo walked out of the store and at the first intersection he left the crowded main street, turned a corner, and headed toward the highway. He hoped to get back to camp before dark.

One block away, as Teofilo waited for a light to change at a street corner, a car abruptly forced him back onto the sidewalk. Teofilo, shaken, cursed to himself and then saw the car stop and back up toward him. Immediately Teofilo recognized Ismael Sifuentes, who leaned over to greet him with a rousing "Ciuvo, cabrón." Before Teofilo could answer, Ismael asked, "Where you headed?"

"Well, I . . ."

"Get in," ordered Ismael. Ismael was well known among field workers in southern Arizona and California. He was specially well known for never being available when needed. Years before, on a Christmas night when a kerosene stove on which tamales were being cooked blew up, killed his daughter and disfigured his wife, he had been drinking with his friends. Thereafter all knew and spoke of how the bones of his daughter's face had been bared by the blast and his wife's face and arms were a purple mass of flesh. She had tried to rescue the daughter from the flames. "I would gladly burn in hell right now if I could change places with my wife and my daughter," Ismael often lamented. Meanwhile he was either getting drunk or gambling.

Teofilo hesitantly got into the car.

"Where you headed?" asked Ismael a second time.

"Back to Williams Farms, Camp Three."

"Good. I'm not far from you. I'll take you back," said Ismael. Then Ismael introduced two farm workers in the car with him. "Meet Tomás García," said Ismael, introducing the first. Tomás and Teofilo shook hands. Ismael then turned toward the other. "Meet Carrot Hands," said Ismael, laughing uproariously.

"I'm Joe Pérez," said the other. Teofilo indeed saw that the man's hands were the color and texture of carrots, the result of pesticides. Pérez and Teofilo shook hands as Ismael drove off.

However, instead of heading toward the highway, Ismael drove around a few streets and into a clearing reserved for the customers of the Los Chingones Bar and stopped. "Venganse," he said, getting out of the car. Teofilo hesitated, got out of the car and was thinking of taking his two cans and oranges and walking away when Ismael put his arm around him and said, "We'll have two, maybe three beers and then we're off to the camp. O.K.?"

"But you see, I . . ."

"Don't say no, cabrón," said Ismael, leading his friends through the door of the Los Chingones Bar. "You're with me. Besides, I'm going to pay."

At that hour, though the juke box was playing "Mary Ann" at full blast, the bar was empty except for a few farm workers. Teofilo followed Ismael and his two friends to a table, wondering how soon they would leave. Too many times two or three drinks turned into a drunk, a drunk into a . . . Teofilo slid into a booth, followed by Ismael and his friends. The waitress came up to take their first order.

Little by little, pickers Teofilo had not seen in years began to greet him. Some merely nodded on recognizing him while others walked over to the table to exchange greetings. "Ciuvo," one said. "I haven't seen you in years. Heard you married a city girl and you learned to use flush toilets."

"Yeah, I was away from the fields for a couple of years," said Teofilo. "I'm back though. I couldn't stay away."

"Once a picker, mano, always a picker. See you later."

"Adios."

"Adios."

The beer in front of them, Ismael toasted to the health of his friends and the bottles went to their lips. After drinking, Teofilo thought:

"Once a picker, always a picker." Still . . .

For almost two years Teofilo lost contact with the fields when during the Korean conflict, an aircraft company moved into Central City. Among the hundreds who sought and received employment, Teofilo, not having any particular skill, was assigned to a department which cleaned the oil and grease from engine cowlings. Hard work? Perhaps. But to Teofilo it was certainly preferable to farm labor. As Teofilo steam hosed and scrubbed cowlings, he became aware that the electricians, mechanics, and sheet metal workers earned more than the scrubbers. What was more, they did not have to wear rubber boots, rubber pants, and rubber jackets to work. Teofilo even thought about night school, then he remembered that he had never had much luck with numbers.

Yet, even scrubbing cowlings had its rewards. On Saturdays and Sundays Teofilo worked on his family's future home. And, with the help of some of his coworkers, the house went up "from the foundations." Teofilo, Natalia, and Adriana moved in when it was partially finished. "My parents were in their late forties when they bought a house after my brother was killed," he said to Natalia. "You and I are luckier."

Meanwhile Natalia gave birth to another child, this time a boy. When she suggested that they christen the boy Teofilo and call him Teo for short, Teofilo reluctantly agreed. "Well, even if he has my name, with his broad forehead he is going to be smart," said Teofilo. Then he added: "He is going to school so he can be somebody even if I have to steam hose and scrub the cowling of all the planes in the air force. I don't want him to pick crops, wrestle ice blocks, or scrub cowlings. No way. Not my son." And while Teofilo might have gone on scrubbing cowlings the rest of his life, the necessity to do so ended with the Peace of Panmunjon.

When the aircraft company handed out the final paychecks and the pink slips, Teofilo sought employment at the ice plant, without success. During his absence diesels had been replacing steam engines. And the diesels, cutting the number of stops on the way to the eastern produce markets, were causing labor cut-backs at the ice plants. Dozens of men waited on corners for spot work, often in vain. Others left Central City, leaving behind possessions, dreams. Teofilo, still drawing his unemployment, began to take the contractors' busses to the cotton fields. Perhaps it was so. Perhaps once a picker, always a picker.

Some time later, while Ismael was away from the table, a camp follower everyone knew as Rana spotted Teofilo. Rana walked over. Teofilo swallowed hard and felt trapped. "Buenas, compa," said Rana, "you gonna buy me a beer?"

Teofilo hesitantly nodded. He had heard of Rana's tactics which included the adept use of the stilleto.

"Mesera," shouted Rana, calling for a waitress. A moment later she came up. "Bring me a cold one," said Rana. "My friend here is gonna pay."

As the waitress headed for the bar, Rana turned to Teofilo. "You were away from the fields for some time, weren't you?"

"Yes," said Teofilo. "But I was out in California earlier this year. I was up North."

"Well, a man can't fight his destiny," said Rana.

When the waitress returned with Rana's beer, Rana took the bottle as Teofilo paid the waitress. "Thanks, amigo," said Rana. "If you need something, a woman, some grass, just call me." Then he moved on.

A short time later Ismael returned to the table. "What the hell did that goddamn Rana want?"

"The usual," said Teofilo. "A beer."

"Well, he better not come back," said Ismael defiantly. "If he does I'll kick his goddamn ass. He's poison."

Teofilo, in turn, was thinking about his destiny.

The men and women who chopped cotton were picked up at designated corners in the Central City barrio. After a twenty-mile ride, they were delivered to various cotton farms. After nine hours of work with half an hour off for lunch, they were paid what was left after the lunch, transportation, and cheap wine was subtracted. Then they were driven back to Central City and dropped off at the corners where they had been picked up.

Teofilo, riding out daily with the unemployed, the desperate, and the hungry, suffered the blistering rays of the sun as he chopped along. He always wondered, as he worked along, if he was taking salt tablets in the right number. Many times he had seen others fall from heat prostration, dragged to the edge of the fields, and revived. On more than one occasion an ambulance was summoned, uselessly. As Teofilo chopped, he knew that he could be earning six or seven times as much if he were in California.

At night, when Teofilo sat with his wife and two children, he thought of how in one or two seasons he might be able to earn enough to pay for some lumber he bought in order to finish the house as well as for some furniture Natalia and he had purchased when the checks from the aircraft company had been coming in. He secretly harbored the wish that the war might have lasted longer.

In the fall, when the cotton picking season started, Teofilo's earnings increased. Four hundred pounds a day were his daily goal and on good days he picked even more. As he sat around with the incoming migrants during the lunch break, Teofilo asked about California. "Don't bother," he was told. "The braceros and the illegals have it all." "Keep out of California unless you want to put yourself in the hands of the coyote contractors who will suck your blood." "We're going back to Texas and I swear we'll never go back to California."

In spite of the warnings, Teofilo felt that for him, for Natalia, and for his two children, California was the answer. "If I go for just two seasons," he explained to Natalia, "I can pay off the materials I bought for the house. We can pay off the furniture."

"I hope something turns up here so you won't go. But if you go, we'll go with you," said Natalia.

"That's out," Teofilo said. "I've seen too many families start on the road and never get off. In a couple of years the kids will be in school and I don't want their education to be interrupted like mine was. In Texas we used to leave for the fields by the end of March and come back in November. That's why I never learned anything. I don't want that for these kids. I want them to be smart so they never have to pick anything. So if anybody goes, I go."

Hours later the Los Chingones Bar was jammed; the chingones were noisy. They bragged about their feats in the fields. "I've picked as many as 800 pounds in one day," said one. "That must have been twenty years ago," countered another. After feats in cotton came feats in celery, lettuce, melons. Then came the boasts of earnings. "I earned over two hundred dollars a week for five weeks," said one. "That's nothing!" The defiant chingones had their day. "I stopped the whole field because of that goddamned foreman." "We kicked the chicken dealer's ass when we found out he was putting the finger on the illegals he was robbing." And so forth.

Ismael, not to be outdone by the other chingones, banged on the table in order to be noticed. "Where is the waitress?" he demanded, looking about. "I ordered beer and some shots of tequila almost half an hour ago." When the waitress arrived with the drinks, Ismael paid, then lifted his shot glass for a toast. "¡Viva México, cabrones!" he said. His companions raised their glasses, then all drank. "Someday I'm going there," added Ismael, putting down his glass and reaching for the lemon. Teofilo put down his shot glass, bit into the lemon and then sat back, dejectedly looking at the bottles and glasses in front of him. Ismael looked at Teofilo and asked, "What's the matter? ¿Que pasa? Come on, Teofilo. Get with it.

Screw sadness, forever." On finishing, Ismael looked around for the waitress in order to call for another round.

Suddenly, some chairs, tables, and glasses were upset and all faces turned toward the commotion. It was none other than Rana and a field worker swinging wildly at one another. After a few more swings, both rolled on the floor, neither landing a decisive blow. Not one man from among those who immediately crowded around to watch the spectacle dared to stop the two contestants. The only encouragement given was for more violence. "Kill each other." "Let's see blood, chingones." Those who knew Rana taunted him. "Is that you on the barroom floor, Rana?" "¿Que pasa?" "What, no knife?"

Rana, bleeding from a scratched cheek, momentarily wrested himself from his adversary, jumped to his feet, and grabbed a nearby chair. Before he could hit his adversary with it, however, the bartender came from the bar and intervened. "Cut it," he said. "Cortenla." Then, directing his voice at Rana, he shouted, "Out. You are the one who is always causing trouble around here."

Rana defiantly threw the chair aside and slowly walked out the back door. The waitress and the bartender straightened the chairs and tables. Then, obviously for the benefit of the audience, the bartender snarled, "If they want to kill each other, let them do it outside."

The short commotion over, Ismael turned to his friends. "Call that a fight?" he asked. "Hell, I've seen cabrones rush out of bars holding their intestines in with both hands. Those were fights." He drained his glass. Then, looking about for the waitress and spotting her nearby, he shouted, "Mesera! Mesera!"

The waitress came over, removed the empty bottles, and took Ismael's order. Teofilo, in turn, was getting drowsy. In spite of the loud music coming from the juke box, the noise of the happy chingones, Teofilo fleetingly thought of his family and wondered what he was doing in a bar.

When the waitress returned with Ismael's order, Ismael looked down the cleft of her blouse, then said, "I've got it good for you, my dark one."

"I'm not your dark one and save whatever you've got for your wife," the waitress snapped. "I understand she was quite pretty until. . . . You owe me a dollar and ten."

Carrot Hands laughed, as did Tomás García. Humiliated, Ismael scowled and countered, "Okay, cabrones. Pay. Pay up. I'm broke." Carrot Hands looked hopelessly at Teofilo, then at Tomás García. Teofilo hesitantly went to his pocket for the fourth or fifth time. The waitress took the money and moved away to attend to others.

Ismael drank, then said, "I don't know what satisfaction everybody gets from reminding me of my daughter's death and my wife's accident. You'd think I set fire to the shack." He took a deep breath and then wiped the tears from his eyes. "After we drink this one we are going," Ismael informed his companions. Then he put the bottle to his lips and didn't lower it until it was empty. "Come on," he said, slamming the bottle on the table. "Let's get out of this goddamn dump."

As Ismael drove out of the parking lot a while later, Teofilo breathed deeply of the fresh air and settled back. He figured that he still had about four dollars and some change in his pocket. It made him wish he had never caught sight of Ismael in the first place, even though the reverse had been the case. He felt around in the back seat and located his two cans and his oranges, his Sunday meal. In any case, he knew he would soon be back in his shack in order to get some sleep. As the car sped up the highway, Teofilo dozed off, the events of the past year coming back to haunt him.

Teofilo made every effort to warn Natalia of the hardships migrant families were subject to. He told her of the foul shacks migrant families were forced to occupy, of discrimination at roadside restaurants where migrants were refused service, and of gas statons whose facilities were closed to them. Still Natalia insisted and in the end. . . .

When Teofilo and his family arrived in northern California, contract workers and wetbacks were everywhere displacing domestic migrants, keeping wages down, and enriching the contractors and coyotes who thrived in all situations. With surplus hands available, periods of work decreased, and an ever increasing number of domestic migrants fled the fields or found themselves broke and hungry and living in squatter camps, under bridges or the stars, and at the mercy of the elements.

At least in the beginning, Natalia hid her displeasure and tried to make the best of a bad situation. Accompanying Teofilo, after all, had been her idea. To improve their situation, she even did a stint in a packing shed, with disastrous results. The young woman she, along with others, entrusted her infants to suffered an epileptic seizure and Natalia returned from her job to find Adriana and Teo dirty, hungry, and crying at the top of their lungs. As Natalia tearfully cleaned them, clothed them, and fed them, she swore never to let them out of her sight again.

On Saturdays Natalia dressed her two children as nicely as circumstances allowed and then all four got into the car and headed for the nearest town. At the stores Natalia looked, mostly, and then bought only the indispensable. At the market Natalia compared prices, examined and weighed every purchase, and stocked her shelves and ice box when the quarters they were occupying made it possible, and then she cooked an ample supper.

On Sunday morning, church. "We must be thankful," she said.

"For what?" asked Teofilo. "The way things have turned out, I should have come alone. Where I'm working there's talk of a strike. If it comes, we'll have to move, or starve."

"Oh, things will change," said Natalia. "Meanwhile we must keep our faith."

A few weeks later, things did change. They got worse.

Teofilo, Natalia, and the two children were on a farm in northern California. Teofilo was working in an orchard while Natalia tried to make a home of a one room shack. They had been lured there by a contractor who had praised the farmer, the housing, and the working conditions. (But the shacks were very dirty and within a week Teo had developed diarrhea.) Anxiously Natalia boiled the bottles, hoping to control the situation. As the days wore on and the situation did not improve, Natalia became alarmed.

In desperation Teofilo and Natalia took Teo to a doctor in town who, after making sure that he would be paid for the consultation, quickly examined Teo and made his diagnosis. "Nothing to worry about, amigos," he said, scribbling out a prescription. "The boy is going to be fine."

In spite of the prescription, Teo's condition persisted. And Natalia in desperation turned to Teofilo. "We cannot live like this, Teofilo. We just cannot. And you ought to have more pride than to permit it. Teo is sick, and if we do not get him away from here, we will lose him. You understand? We will lose him." Teofilo saw that Natalia had reached the end of her patience.

That night Teofilo and Natalia piled their belongings into the car and, with their two children, started home. Two days later they drove into Central City and the reassuring walls of their as yet unfinished house. Teo was feverish. But, in spite of doctors, the hospital, and prayers, he passed away. "I'm sorry," said Teofilo to a sobbing, bitter Natalia after the funeral. "I'm sorry." However, an inconsolable Natalia was not listening.

A week later Natalia found a job in a store. Teofilo, frustrated and bitter, took the bus out of town. He would write as soon as he earned some money.

Some time later Teofilo woke up when Ismael's car hit a deep rut.

"Damn these roads," shouted Ismael. Teofilo sat up as Ismael brought the car to a stop. Teofilo rubbed his eyes and, looking out the window, failed to recognize the surroundings.

"But this is not . . ." he began.

Ismael quickly reassured him that as soon as they ate a bowl of menudo he would drive him to Williams Farms. "You are with me, cabrón," said Ismael, getting out of the car. "Your woman is not going to beat you up if that is what you are worried about. Come on." Meanwhile, Tomás García, without taking his leave, walked away, leaving Carrot Hands in the company of Teofilo and Ismael.

The three then waited in a long line of field workers in front of a large shed where the menudo was being ladled into tin bowls from large boiling cans. Teofilo paid for his own and Ismael's, hoping it would be the last time he would reach into his pocket. Carrot Hands paid for his own. Then they sat down on some make-shift benches to eat the hot menudo and some cold corn tortillas. Eating the menudo without the benefit of spoons, the customers slurped the menudo directly out of the bowls.

As the hot menudo went down his throat, Teofilo wondered what his wife and daughter, far away, had for supper. He comforted himself with the assurance that Natalia would somehow provide. And right then and there, with the hot menudo singeing his palate, Teofilo decided to leave Ismael and head for Williams Farms, Camp Three, wherever it was, even if he had to do so on foot. Ismael, he reasoned, never knew when to stop.

No sooner had Ismael's head been partially cleared by the menudo than he announced to Teofilo and Carrot Hands that he must look into a little game. "We won't stay long," said Ismael. "Then I'll drive you both back to your camps and I'll tuck you in for the night, cabrones. Besides, if you go on the road now, you'd probably get beat up, robbed, maybe raped." Ismael laughed loudly at his own statement.

Teofilo winced and trembled as a man chained to an inescapable fate. "But you see . . . I have no money, Ismael. I . . ."

We're just going to look, that's all," said Isamel, walking ahead. "We won't be long."

A few yards away, Ismael came to a shack and knocked on the door. The door opened slightly and a suspicious face peered out at Ismael, Teofilo, and Carrot Hands. "These two are with me," said Ismael. The door opened and the three walked in. At a makeshift table dice were being rolled by the light of a lone light bulb. Around the table were six or seven players, their anxious faces awaiting the stop of the thumping, rolling dice. The shack reeked with the smell of human perspiration and smoke.

The immediate situation soon became obvious. One farm worker, a thin, toothless individual everybody called Wilo was on a winning streak. He kept rolling, passing, and calling for new points and making them. Ismael took some money out of his pocket and began to bet with the lucky player. At the end of a series of passes, the dice changed hands. Ismael showed Teofilo a fistfull of crumpled bills. "We are in luck," he whispered to Teofilo. "Get on this skeleton when he gets the dice again. He will be our salvation, unless he drops dead."

Teofilo, now down to two dollars and some change after having paid for the menudo, hesitantly decided to play just one dollar, only one. If he lost . . .

When Wilo got the dice again, he made another string of passes while calling for new points. Teofilo nervously bet with him. And, much to his surprise, Teofilo began to pick up bets. He was nervously counting dollar bills and putting them in his pocket when Wilo lost the dice.

When the dice came to Teofilo, he declined them. Ismael, in turn, put down five dollars, rolled a nine and lost the dice in four rolls. "Cursed luck," he muttered.

When Wilo got the dice again, Teofilo, betting with him, doubled the size of his bets. Then, feeling Wilo's streak couldn't last, brought the size of his bets down. Wilo's streak cooled. The dice changed hands and came to Ismael. He put down three dollars and muttered, "My luck has got to change. It's just got to." He rolled an eight and doubled his bet while calling for a new point. Covered, he came up with a four. Two rolls later the dice passed from his hands.

As it was late, a wine merchant came in. Ismael, desperate, shouted to Teofilo for five dollars, bought two half pints of cheap port, and covered a bet in front of him. He lost. "¡Chinge a su madre!" he roared. Looking about for Carrot Hands and failing to spot him, Ismael shouted to Teofilo for another five. Teofilo hesitated. "Ora, cabrón," he said. "I'll give 'em back. Come on." Teofilo hesitantly gave Ismael another five from his winnings, now decreasing rapidly, hoping . . .

At that moment three whores came through the door, bringing into the crowded shack the smell of cheap perfume. The Mexican queen, a young girl in a flowered dress, found her way to Teofilo's side. Ismael, in turn, embraced both the blonde and the mulatta who completed the trio. "Now my luck is going to change," he said. "Teofilo, another five. This little game is about over." Teofilo complied.

Ismael drank heavily of the wine, kissed the girls, and then eyed the dice awaiting him. He put down the five dollars, rolled, and disgustingly looked, when the dice stopped, at a pair of snake eyes. Once more Ismael looked toward Teofilo. The other hands looked at Teofilo too. They knew he had won twenty, perhaps thirty dollars in addition to what he had given Ismael.

Teofilo, in turn, eyed the girl. He would use her, he decided, as a pretext to leave the game. Once outside the door he would pay her and disappear. Surely he'd find Williams Farms, Camp Three, Ismael or no Ismael. He drank deeply of the wine to fortify himself, then put his arm around the girl and started for the door.

At the door, however, one of the pickers who had been losing, stepped in front of Teofilo. "¿A 'onde vas?" he asked.

Teofilo felt the picker's hot breath. "I am leaving," he said.

"You're not going anywhere with all that money," the picker said.

"Hell I'm not. I won it fair and square."

The picker pulled out a knife. Teofilo stepped back.

"Why can't he go with me?" the girl asked. "Why not, hijo de la . . .?"

"He can go with you, but later," the loser snarled.

Nervously Teofilo returned to the game. He drank deeply of a bottle of mezcal somebody put in his hands. When the dice got to Ismael's hands, Teofilo bet with him and lost. When the dice came to Teofilo, Ismael said, "Come on, Teofilo. This is it." Teofilo rolled a six. As Teofilo picked up the dice, he was presented with the butt of marijuana by a picker who said softly, "Drag on it. It will calm you down."

Teofilo took a deep drag, passed the butt on, and failed to come up with the needed six. Thereafter, the bets Teofilo covered, he lost. In addition, Ismael took another five from him and put them into the game. Teofilo saw his winnings disappear. The girl at his side remarked, "You and your friend are salaos tonight." Then she moved next to a picker with more luck.

Teofilo, his money almost gone, his mind reeling from the beer, tequila, vino, marijuana and the smell of perspiration, smoke, and cheap perfume, said to Ismael, "I must go. I'm sick. I . . ."

"Wait for me in the car," said Ismael, still harboring illusions with a few crumpled dollars. "I'll take you back to your camp in just a few minutes."

Teofilo staggered out and headed in the direction of Ismael's car. He had not gone far when he bent over and emptied the entire contents of his stomach. Then to complete the job, he opened his fly and relieved his kidneys. Straightening up, he breathed deeply of the night air and momentarily felt better. As he looked about, however, he failed to recognize Ismael's car. He decided, his head and temples aching, to find an empty shack.

At the first shack which Teofilo stumbled into he was rebuffed: a man and a woman cursed his unexpected entrance. Teofilo hastily exited. As he crept into a second shack thinking it was empty, a youngster began to cry, a mother to shriek. Once more Teofilo stumbled out into the darkness. Unexpectedly a dog attacked him and gashed his leg before Teofilo was able to kick him away. At last, on the third attempt, Teofilo pushed open the door of a tiny shack, slammed the door shut, and fell to the dirt floor in a heap, his thoughts, his dreams, his fears in disarray. Then silence . . .

Gazing at the cotton field before him, Teofilo was aghast. Never had he seen such giant cotton bolls, ripe for picking. What was more, he was alone. He had no competition from locals, "braceros," "ilegales," or other migrants. Teofilo ran toward the waiting field, his sack ready, when, all of a sudden, he heard the roar of the mechanical pickers. They came into view, dozens of them, quickly picking all the cotton in their path and leaving the field bare.

Then the mechanical pickers headed for the tomatoes, grapes, melons, lettuce, and . . .

Hours later Teofilo came to when he heard someone rapping on the door. Teofilo momentarily raised his head to listen. His head spun; his temples seemed about to burst. Looking about, he wondered where he was. Soon there was more rapping on the door. "Wake up, sinner," a voice said. "Wake up and hear the voice of God. Hear the voice of God."

Teofilo once again raised his head. The voice faded. Teofilo then rolled over on his back. Even though he was perspiring, he shivered uncontrollably. He managed to raise his head, prop himself up on one elbow, and struggle to his feet. He stumbled toward the door, fighting to keep his balance. He opened the door and surveyed the quiet shacks nearby. Then his memory cleared. He remembered he still had some money left when he had stumbled out of the dice game. He felt for his pocket. It had been turned inside out and it now flopped outside his torn pants leg. Ismael, he thought. Ismael? He had lent at least three fives to Ismael, perhaps four. That he knew. That he remembered.

Since the camp seemed empty, it was probably because it was still too early in the morning. Teofilo closed the door and fell to the ground to get some more sleep. This time, to keep from shivering, he curled up into a ball.

Hours later, Teofilo woke up again. This time he woke up to the noise of children running outside his shack. He was thirsty, so much so that his mouth and lips felt like sand paper. Teofilo got up once more, steadied himself to keep from falling, and went outside and down a row of shacks to find some water to drink. In front of one shack Teofilo saw a young girl. "What camp is this?" he asked.

The young girl looked at Teofilo momentarily, then shrugged her shoulders.

"Do you know what time it is?" he asked.

This time the young girl ran off.

At that moment the door of a nearby shack opened and an older woman came out. "Perdon, señora," said Teofilo. "Could you please tell me what time it is?"

"Almost six in the afternoon," the woman said. "Can't you see the sun?"

"Yes. Yes," said Teofilo. "You see, I'm looking for Williams Farms, Camp Three . . ."

"Well, this is Acme Farms. Williams Farms, Camp Three, is over there a few miles," she said, pointing west.

Teofilo, his step unsteady, his head aching, and his throat parched, stumbled toward the setting sun. He had to get to Williams Farms, Camp Three, by Monday.

A Very Old Man

Jesús Salvador Treviño

The morning smelled of onions.

Vicente sat upright in bed and watched the soft line of sunlight move slowly up the white sheet, over the fold, and flow over Yolanda's moist breasts. She slept smoothly, her young breasts rising and falling lightly in the quiet of the early morning. Once, awkwardly, she moved as if to wake, turning abruptly, pinched by an angry dream. Then she was still once more— the rhythm of her breathing kept pace with the beginning of day. He had been watching the careless drama of her sleep for more than an hour. He wondered how to tell her.

It had been several months since they had first met. She had seemed so childlike then; shy and fleeting, a gawky girl in a faded green dress. He remembered his first glimpse of her, behind the clothesline, as she carefully folded the wash into a large woven-straw canasta inherited some months earlier at the death of an aunt. One by one she took down each towel, each stocking, each shirt and folded them into the canasta. The rhythm of her movements bespeaking childlike play, the reaching and bending betraying her young womanhood. Naturally, she had taken no interest in him. And why should she? "Scavenger," they called him, "the crazy old man." There were rumors in La Loma that he had committed hideous crimes long ago. That he carried with him the sign of evil. That he was queer. That he liked young men. That he was a thief, a heretic.

At first she had not noticed him at all.

And he? In his careful, practiced manner, he had watched over her for several weeks. She was the one, he was sure. And he must not blunder this chance. He had invented excuses to walk by her house, as might a schoolboy spying on his first love. He had engaged her father, the caretaker at the campo santo, Julio Domínguez, in random conversation. As they spoke, he kept a careful eye alert for her moving inside the white adobe, her father quite unsuspecting.

—Your fence needs mending, Don Julio.

159

—'Sta bien, Don Vicente. It'll keep another year.

—You can't be too careful, you know. Remember the storm of '52? Water took fences like this, and a house just like yours, in one *chorro*.

—Well, if it rains that much, a new fence isn't going to make much difference. Is it?

—Next year, then?

—Sí, next year, Don Vicente.

A week later he had sat through a terrible rainstorm under the dripping awning of Renteria's store, across the street from her home. He had counted the times she passed by her front window to stare out at him. She was now aware of him. The fence had survived the storm.

It had finally happened on a cool spring day, with the air still wet from an afternoon rain, and the smell of soil and water mixing in his nostrils. His heart had stirred as he approached her house, and despite the fact that he had rehearsed the scene so many times before in his mind, he still could feel the sweat forming on the palms of his hands. His sense of humor rippled as he thought of what he looked like: a gaunt, tired old man, his back arched with age, his faded, worn jeans settling over mud-caked sneakers and, of course, the preposterous, identifying yellow baseball cap with the large "G." It was enough to cause outright laughter, and more than once he *was* laughed at openly by the townspeople. But meeting him for the first time, the young woman, scarcely beyond adolescence, saw no humor in the old man, only mystery.

There he is again, that viejito Vicente, watching, always watching. What does he want from me? Is it what mother says: that he thinks of me as the boys do? And what do she and father whisper about so much when they think I'm asleep. Does it have something to do with the old man? Now what can he want? He's coming this way. Cross yourself when you pass near him, mother says, to ward off the evil that surrounds him. What can he want? Mother said to ignore him if he should ever speak to me. He is crazy and full of strange ideas. Cross yourself, child, and walk away from him. Cross myself? That's silly . . . he's just an old man, probably lonely. He just wants to talk. I'm sure. Look . . . yes, he's going to speak to me. He has such clear eyes.

—Buenos días, he had smiled.

She walked lightly, a dance—the wind rustling the loose skirt around her slender legs—to the worn, wooden fence. She smiled back at him, wondering at his sparkling eyes.

—Buenos días, Señor.

But what does he want? He just stands there fingering the fence, and

. . . Oh there I go. I can feel myself acting like a child again. Why can't I be calm, adult, like the other girls when they talk to boys. Of course, the old man Vicente is hardly a boy. Mustn't laugh, he'll be offended.

—You are Yolanda?

—Yes.

—Your father, Don Julio. He's spoken to me about you. I know your father, a good man.

—Sí, Señor?

What *does* he want? The way he looks at me! If he doesn't say something soon, I'll run inside.

—I thought you might like this flower.

From behind him, like a much practiced song, he had pulled a lonely daisy—hopelessly silly to anyone but the young girl.

—Gracias, Señor.

She had accepted.

Carefully, ever so carefully, he had summoned the experience of his years. In the few hours left of the afternoon, he had talked magically to her, nudging tenderly the desire in her body. "Listen to me Yolanda," he had said. "Watch me," he had touched. Within moments her child spirit was enticed, lured by secret notions of fire hidden deep beyond his wrinkled eyes. Her spirit followed, naively. He whispered promises from his tired old man lips.

Listen, Yolanda, listen to the story of this body and these hands. They are older than you think. Older than time. They'll speak passion to your body in ways you do not know. Listen, they'll set free your mind, Yolanda. Do you see, child? Do you understand? Can you feel what I am saying? No, not here, not these weathered hands on this wooden fence. Not this cluttered ragweed yard to which you were born. Not this hell-hole town, with its fate obsessed, cowardly people. The special magic, Yolanda. That's what I offer, the special magic.

The radiant flower remained in her hands. The weed grown yard, the adobe house, the empty fields beyond, became backdrops to the desire latent in their bodies. When, at sunset, the wind had raised goosebumps on Yolanda's shoulders—and her mother, finally noticing that she was speaking to the old scavenger, had called her twice to come inside and let the old man be—he departed.

He had left her with the promise to explain how it was that he knew so much about the days before copper had been discovered outside of La Loma. And how it was he could describe the early settlement of the mining town, and even more wonderously, how he could remember the names of the men who had come to America with the conquistador Hernán Cortés, and how he learned to tell the weather by scent, the time of day by squinting into the sun, and age by the color of a person's skin. As he walked the path back to his house, on the other side of town—where the railroad tracks joined with the new irrigation fields bordering the Arizona desert—his mind had filled with the knowledge that she was the one and that she would come to him soon.

—Be still.

—Come with me.

—No, be still.

—You can do it now, join me.

—Ambrosia, leave me alone, Leave now!

—Remember me, always remember me.

—Yes, yes, I'll remember. But leave now. Go!

—Remember me.

It was dusk. An uncomfortable silence settled over Vicente's thoughts. The echo of voices lingered momentarily and then was gone. Across the fields in front of the porch, Vicente could see a few fieldhands silhouetted against an orange sunset. A cool wind blew in from the desert behind the house, whipping around the front porch and bringing the smell of coarse desert sage and sand to Vicente's senses. Summer was finally over and even autumn would soon be ending, leaving Vicente once again alone to face the desert winds from the east.

Why does it happen so often now? It didn't used to. He had been asleep for several hours, and as was more common these days, his mind had drifted to the memories of the past. To Ambrosia, to the bitterness.

—Even in my sleep you're a bitch. Damn it, can't you leave me alone? Not even in sleep. Damn you . . . Leave!

Slowly he awoke. His senses reviewed the weathered armchair in which he sat; the tired creaking of the front door as it opened and closed on its rusted hinges; and the broken slate on the wooden flooring—was it last year or the year before that he had broken through that slate? He caught sight of the familiar onion fields, the fields which even in the barren winter months were silent friends to Vicente's solitary vigils.

—Vicente, come inside!

It was Ambrosia, of course. Bitter and demanding, as always. And as always, there to disturb his thoughts.

—Damn it, leave me in peace.

—Come in, you've been out there too long. It's time for dinner anyway.

Vicente rose and entered the house. Inside, Ambrosia was waiting. She was standing with her back to the window, as strong and robust as in the first years of their marriage. He paused at the door for a moment, his eyes playing along the strength of her large hands as she kneaded the dough for tortillas. Massive hands, he thought. That was the first thing he had noticed about her. And that was also the last thing. Massive, large hands, strong fingers. Ambrosia, how preposterous for you to have those hands! And how silly of me always to forget them, to be amazed when I see them again. She turned to speak to him, not missing a stroke with the dough.

—You're awake.

—Yes, I'm awake.

—And in a bad mood, too. I heard you talking outside.

—Yes, I was dreaming.

How long have we gone through this game? I know already what she'll say, and how she'll say it, and yet I allow her to go on. How long? She's already planning her defense, and she'll say it, no matter what. And I'll wind up saying the same thing as well, playing my part, no matter what. How long?

—You're in a bad mood.

—There is someone coming; I want you to leave.

—It's her again, isn't it? The young one?

—Yes, it's her again, so what?

—You never change.

—I want you to leave.

—No.

—You must leave.

—You're always in such a bad mood when you sleep in the afternoon. But you never listen to me, and then you wonder why you get angry over little things.

—You will leave . . . now.

—Not when you're in a bad mood. Come have some tea.

—I don't want tea. Leave.

—Damn you, why not me! Why her all the time?

—Now!

Vicente was quiet as she poured the tea. The cup filled slowly with yerba buena, the yellowish liquid overflowed the cup and then slowly faded from view. He looked up to Ambrosia who also had disappeared. In her place was the rough surface of the table top, beyond the dull tarnish of pots seldom used, hanging on the cracked wall. The pots reflected the last of the twilight into the empty kitchen. The apparition was gone.

Outside, the chair creaked and Vicente stirred once again. The dreams came and went. He especially disliked the Ambrosia episodes because they were always filled with the guilt and pain of too many hasty words and much past anger. That's how it had always been with Ambrosia, even when she was alive, one argument after another. Even at her deathbed she had cursed him. "You'll be free of me now," she had said. "Go with your young ones now! May God damn you forever.! Cabrón!"

Vicente turned uneasily in his worn armchair, brushing aside an un-unsuspecting spider. Through half-opened eyes he could make out the last of the fieldhands slowly moving in the distant fields. He imagined their words and remembered the days when he used to spend long hours under the sun.

—Half-an-hour and we'll be through.

—Watch me tie one on tonight!

—Sure, like the last time, eh? When the whores came out, couldn't even get it up!

—Shut up, that's not true!

—Hah!

—Well, watch me this time.

Vicente mused at the idea. At least Ambrosia was gone now. He turned and noticed a figure walking toward the house. It was Yolanda.

It had taken several weeks before he could convince her that she should visit his house. Yes, it's the adobe on the road south of town, near the fields. Of course, it was prohibited. What would her parents say? The thought of it, if they ever found out! Need they know? They'd say that old man Vicente was seducing young children! They had laughed at that. Yolanda, do you think me that old? "No, of course not," she had lied, but she did want to protect *his* reputation. Seducer of children! Again they had laughed, her yearning was coy and childlike. Why, if her mother ever found out. . . .

—Yes, I can come today. But it won't be until late in the afternoon. I'll tell my mother that I'm visiting Doña Cuca; she's a friend, you know.

—Yes, child.

—But you musn't tell anyone, not anyone!

—Child, who would I tell?

So he sat, waiting, rocking in his chair, after years of being the legend, the joke ridiculed by the young men who sat outside Ernie's garage and made fun of him as he passed.

—¿Viejo, que ya no se te para el chile?

—¡No se le para porque ya no tiene!

Yet she had come. To visit this old man, ancient relic. Yolanda the young, the virgin, the innocent, and the old man, the very old man, Vicente. He who had been the first in town, who had fled the Cananea massacre and was near death of thirst before he stumbled on the natural springs, which later were called Maldonado. He who had worked the copper mine that grew up when the railroad came through town; and he who had faded from people's memories, until no one remained alive who remembered that a hundred and more years ago he had founded the town.

—I want to know about it.

—I told you I would tell you.

—That was months ago. I want to know now.

—There is time.

—Tell me!

—Come in.

She hesitated at the door, her clever eyes quickly taking in the bare, clean kitchen, the adjoining bedroom, the storage space full of its aged artifacts and junk. And most of all the windows, the many, many windows that threatened to make her visit here so public. He sensed her concern and moved to pull the tattered shades. She moved suddenly then, as if to stop him; instead she merely sat down at the table. He finished closing the shades and in the semi-darkness that engulfed them, turned to her with a silent smile. They were still, embarrassed. In the darkened room he could sense that she was blushing. It was so different from what she had expected. Am I really here? The magic of the afternoon conversation was gone. I am here with the old man Vicente!

—Why not?

He's reading my mind. Old man. Why, if her parents found out!

—Tea?

Yes, something safe. Vicente quietly began to boil water on the ancient black stove. Like the kitchen, the stove gave off a faint smell of old things. The paint along its yellowed sides was flaked, curling like wet paper left too long in the sun. Here the scent of age, of use, of time. And Vicente, with his faded shirt and jeans, and the tennis shoes, and the funny baseball cap.

—This is the first time for you, Yolanda?

—Such a question to ask!

She was silent, embarrassed; she wouldn't look into his eyes. She moved to change the subject.

—What do you think about when you sit out there on the porch?

—On the porch?

—Yes. Well, people think you are strange because you sit so much. I mean, the people in town say all you do is sit.

—That I'm senile?

—No you're not! It's what they say.

Warmly, she was glowing now. They smiled again.

—Then?

—Then, let them say what they will say.

Pause, distance. He turned to her.

—What do you say?

She laughed, he laughed. Lessons of fear began to leave her as Vicente continued with his talking.

—See the flowers outside, on the nopal. There . . . lift up the edge of the shade. See it? That nopal was grafted from a plant over a hundred years old by an uncle of mine.

He lied. He had really brought it over with him from Cananea, as he had taken it to Cananea so many years before that.

—See how it is blooming? Yes, it's beautiful. That is always a good sign, when it blooms. I watch that plant; when it blooms, it's a sign of good things. That's why I knew you would come today.

She was silent.

—You don't believe me?

—You knew because I told you I would be coming . . . that's how you knew I was coming today!

Laughter. Vicente went on. Leading her from fear and modesty to the desire in her body. He talked on and on. Of a daring sunrise he had once witnessed after a stormy night of rain and hail, of sitting through afternoons of white clouds that formed themselves into strange animals and birds, of drinking from mountain streams she had never known, and of swimming in the ocean to the West that to her was only a legend. He spoke of lifetimes of living, sharing centuries of visions and dreams and poetry with her. She had not even noticed how the old man moved her, only that his words had taken them both to his bed, where a younger, smoother, more tender image of the senile face was suddenly kissing her breasts, and young delicate hands were touching her. The gnarled skin had changed, the old-man bones had changed, the old-man beard and old-man lips and old-man eyes had become transformed. Here suddenly was a match for her young body. She had not questioned, only allowed herself to be mesmerized by the magical sound of his voice. "Listen to the sound of lovers dreaming," he had said, "listen to the magic."

—Will you tell me?
—After we make love. Everything.
—Yes?
—Yes.

Outside the Church, Vicente rested in the warm midmorning sun. The yellowed adobe walls reflected the heat on the dusty, unpaved road ending several yards from the Church entrance. A sudden wind sent whirlwinds of dust scattering across the courtyard. As the dust settled around Vicente's feet, a youthful, plump, woman emerged from the crowd leaving morning mass. The woman approached Vicente with a frown on her face, the same frown she had worn so often when she was alive.

—Why are you sitting out here?
—Ramona, you *were* in Church! I thought I had just imagined.
—Well of course I was there, and why not? But what's all this—sitting in the sun—you'll get a stroke, at your age.
—I enjoy the sun.
—Hah! Get inside now.
—You're so young.
—Like when we first met?
—I'd forgotten.
—A memory. Why not be young?
—When I think of Ambrosia, she's always older, much older.
—Don't speak about her, I didn't come to hear you talk about her. I'm not happy about it you know. But I understand.
—Just now, I was thinking about the old wire mesh screens, in the windows, do you remember?
—I don't like her, but I can forgive you. I've told you that before. I was gone by then anyway. It's this young one I want you to be careful with.
—I was saying about the mesh screen windows.
—Yes, of course I remember the screen windows, dandy windows and the talk of the town. Did you hear me about the young girl?
—I had ordered them from St. Louis. Not even the supervisor's wife had screen windows!
—Leave her alone.
—You know I can't.
—You're pitiful—sitting in the sun with old memories and seducing children.
—That hurts me, don't say it.
—I'm leaving.

—Stay for a while please. It's so good to remember you this way—
before you began to hate me. Please stay.

—Stop your crying now and get out of the sun. Here comes Father
Regalado. Be still or he'll think you *are* crazy.

—Ramona, please.

The woman was gone, leaving Vicente speaking to himself. Father
Regalado approached, large patronizing smile, heavy sweaty brows, black
suit already white from the morning dust, half-moons of sweat collecting
at his underarms.

—Buenos días, Vicente.

—Buenos días, Padre.

—Taking in the sun, now?

—Yes Padre.

—Beautiful morning, beautiful. Listen, be careful you don't over do
it, eh. A man your age.

—Yes, Padre, I was just going inside. Good day.

—Good day, Vicente. God be with you.

Yolanda turned in her sleep again. She'd be awake soon and how to
tell her? A fable perhaps. That's what he'd do. A fable about a man who
never aged. A man who was now over four hundred years old, who was
born the year of the conquest, the bastard son of Spanish rape. She would
think he was lying. The fable would go on, about how the man had survived his first life, as a peon working on one of the great churches of the
new colony, and of his second life, spent hiding from the inquisition, and
the third, and fourth and fifth until he had forgotten how many—each
with its own history, its own wives and friends, and battles and wars and
deaths.

Death, except for him.

And each lifetime without children. That was the price for life ever-
lasting. To never grow old. To never know children.

· The fable, he would continue, was about a man who could not die, a
man had to sit by and watch while the rest of the world died around him,
by him, for him. Madness? Yes, he had gone mad. Once, after his second
lifetime, when he could not understand it, and the pain of losing two lifetimes of loving and living was much too much for him. The fable of a
man who finally worked out a way of living with himself, because he found
a link that kept him sane. The magic that linked him to all of his lives.
The magic of appearing to be old or young at will. The magic of Ambrosia,
Ramona and the others before. And now Yolanda. That's how he would

tell her. That's how he'd get her to understand. And afterwards, he would take her again to his bed, and rather than crying out or calling him madman again, or running from the house, he knew she would once again be silent. That was her way, since their first time together.

The rocking had stopped. Vicente lifted himself from the chair and quietly took the baseball cap from his head, moving carefully so as not to disturb the graceful sunning of a lizard. With one swift move, the hat fell on the lizard, the head caught by the brim. Inside he could feel the body, the fast lizard tail thrashing about for escape. Hah! He watched the lizard struggle. He examined it, the lizard vainly trying to bite his bony fingers, the only entertainment of the day. Since the morning he had been rocking and watching the sky. Early the wind had started up, and by afternoon he had caught the scent of dust from the desert, mingled with a hint of rain. Later still, he had awakened to find the sky full of cloud shifting shapes, coming quickly like legionnaires preparing for celestial battle. By now rain was certain.

—What are you doing?

She has arrived and caught him. Fool! He quickly let the lizard go.

—Nothing, just watching the lizard.

—You were bothering the poor thing, Vicente, really! And then you wonder why people talk!

—I was just having some fun, I wasn't going to hurt it. I got tired of waiting, thought perhaps you weren't coming.

—I told you.

—Yes, I know, of course I knew. Come in.

Inside Yolanda sat casually on the bed and began to take off her blouse. It was a daring experience for her. She enjoyed walking about without a top. Her young breasts exposed for him to see. During the first days of their loving, the magic had stayed with her. And if her mother had bothered to notice, she would have noted a subtle change in Yolanda: in the way she carried herself, in the new way she approached life, with the wisdom of one who suddenly knew why the moon rises early on dusty evenings and why the barking of dogs in the midday sun is poetry.

She had learned so much from him, including how not to be timid. She undressed and waited for him in bed. Outside the clouds had begun to curl upon one another like giant stuffed pillows. It began to rain.

—It was another time, she says, and we were different people.

He turned to discover Ramona standing behind him in the garden.

—You heard me.

He had met Ramona several years after Ambrosia had died. By then he had already returned to La Loma from California. By then the town was well grown, the mines were dug, and already there were people whom he had never met, strangers in La Loma, strangers who came in such numbers that he could not know them all. He had found her waiting outside the Church one day, as if expecting him. She was young, naive.

—How you changed that!

Yes, she was also there several years later, in the early morning shadows, waiting for him to return from the night drunk. He would storm in, often angry, the smell of mescal signaling the violent retching that would follow. She sat in the dark corner, waiting for him to stumble into bed—he was too big for her to handle—only then did she begin to undress him, now and then dodging a wild swing from his hands. After she undressed him, he'd fall into a deep sleep, waking late the next day to relieve himself on the bare desert earth outside.

—It was bad for you, I'm sorry.

—It was my own fault for putting up with it.

—We were different people then. It was a different time.

—Always excusing yourself.

—I suppose that's true. Nonetheless, you know I'm sorry. I am sorry about it all.

—Save your breath. What about this new woman. Are you in love with her?

—Yolanda?

—Yes, of course. I've seen you with her. I know it all. Do you love her?

—Love. I'm not sure, it's been a long time since I've been in love.

—Save me the philosophy. You won't treat her badly, will you?

—I suppose not. As you say, we are different people now. Hell, I'm not sure I know how to get angry anymore.

—Well, angry or not, be kind to her. Don't destroy her. Tell her to leave.

—You and Ambrosia are in this together, eh?

—And several of the others, we've all discussed it. She's got to find out sooner or later. Send her away now, or at least tell her about it, so she knows now.

—She already knows; I told her. You must be aware of that.

—She doesn't believe you. Tell her again. Tell her about it *all*. It matters, understand? It will mean something to her. Tell her.

—When she wakes.

He sat with Ramona in the garden for a long while, like they used to before she died, staring out at the desert beyond the eastern hills, following the ribbon of endless railroad tracks to the horizon.

—Are you angry at me, Yolanda?

She had been lying in bed without moving since he had told her. He had already gotten up for a cigarette. He smoked it and lay next to her again, and still she said nothing. Did she believe him, or was she certain now that he was mad? The smell of onions once again wiffed through the room.

—What is it then?

Silence. She turned from him, facing the wall.

—You're going to leave? Is that it?

—What you said about never having had children? Is that true?

—Yes, everything.

—Haven't you ever wanted children?

—I suppose so, I don't know. It hasn't really bothered me much.

Of course I wanted children. Of course I wanted life, from Ambrosia, from Ramona, from the forgotten others before.

—Is the problem . . .

—It's with me.

It's the seed I don't have. Yolanda, if only you could know. If only I could tell you what it's like to live many lifetimes alone. To see the ones you love so quickly age, to quickly die, leaving you once again alone. Always alone. The children would have helped, would have given some hope, some reason to this strange destiny.

—No, I've never fathered children.

He had gotten up to relieve himself outside. When he returned, she was sitting on the bed, she had dressed.

—Some tea?

—Yes, please.

He began the ritual, bringing the water to a boil, selecting the yerba buena from the cupboard. When he turned, she was standing by the door. She had a look he had seldom seen, as she had looked by the clothesline when they had first met, or once when he had accidently met her and her mother on the main street and she had pretended not to know him.

—I'm going.

—The tea's not ready yet.

—It's time for me to go; you drink the tea.

—So soon?

—Come with me, Vicente.

She had taken him by the hand like a child. Outside, the wind was starting up again, blowing on them lightly.

—Vicente, I'm very happy today. And tomorrow, tomorrow I'm coming back here to stay, to stay with you, Vicente. That's what I want to tell you. Do you understand? Forever.

She thinks she's in love with me, that's it! She thinks we can have a life together, just like other people, a seventeen year old child and an old man. Of course. She thinks she loves me.

—Vincente, I'm pregnant with your child.

She had kissed him then, tenderly, not the kiss of parting lovers, only that of friends who will be seeing each other soon. Then she had gone, smiling, from the house, leaving him alone once again on the porch thinking about her words. Much later, he had gone in to drink his tea, and after that, feeling himself very tired he had lain down to nap. That afternoon, with the autumn smell of onions still lingering in his nostrils, he died.

The Corpse

Kika Vargas

Matilda lay in the room next to the kitchen in the coffin that her senile grandfather had built out of rough planks of pine. Attracted by the sweet smell of the tobacco juice which had dribbled out of his mouth as he worked, flies now buzzed above the white veils that protected her head.

Since there had been no money for a formal embalmment, Matilda's sister, Crazy Jane, had been allowed to prepare the body for burial. It had been a mistake to let her do it, for in her inspirational frenzy she had concentrated on effect rather than practicality and had missed some of the most obvious things: bits of gravel, splintered glass, and small clots of dried blood were imbedded in the matted hair, and the fatal gash at her hairline had not been properly washed nor an attempt made to conceal it. Instead, Matilda's lips were painted a deep, ruby red, made even redder by a black beauty mark which Crazy Jane impressed upon her rouged cheek; another beauty mark just below her swollen lips served to accent their petulant fullness to an extreme, giving her an air of voluptuous sensuality. The eyes—whose lids were smeared blue with eye shadow, eyebrows plucked and arched haughtily with eyebrow pencil, lashes curled and caked with black mascara—perched like two jet-black crickets on her otherwise pallid face.

Lastly, Crazy Jane had dressed Matilda in an outgrown hot pink chiffon and taffeta prom dress which the bulges of two pregnancies, one right after the other, prevented zipping all the way up the side, so that part of her bruised body was visible. A garish rhinestone brooch, stolen from her grandmother's dresser, adorned the ruffled bodice, drawing everyone's attention to Matilda's emblazed swollen breasts as it attracted the tiniest bit of light which penetrated the curtained room.

"Shameful!"

"My God . . . !"

"What insanity?"

"Why did they let her do it?"

"Madre de Dios . . . !"

All of these utterances were audible to the family as the mourners approached the coffin and were confronted with the corpse before which they knelt, gaping. As they moved away from the coffin, they crossed themselves as if to ward off an evil spell, horror and disbelief displayed in their eyes as they moved to the family to offer condolences.

But it was too late to do anything about it; the body was beginning to exude the smell of death.

"Ah, shit! Never mind! It's not that big of a deal. Just bring more lilacs if you don't like it. Cover it up, if that's what you want," Crazy Jane responded with hurt to her grandmother's repeated, "Shame on you!"

By the morning of the funeral, the room was filled with the bittersweet fragrance of lilacs, and each newcomer brought still more of them to lay on the coffin and cover up the spectacle and the smell, word of Crazy Jane's doings having travelled quickly through the neighborhood.

But Crazy Jane, standing sentinel at the head of the coffin to make sure that the face at least was not concealed by the mounting array of flowers, was proud of her creation. In one mighty flight of inspiration, she, who had always been clumsy and devoid of physical grace, had brought to her dead sister's impassive face all her wildest fantasies of seductive femininity and womanly beauty.

On the third day, the day of the funeral, Carmela arrived to add the final touch: a starched butterfly, which she pinned to Matilda's veil, finally concealing the gash. She had worked on this butterfly since she had been told of Matilda's death two days before. It was unlike any of the other butterflies she had crocheted; it was a strangely-formed butterfly, a composite butterfly, as much a spectacle of a butterfly as Matilda was a spectacle of a corpse, crocheted out of all the assorted colors in Carmela's yarn bag.

Starched and ironed, varicolored threads ran through the butterfly's body like the veins on the translucent wings of a cicada, giving the visual illusion of perpetual undulating motion to the friable wings, which grew out of secret recesses of darker color, unfolding and billowing out into expanding myriad rainbows wherever the eye tried to settle.

Perched on Matilda's head, the butterfly, other-worldly and delicate, looked as if it would scatter like ashes if anyone dared breathe on it.

The butterfly's presence comforted everyone who gazed upon it, bringing an immediate suffusion of peacefulness to the troubled eyes of the mourners as they looked upon Matilda. Somehow, it effaced the grotesqueness of Crazy Jane's creation, and it made everyone feel more secure about

Matilda's final journey to know she was to have such an emissary and companion through the dark regions where she was bound.

"It was the Devil who made me do it," she told the mourners months later. "And once the act had been accomplished, there was no way to evade my punishment and what was to come to pass."

Everyone remembered, as she recounted the tragic story, how Marica changed. After that, there were no more parties in her house and, as if in mourning, she began wearing black, a habit she was to continue for the rest of her brief life.

They remembered, too, how on Holy Friday, she had joined the throngs of sinners on the Path of Sorrows for the yearly climb to the summit of the hill behind the cemetery and morada. She had prayed so fervently the whole time that even the holiest among the group wondered why, other than for show, she was castigating herself so. Now they were to know.

"It was close to the end of the month; there was no money for cigarettes, not even fifteen cents for a box of Prince Albert. Imagine that! I'd been able to borrow a few cigarettes here and there, but I knew the neighbors were beginning to talk about me and my bad habits, like they always do—especially my aunt. Well, God knows best. Anyway, with Matilda, Juana, Domingo, Mundo, and Teresa all smoking, it was hard to keep my children supplied with cigarettes. Poor Jane! She even went out with Santiago, a guy she couldn't stand, just to get the price of a pack of Camels for her brothers and sisters. Bless her heart. . . .

"That was on the 20th of the month. There were still ten unbelievable days before the 'cheque' was due to arrive at the first of the month.

"That was when those irreligious girls showed up, each one desperate to know if 'he' was thinking of her; did he really love her in spite of her pock-marked face; what did it mean if a person dreamt she had caught a wedding bouquet from the hand of a dead lover? I should have known they were the Devil in disguise trying to tempt me into wrongdoing, especially when they upped their price from $1 to $2 plus a new deck of cards and a pack of Luckies. That made $10 for all five of their fortunes! God forgive me! I did it for my children!

"Ten dollars, I remember thinking, is it worth ten dollars?"

Her brown-spotted hands trembled even now as they held the match to the cigarette that Mano Alfonso consolingly extended to her. She inhaled the delicious smoke and exhaling, whispered softly, remembering the incident of a year ago. "Padrecito mío, perdonéme," she said as she made the sign of the cross from forehead to heart to breasts and across her chest.

"The candles on the dresser flickered and were almost extinguished as I went to the dresser to get the old cards. But I had let the Devil go too far. I ignored the sign. God, forgive me. I sinned."

After reading Elvira's fortune, her fears abated somewhat, for the message divulged by the cards was a happy one, a prophecy of travel and good fortune. She moved on to Rose, Elvira, Aurelia, Josefa, and Louisa.

"I read all five fortunes and my fears quickly melted away. I was totally unprepared when Matilda asked me to read her fortune for the second time that month. Although I knew the cards did not change, I wanted to relieve my daughter's sadness by consoling and supporting her in her hopes that the stars had miraculously shifted their course for her and favored Julian's return to her.

"I just couldn't see how it would hurt to reread them, even if the message had not changed." She paused and looked up at the mourners gathered around her, an expression of incomprehension and pain in her eyes. "My God, it was the Devil! Why didn't I see it then?"

There were no tall men who would come to their house. There were only dark, somber men with papers, bearing news. There were no weddings that would take place in that old house where men entered furtively only after dark and passed through the back door long before the sun and neighbors arose. There were no romances with curly-haired, fair-complexioned men of business who carried briefcases and brought money. There were no letters from long-forgotten sweethearts. There were no dark women of whom to beware. There were no surprises.

"There were only two nines of spades blackening the table, casting their shadows across my life. No one knew what those cards meant. Only I. Only I. . . ."

As soon as the cry was out of her mouth, the mourners remembered Marica crawling up the mountain on her bare knees with the Penitentes. It was the same cry that had escaped from her that day, a cry which filled them with dread. They had all reached the top of the mountain and were gathered in a circle praying. People started to file past Marica's kneeling form to approach the cloaked image of Jesus and kiss the holy ring. They were on their way down the mountain when Marica at last rose to kiss the ring. Mano Levi was the one who witnessed the incident and he later repeated it to some of his friends.

Marica had bent low to the ground, and just as she reached up to touch the holy velvet robe, a great wind rose, so that the statue tottered and toppled, as if recoiling from her touch. Marica's shriek, as she watched it fall, echoed through the canyon, an eerie sound which bounded off the rocks, scurried along the arroyos, lonely, searching and mingling with the wind, finally consumed by the earth that also cradled the collapsed form of Marica.

With supreme kindness, they remembered, Mano Levi had helped Marica to rise. Together they had stumbled down the rocky path, knees bleeding and burning. Marica's black skirt had come undone at the hem and kept getting entangled among the dry pine cones and tumbleweeds. As they progressed down the mountain, the other Penitentes came to help her. It was one of the few times the Brotherhood had allowed a woman within its circle.

"I gathered the cards up quickly, reshuffled them with trembling hands, cut them and slowly, praying the whole time, laid them in a circle," Marica continued with reddened eyes. "I read the message silently, gathered up the deck again, cut it, and again laid down twelve stacks of cards for the twelve months of the year. Having read their message, again I reshuffled, recut them into two equal stacks, turned them over and met the two black nines again. Out of the corner of my eye, I saw the candles flicker as before, but this time, one candle expired. In the dimmed room, I envisioned an endless winter stretching into the distance, way beyond. . . ."

Matilda had heard enough of her fortune to know that her mother had no new message for her about Julian. She didn't insist that her mother finish the reading.

"A believer in miracles and dreams and God, she thought that prayer would work where all else had failed. My dear daughter! Dead! Gone! Gone. . . . Elvira, Rose, Aurelia, Josefa, and Louisa, each preoccupied in her own fantasy, went home to their own form of waiting. Josefa, unmarried at 40, went to await the surprise the cards had promised for June, the month eternally tied up in her mind with weddings; Rose's pock-marked face was flushed with expectation; Aurelia inwardly shrinking at the thought of the men of important business who, very soon, were to knock at her door late in the evening; Elvira broke out in a sweat and giggled as she remembered a face in a crowd that had smiled at her, once, in a dream, which bore a resemblance to the cards' description of a secret admirer; Louisa wondered what short, fat, dark man had been weaving romances about her while she slept. And I? I knelt alone in the back room and prayed long into the evening refusing even the Luckies which Juana brought me, though I had paid so dearly for them."

De Sol a Sol

Tino Villanueva

. . . y a poco creyen que yo no me fregué la vida yo tamién. Yo me la
fregué bien fregada, ya desde muy chica andaba en la labor cuidándolas a
ustedes chiquillas y muy de mañana. Yo hasta le ayudaba a amá en la
cocina y nos levantábamos bien temprano en aquel ranchito del Hofheinz.
Y 'hora me dejan aquí sola sin quererme ayudar. ¿Dón'tán? Vengan acá o
si van a salir afuera ya les he dicho que no dejen de regar las matas, por lo
menos los tulipanes y el mirasol que tanto le gustaba a amá. No dejen que
se muera ¿oyeron? Pero vengan aquí primero. Si yo pudiera levantarme
de aquí no les 'tuviera pidiendo nada, yo al trabajo nunca le he tenido
miedo, me acuerdo que tan pronto crecí yo tamién le metía duro trabaje y
trabaje de sol a sol, cuando no desahijando entonces piscando lo que fuera,
y hasta aprendí a cuidar y ordeñar las vacas y a dales de comer a los
marranos y gallinas. Y jue apá el que quiso moverse p'acá p'al pueblo a
ver si nos iba mejor, y quién lo iba a culpar por eso, ya 'taría cansao de
trabajar las tierras aquellas tan duras y llenas de piedra. Amá y apá habían
ido a dar allí buscando trabajo unos días después de haber cruzao el Río y
se habían quedao. Apá después nos dicía que le había dao muncha pena
haber tenido que abandonar el ranchito porque ya tenía veinte años con
el mismo patrón. Pero salió mejor que nos moviéramos porque yo sé que
el carancho viejo alemán nos hacía chapuza los días de pago y esto después
de que nos jalábamos bien jalaos, especialmente apá. Ya desde muy
temprano andaba con su tiro de mulas y no es fácil trabajar a medias y
tener que mantener a una familia de nueve, pero bueno, mercó este solarcito
y vinimos a dar aquí. Ustedes 'taban todavía muy chiquillas y no se acuerdan
pero ya les he dicho que en aquellos primeros meses ya mero nos moríamos
de hambre. Cómo iba apá a conseguir un buen trabajo si ni sabía inglés.
Hizo como pudo y consiguió por fin un trabajito en el traque pero luego
pa'cabala de amolar vino la Depresión y ya nos andaba. Pudo trabajar
unos meses con el *WPA* arreglando paipas de agua y barriendo calles pero
eso no era suficiente y tenía que andar buscando algotros trabajitos, a

veces s'iba a cortar cedro o a limpiar las yardas de los gringos, lo que consiguiera. Y en esos días los gringos eran más desgraciaos que 'hora, a veces ni le pagaban fíjate, y eso tamién le pasó a don Chencho y a munchos otros. Pero bueno, hicimos como pudimos por algún tiempo y de ay en adelante comenzamos a salir al *wes,* allá por Suitguara, Odesa y Lóbica para por lo menos poder hacer los pagos, y ya pa' entonces 'tábamos bien endrogaos con esta casa que habíamos hecho un poquito antes de la guerra, ustedes se acuerdan, ustedes 'taban ya grandecitas. 'Hora miren, ya se 'tá caindo y miren ay las rendijas por 'onde entra el frío, y cuando llueve ya saben que se liquea a veces este cuartucho. Una de ustedes venga aquí a darme aquel magazín siquiera, yo me levantaría a agarralo pero con esta humedá a uno se le tullen las piernas y hasta siento que me dan calambres. Miren que ya ha comenzao a lloviznar, ójala se pare y salga pronto el sol, si no, aquí me voy a 'tar todito el día sin moverme. ¿No ha anunciao el radio si se va a limpiar más tarde? *Estas caranchas 'ónde 'tarán.* Silvia . . . Felia . . . , una de ustedes venga acá, no sean tan ingratas que esta silla 'tá tan dura les digo, 'hora hasta creo que me 'tá dando sueño ¿por qué no me acuestan mejor? Creo que 'taría más a gusto tirada en la cama. Estos condenaos dolores que dispiertan a uno tan de mañana hacen que le entre sueño a uno después. Eso sí que vi salir el sol y tan lindo que se vio, hacía tiempo que no veía una madrugada, pero luego se nubló. Bueno pos ¿'ónde andan? Silvia ¿andas barriendo la sala o qué andas haciendo que no puedes ni contestar? Si no les 'toy exigiendo que se 'tén aquí conmigo todo el día, yo nomás quiero que me den una ayudita cuando yo no pueda. ¡Qué vergüenza que uno tenga que rogales a sus propias hermanas! Como esta mañana por fin me vistieron y me trujieron el almuerzo, a fuerza pero me lo hicieron. Ya saben que cuando 'tá mojao afuera me dan riumas, si no, anque batallando yo me levantaría de aquí. Quisiera levantarme y poder hacer algo, ir a la cocina y sentarme allá o ir a sentarme en la sala, de allá se ve muy bien el patio y los carros que pasan. Ayer no me dolían tanto las coyunturas y pude por lo menos moverme un poco pero hoy no, estas piernas ya no me ayudan como antes y pior estas manos. Mira nomás cómo las tengo. Quisiera que algún día se me quitara este artiritis o no sé qué para poder coser otra vez. A veces me dan unas punzadas pero punzadas y con esta hinchazón uno no puede ni rascarse a veces. Yo no sé por qué estos dotores no han inventao una medecina que cure estas condiciones, por lo menos así podría hacer delantares anque no vestidos y colchas porque eso se toma más tiempo y cansa, pero por lo menos así podría hacer un poquito de dinero. *'Onde diablos 'tán que no contestan 'hora sí que 'toy arruinada con estas dos caprichudas que no hacen caso. ¿Pa 'ónde se jueron,* 'tán allá en el portal que no me oyen? Ya van pa' las tres me imagino ¿verdá? ¿Qué diantres 'tán haciendo, a poco 'tán en la sala bien aplastadas chismiando en el sofá? Quisiera poder levantarme de aquí pa' ir a dales unos coscorrones que es lo que necesitan. Ustedes sí que le sacan al trabajo, no se parecen nada a lo que jue amá ¿por qué no se ponen a sacudir los muebles? Y todavía así quieren casarse. Quién diablos va a querer a dos viejas cuarentonas, los hombres buscan trabajadoras, alquien que les haga la comida y les planche y que les sepa cuidar los niños y asear la casa. Yo no me casé anque tuve munchas chanzas, pero bueno. Si no 'tuviera como 'toy yo me las hubiera llevao conmigo a las piscas que es lo que haría apá si 'tuviera vivo. Ay 'taban anunciando el otro día que don Maximino el troquero andaba buscando manos 'pa salir pa' Wharton. Si a mí no me gusta 'tar aquí dioquis y arrumbada, quisiera salir afuera. Aquí me siento toda desolada. Y ya saben que a mí nunca me ha gustao recibir ese dinerillo del Welfare, o como dicía apá: «da pena recebir dinero de ese güero Félix», y a mí tamién. Si no 'tuviera como 'toy 'horita anduviéramos en la labor bien metidas en los surcos. En Wharton y en El Campo siempre se dan buenos algodones y yo bien me podría echar mis ochocientas libras por día y no le hace qué tan caliente 'tuviera el solazo. Yo les apuesto que ustedes no podrían piscar tanto así pero algo es algo. Durante la guerra cuando íbamos a Míchigan yo tamién era la que piscaba más cherry que ustedes, ya para mediodía yo tenía mis trescientas cajitas piscadas, o cuando anduvimos en el tomate y cebolla y ejote en Joliet, y qué friazos pasamos, pero allí tamién me sacaba una buena raya en los sábados, y una vez hasta oí a alguien que dijo: «¡Jiiijo, Lucía sí que le entra parejo!», pero porque sabían que yo piscaba casi tanto como un hombre. A Saúl, Oscar y a Chano se los había llevao el arme y por eso Sonia, Tila y Lidia antes de que se casaran, y ustedes y apá y amá y yo teníamos que hacele la lucha. Hacíamos suficiente en cinco meses pa' todo el año, y 'hora este chequecito que me mandan no es suficiente pa' las tres. Nomás vale pa' pagar dos o tres biles y pa' mercar unas cuantas cositas y ya. Tan caro 'tá 'hora todo que lo'o lueguito se va el dinero, por eso les digo que aprendan a coser mejor pa' que puedan siquiera hacer ropita pa' niños y que salgan así al barrio a vendela. Porque eso de lavar y planchales la ropa a los americanos nomás de vez en cuando no les deja casi nada. Y no podemos 'tar dependiendo tanto así en Saúl y Oscar, por eso se educaron y se fueron pa' Chicago y por allá todo es caro. Y de Chano olvídensen, él tamién tiene sus biles y de todos modos un plomero no gana tanto así. Ay 'tá la máquina haciéndose vieja, como nadien la usa. Y es una buena máquina y me ha servido muy bien, la Singer es una buena marca, nada más el otro día salió anunciao el

último modelo en el pediórico. Silvia . . . o tú Felia . . . mira que parece
que ya paró de llover y hasta creo que quiere salir el sol, una de ustedes
venga a subirme más las ventanas que se 'tá poniendo bochornoso aquí y
no quiero 'hogarme de calor. Silvia . . . una de ustedes venga aquí un ratito,
no sean así. Qué modo de tratar a uno después de que uno las ha mantenido
matándose como una burra en los files, ójala que las castigue Dios por
hacerse sordas. Si no me dolieran tanto las coyunturas no les pidiera nada
y yo misma me levantaría a tirarme el la cama. Mira cómo se ha pasao no
sé cómo el día, vengan 'horitita a bajar las cortinas que me 'tá dando el
sol en los meros ojos y me molesta, y que no me pegue la resolana tampoco.
¿Ya 'tán haciendo la cena o qué? Tengo más sueño que hambre. Silvia . . .
Felia . . . ¿por qué no me train un vasito de agua siquiera? . . .

ACKNOWLEDGMENTS

We gratefully acknowledge permission to reprint the following: Francisco Jiménez, "The Circuit," *The Arizona Quarterly* (Autumn 1973), by permission of the author; Lionel G. García, "The Wedding," *Dialog Literary Magazine* (1983), by permission of the author; Mario Suarez, "The Migrant," *Revista Chicano-Riqueña* (Fall 1982), by permission of the author; Tino Villanueva, "De sol a sol," *Insula* (October 1974), by permission of the author; Rudolfo A. Anaya, "B. Traven is Alive and Well in Cuernavaca," *Mother Jones* (July 1982), reprinted in *The Silence of the Llano* (Tonatiuh-Qunito Sol International, 1982), by permission of the author; Marta Salinas, "The Scholarship Jacket" is reprinted courtesy of the publisher of *Nosotras: Latina Literature Today* (Binghamton, NY: Bilingual Review/ Press, 1984).

Contributors

Rudolfo A. Anaya is the author of *Bless Me, Ultima, Heart of Aztlan, Tortuga, The Silence of the Llano, The Legend of La Llorona* and various other works.

Ron Arias is a native of Los Angeles, California. He received his B.A. in Spanish and his M.A. in journalism from the University of California at Los Angeles. His fiction and nonfiction have appeared in many journals and magazines. His novel, *The Road To Tamazunchale* (1975), was nominated for the National Book Award. He is associate professor of English at Crafton Hills College, Yucaipa, California.

José Armas is a publisher (Pajarito Publications), managing editor of *De Colores; Journal of Chicano Expression and Thought*, and a widely published critic and fiction writer. His criticism and nonfiction have appeared in *La Luz, Nuestro, Caracol*, and *De Colores*. He is currently working on a novel.

Kathleen M. Baca is an undergraduate student in creative writing, journalism, and broadcasting. She is from northern New Mexico.

Bruce-Novoa was raised in Colorado. He is associate professor of Spanish at Yale University, and writes academically and creatively without differentiating between the two. Widely published in the United States and Mexico, he has written extensively on Latin American literature and Chicano literature. His latest book is *Chicano Authors: Inquiry By Interview* (University of Texas Press). He is now on a Fulbright Fellowship to West Germany.

Nash Candelaria is a descendant of one of the pioneer families that founded Albuquerque, New Mexico. He is the author of a New Mexico trilogy of novels: *Memories of the Alhambra* (1977), *Not by the Sword* (1982), and *Inheritance of Strangers* (to be published in 1984). His short stories have appeared in *The Bilingual Review/La Revista Bilingüe, De Colores, Puerto Del Sol, Revista Chicano-Riqueña,* and *Riversedge.*

Ana Castillo was born and raised in Chicago. Her poetry and fiction have been anthologized in *Women Poets of The World, Canto Al Pueblo, The Third Women: Minority Women Writers of the United States.* Her work has also appeared in *Spoon River Quarterly, Letras Femininas, Nuestro,* and *Revista Chicano-Riqueña.*

Denise Chávez is a poet, playwright, and actress. She received her B.A. in English and drama from New Mexico State University and her M.F.A. in drama from Trinity University. Her poetry has appeared in *The Indian Rio Grande, The Writer's Forum,* and *El Cuaderno;* her short story "Baby Krishna's All Night Special" appeared in *Southwest: A Contemporary Anthology.* In 1982 she was awarded a creative writing fellowship at the University of New Mexico.

Sergio Elizondo is professor of Spanish at New Mexico State University. Previously, he taught at the University of Texas at Austin and at California State College, San Bernardino; he was also Dean of the College of Ethnic Studies at Western Washington State College. The author of *Perros y Antiperros* and *Libro Para Batos,* he is a widely published scholar and critic.

Carlos Nicolás Flores teaches Chicano literature at Laredo Junior College (Texas). He is the former editor of *Revista Río Bravo,* and is currently working on a series of short stories set in South Texas. "Yellow Flowers" is from his unpublished collection of stories, *A Ganglion of Seeds and Other Stories.*

Lionel G. García attended Texas A&M University and received a degree in veterinary medicine. His novel, *Leaving Home,* received the PEN Southwest Literary Award in 1983, and he has been published in several literary magazines throughout the United States. Dr. García is now in private practice in Seabrook, Texas.

Juan Felipe Herrera was born in Fowler, California. He has degrees in Social Anthropology from Stanford and from the University of California at Los Angeles. He has published two books of poetry: *Rebozos of Love* (Tolteca Publications, 1974) and *Exiles of Desire* (Lalo Press, 1983). His forthcoming book is *Akrilica* from Alcatraz Editions, Santa Cruz.

Francisco Jiménez is professor of Spanish and director of Arts and Humanities at the University of Santa Clara. He received his M.A. and Ph.D. in Latin American Literature from Columbia University. He has edited several anthologies, including: *The Identification and Analysis of Chicano Literature* and *Hispanics in the United States: An Anthology of Creative Literature.*

E. A. Mares received a Ph.D. in History from the University of New Mexico. He has taught at New Mexico Highlands University, Colorado College, and at the University of New Mexico. He has written scholarly articles in history and social sciences, and his poetry and fiction have been published in *Voices From The Rio Grande, Festival de Flor y Canto, Southwest: A Contemporary Anthology, La Confluencia,* and *Rocky Mountain Review.* His latest book is *The Unicorn Poem,* a collection of his poems. Dr. Mares is curator of education at the Albuquerque Museum.

Robert L. Perea received his B.A. (1968) and M.A. (1978) degrees from the University of New Mexico, where he studied creative writing. He is a Vietnam veteran and is researching materials for a book on Vietnam. His fiction has appeared in *Mestizo: Anthology of Chicano Literature.* He currently lives in Mesa, Arizona, and is an instructor at the Neighborhood Youth Corps in Phoenix.

Alberto Alvaro Ríos received the M.F.A. in creative writing from the University of Arizona. His latest book is *Whispering To Fool The Wind* (1982). He lives in Arizona.

Marta Salinas was born in Coalinga, California. Her stories have appeared in the *L.A. Herald-Examiner* and in *California Living.* She is a graduate student in the M.F.A. program in creative writing at the University of California in Irvine.

Mario Suarez was born and raised in Tucson, Arizona. He has written various sketches and stories about the region; these include "Las Comadres," "Los Coyotes," and "El Hoyo." The latter is anthologized in *Literatura Chicana: Text and Context* (Prentice-Hall). He teaches English, history, and folklore at California State Polytechnic University in Pomona, California.

Jesús Salvador Treviño is an award-winning writer, producer, and director of television and motion pictures. Among his film credits are *Yo Soy Chicano, Raices de Sangre,* and *Seguin.* His nonfiction articles have appeared in *Film Quarterly, Jump-Cut, Caminos,* and *La Opinion.* His fiction has appeared in *Nuestro* magazine.

Kika Vargas, a native of Taos, New Mexico, graduated from the University of New Mexico. "The Corpse" is her first fiction publication (her poetry has been anthologized), and she is currently working on a novel.

Tino Villanueva is from Texas. He is the author of *Hay Otra Voz Poems* (1972), and editor of *Chicanos: Antología histórica y literaria* (1980). He teaches at Wellesley College and has published in such journals as *The Ontario Review, Latin American Literary Review, The Texas Quarterly, Insula,* and *Cuadernos Hispanoamericanos.*